The
Other Half

Door Peninsula Passions Books One

Katherine Hastings

Flyte & Publishing

THE OTHER HALF
Copyright © 2019 by Katherine Hastings

For information contact :
http://www.katherinehastings.com

Ebook ISBN: 978-1-949913-12-5
Paperback ISBN: 978-1-949913-13-2

First Edition: June 2019
Editing: Tami Stark
Proofreading: Vicki McGough

www.katherinehastings.com

Door Peninsula Passions

THE OTHER HALF is the first romantic comedy in the Door Peninsula Passions series. While each book can be read as a standalone and features its own love story with a HEA, they feature reoccurring characters on a continued timeline. If you don't want any spoilers about a previous couple, then start at the beginning and enjoy them in order.

READING ORDER

The Other Half

The Other Room

The Other Plan

CHAPTER ONE

Cassandra

The music pounded, and I closed my eyes, letting the bass pulse through me while I moved to the sound. Even though I shared the dance floor with a hundred other people, I felt totally alone while the tunes thumped and the floor beneath me vibrated from the dancing crowd. Enjoying the solitude in a sea of people, I forced the weight of my problems off my shoulders and let the music transport me away. The DJ worked his magic once more, and the crowd roared their approval, but my eyes remained shut against the din.

"Cassandra!"

Though I heard Liza calling my name, I ignored her, remaining in the bubble I slipped away to each night I hit the clubs and danced.

"Cassandra!" Liza shouted with more force, and my eyes snapped open when she gripped my arm.

"What?" Turning to see her, I shouted over the loud music.

"Donovan is looking for you!" she yelled into my ear, trying to win out over the music.

"I'll find him later!" The irritation in my voice didn't go unnoticed, and she widened her eyes in response.

"He's looking for you *now!* Come on!" With her tugging on my arm, I groaned and followed behind, reluctant to leave my prime spot in front of the DJ. The crowd swallowed up the space I'd abandoned and I knew it would take an hour to push my way back in.

Leaning up into her ear while we pushed through the people, I moaned my displeasure. "Couldn't he have waited five more minutes? That was my favorite song!"

She grinned over her sequin-covered shoulder. The gold dress she wore tonight was the one we'd picked up in Milan last week. "He's got a surprise for you!"

A surprise. Knowing my boyfriend, Donovan, I knew exactly what that surprise would be, and it wasn't interesting enough to pull me off the dance floor. At least not tonight.

Liza lead the way up the stairs and past the bouncers guarding the VIP area. With only one look at me, they stepped out of the way. One of the many perks about life as a New York City socialite... my face worked like a magic key and opened any door or rope that shut out the rest of the world.

"Cassandra! Over here!" Donovan called, and I scanned the glass tables and velvet booths filled with people I partied with every night. There he sat in the center of our posse with his blond hair brushed back in a swoop and that new Armani suit making him look as stylish as ever. Jessica, James, and Richie sat around him. Besides Liza, Donovan, and I, they were the other half of our group. The papers called us "The Six-Pack" and they loved chronicling our wild jet-setting adventures.

"Come *on,* Cassandra! Liza! Hurry!" Jessica waved, and her vodka slid over the lip of her martini glass.

"Coming!" Liza called, and she quickened our pace through the VIP area. Only the most elite of our society were allowed up here, and they all greeted me with a nod as I meandered through them.

"Hey, Cassandra. Hot shoes," Becky said as I passed by.

"Thanks, Becky. Love the new Louis."

"Thanks, babe!" She swept her hand over the newest purse not yet released to the masses.

"Cassandra! Hurry up!" Donovan called again, and I hurried behind Liza until we arrived at his table. "Baby, I was waiting for you!"

"Sorry, I was dancing," I answered, and he responded by yanking me down into his lap.

"My little dancing queen."

"That I am," I answered after he planted a kiss on my lips. Dancing was my solace, my escape, and it still irritated me that they'd ripped me away from it.

"I've got a surprise for you."

"Do you, now?"

With the wave of his hand he gestured to the glass table in the center of our group. There, between the half-empty cocktails, purses, and cell phones was an assortment of pills.

"Your choice, baby." His brown eyes danced with excitement and he investigated mine, waiting for my reaction.

"Not tonight, Donovan," I said, brushing a stray piece of golden hair from his face and pressing my lips to his, hoping it would distract him.

Breaking our kiss, he leaned back and scrunched up his brow. "Come on, Cassandra! Don't be a party pooper."

"Party pooper? What are we... five?" My brow furrowed to match his.

"Every party has a pooper. That's why we invited you," Richie sang-song and my small group of friends burst into laughter then joined him in the taunt.

"Seriously, you guys. I'm just not into it tonight."

Lately I'd been questioning all my recent decisions. The parties. Drinking. Drugs. *Even all of you*, I thought while I looked at the five faces that accompanied me out to the clubs every night. Sure, we had some laughs, the paparazzi loved us, the music was great, and from what I could remember of our outings, I had fun. But each day when I awoke with a pounding headache, the ache in my gut I had tried to booze away returned with a vengeance and it seemed to deepen even more, cloaking me in dark energy. It had taken two years, but I was starting to realize that numbing the pain didn't erase it. In fact, it only seemed to amplify it.

"Come on, baby. Just have some fun." Donovan leaned forward, careful not to topple me to the floor, and plucked a blue pill from the pile.

"That one's my favorite!" Liza said, clapping her hands, and I noticed the diamonds on her manicure for the first time tonight. They glittered in the colored lights pulsing around us. "Come on, Cassandra. What gives?" Pushing out her over plumped red lip, she batted her lash extensions.

"Sorry, guys. I'm just not in the mood."

Donovan pressed the little pill to my mouth, and I pursed my lips tight. I didn't want it.

I didn't want *this*.

But despite my best effort to resist, the promise of escape called to me and I felt my resolve loosening along with my lips. With a push the pill popped inside, and I swallowed. My posse cheered their approval and glasses raised in the air. Shoving a glass of champagne in my hand, Donovan kissed me on the cheek, and I swigged the rest of it down. Before I could blink away my regret, I felt the weight I carried with me lift off my shoulders and float away on the notes of the new song.

"Ouch!" I grunted as I landed on the curb outside my New York high-rise. My friends roared with laughter as I tried to right myself, one leg still in the limo, my dress up over my waist, and my purse contents scattered out on the sidewalk. "That hurt!"

"Oh my God, Cassandra! You fell!" Jessica laughed, and Liza choked on her drink.

"I tripped." With a snort, I rolled over onto my back, and lay on the sidewalk while the upper-east siders passed by and stared down noses wrinkled in disgust.

"I love you, baby!" Donovan said, freeing my stiletto from the door and folding my leg out of the limo. "I'll call you!"

With my limbs now clear of the limo, he closed the door, and I heard the volume go up. With throbbing bass and shaking windows, the car pulled away into the traffic already thick at ten in the morning.

"Ow," I grumbled and crawled to my knees, scooping my spilled belongings back into my Birkin. A woman walking a dog side-stepped me and clutched her pearls. The look of pity in her eyes stripped away my buzz, and I realized how ridiculous I looked this late in the morning, crawling along Fifth Avenue. Hurrying to get inside, I tripped on the stairs leading to my building and Archie, the doorman raced to support me.

"Good morning, Miss Cassandra. Let me help you." His arm slipped around my waist and I leaned on him for support. It wasn't the first time he'd needed to help me into my apartment building, and I reminded myself to get him something really good for Christmas this year.

"Thanks, Archie. You're the best." A hiccup punctuated my sentence and drew a smile from Archie.

"Looks like you had another fun evening, Miss Cassandra. I'll help you up to your apartment."

"That won't be necessary." The judgmental voice coming from the lobby ripped the smile from my face, and I cringed against it. Looking up, I saw Eleanor's stern face with those eyes burning from behind her glasses. As my grandfather's assistant and head of our household, those keen eyes seemed to see everything. "I'll take her up."

Archie and I exchanged a glance like two busted school children, and I straightened myself up, lifting my gaze to meet hers. "Good morning, Eleanor. It's not what it looks like."

"It never is with you, is it? Follow me." Without another word she spun on her kitten heel and click-clacked her way to the elevator. Looking at Archie, I sucked the air through my teeth at the exact moment he did. We dissolved into laughter and the click-clacking heels stopped. Eleanor spun around and leveled us with a glare.

"Oops. Busted," I whispered to Archie and stumbled off after her, blowing my savior a kiss over my shoulder. "Again."

When I reached the elevator, we stood beside one another in silence. The gold arrow counting the floors ticked toward the left as it descended, and both sets of eyes remained fixed on it. I knew she wanted to give me an earful, but the last time she had a few weeks ago, I reminded her she wasn't my mother. Not even close. Eleanor was just a housekeeper who had no right to speak to me that way. Going off on her wasn't my proudest moment, and since that day she'd kept her lips sealed when I crawled home each morning. I'd apologized for the outburst, but I could tell she hadn't forgiven me yet. And I deserved her bitterness. After being there for me through some of the worst days of my life, I'd treated her like nothing more than a servant.

When the elevator dinged, and the doors opened, she stepped in and I followed like a scolded child. With my blonde hair in tangles and my disheveled appearance, I wouldn't be surprised if I looked more like a kid who'd just come in from playing outside than a twenty-eight-year-old woman.

"Your grandfather is waiting to see you," she said when the doors closed.

"What?" Whipping my head around to look at her, I searched her face. "Isn't he at work? What does he want?"

"To *see* you." Where her tone had once held warmth, now only an icy chill remained, sending a shiver up my spine. The warmth had disappeared the morning I insulted her, and she'd finally given up on me. She'd been with my grandfather as his right hand since before I was born. She was his assistant, his head of household, and the woman who held everything in our lives together. After my grandmother passed when I was twelve, she'd felt like one when I needed comfort. And now she felt like a stranger riding beside me leading me to my grandfather as he waited in our apartment upstairs.

To see me.

Before I could ask another question, the elevator reached the penthouse and the doors opened to the long corridor that led to our home. On one side was my grandfather's half of the expansive floor, and mine was on the other. I started after Eleanor and turned toward my bedroom door.

Her stern voice stopped me in my tracks. "No. Your grandfather wants to see you."

Part of the reason I stayed out so late, or I suppose early since it was already ten in the morning, was to avoid his critical glares. Most mornings he left for the office at eight on the dot and I could stumble in as I pleased and fall into bed. Nancy, the cook, would send eggs and fruit to my room and my dog, Poppy, would snuggle up beside me and we'd sleep all day then join him for dinner when I didn't look like something that washed up in the Hudson River.

"Let me clean up and change and I'll come–"

"Now." Eleanor's razor-sharp tone ripped through me. Though she had been curt with me lately this was colder than her new normal. I couldn't help but wonder why.

With a nod, I followed her toward the tall doors at the end of the hallway leading to Grandpa's office. I wondered if this is what it felt like getting marched to the principals' office. When I was in high school, I never broke a rule or stepped out of line. Though no one who saw me today would believe it, I was a straight-A student, always home by curfew, and I graduated the class valedictorian. But as we approached the towering doors before me, I finally knew what those naughty students felt like.

"Good morning, Miss Cassandra!" Lily, our newest housekeeper, called from behind us. When I turned to see her, I lit up when I saw my dog bouncing on a leash beside her.

"Good morning, Lily! And look who it is! Princess Poppy!"

Dropping to my knees, I opened my arms and Lily released the leash. Poppy sprinted down the hall toward me, running so fast her tiny little ears pressed back into her head, and then she launched all seven pounds of her brown body into my arms.

"Princess Poppy! I missed you!" Her flat face pressed into mine while she snorted and covered me with kisses. "Are you the most beautiful girl? Like a model! You look just like a beautiful model!" Those big, bulging eyes got wider when I cooed over her and the kisses and snorts continued.

"I just got her back from her morning walk. She saw a little bulldog on the street she was quite taken with." Lily smiled.

"Oh, is that right, Princess Poppy? You met a boy? You little fox!" Poppy wiggled around some more then settled down in my arms. "Thank you for taking her out, Lily."

"You're welcome, Miss Cassandra. She's just the cutest thing!"

"Did you hear that, Poppy? She agrees! You're the cutest thing ever!"

While I reunited with my little dog, Eleanor cleared her throat and the sense of doom pierced my gut once again. My grandfather waited inside, and from the seriousness of her look and tone I had every right to be worried.

"I'll take her from here, Lily. Thanks again."

Rising up and clutching Poppy tight, I inhaled a deep breath and tried to look as sober as I could while the doors swung open. Eleanor stepped aside and the fact she remained outside drove the doom a little deeper as I stepped past her. Our eyes met for a moment and I wasn't sure if it was pity or condemnation I saw in them, but it only lasted for a second before she bowed her head and stepped out, slamming the doors shut behind me.

"Good morning, Cassandra," my grandfather said, and I looked up to see him sitting at his mahogany desk wearing a similar expression to Eleanor's. His grey eyebrows, the only hair left on his head, pressed together while he gestured to the chair across from him.

"Hi, Grandpa," I said, my voice rising a few octaves with my nerves. "This isn't how it looks." I tried that once again, but his scowl deepened, and it worked no better on him than it did on Eleanor.

"Sit."

"Yes, Grandpa." Hurrying across the room on my stiletto heels, I swiped my miniskirt under my butt and sat down, trying, and failing, to look less like a hooker and more like the granddaughter of one of New York's most influential men.

The silence settled over us and I shrunk under the weight of his stare. When my grandfather used to look at me his cheeks would swell with his smile and those green eyes of his I'd inherited would ignite like I was the light of his life. Now, those emerald orbs appraised me with revulsion and wrinkles formed on his nose while he noted my appearance. This wasn't the first scolding I'd had in the last two years, but something felt different today.

Serious.

"Cassandra. Look at yourself."

"I can't. No mirror," I joked, but it only caused his face to deepen to a shade of crimson.

"This is no laughing matter, Cassandra!" he shouted, and I pressed back into my chair under the weight of his words. Poppy cowered in my arms and I held her tighter, both of us startled by the force coming out of the man who rarely raised his voice. "Look at yourself! What has become of you?"

"Grandpa, please. If you'll just let me go get cleaned up, we can sit down and—"

"Go get cleaned up? You shouldn't *need* to go get cleaned up! You're a Davenport! And look at you! You look like a streetwalker!"

His confirmation of how I felt I looked did nothing to ease the discomfort I felt beneath his penetrating gaze. "I know. I'm sorry. I didn't mean to stay out so late."

"You never do, Cassandra. Yet, every night. Every. Single. Night. You are out drinking and doing drugs with those hoodlums you've gotten yourself trussed up with. *The Six-Pack*." He spit out the name of my crew and scoffed as he tossed the morning paper on the desk. It was open to the social page from this morning's paper and I saw a photo of myself and Liza standing on a bar with a shirtless man sandwiched between us.

"Oh, God." Pressing my palm to my face, I felt the last of my buzz fade away as cold, grim reality seeped into every cell of my body. My grandpa was staring at a photo of me requiring a censor label to block out my crotch.

"*This* is what you've resorted to? *This* is the lifestyle you're living with the money *I* made from the company *I* built from the ground up? I didn't work this hard to have my wealth turn my legacy into nothing but a… a… boozy whore!"

"Grandpa!" I gasped.

"I won't have it, Cassandra! I won't watch you destroy yourself for one more day. I've sat idly by, hoping and praying you would find your way back to the woman you used to be. But each day I watch you drift farther and farther away. One of these days you're going to wind up dead, and I won't sit by any longer as it happens."

"Grandpa, I know it looks bad. I know I've *been* bad, but I swear I'm done now. I don't want this life anymore." I said it and I meant it. Something in me had shifted lately.

I knew my current ways weren't the answer, but I struggled to find my way back out of the abyss and onto solid ground. Maybe, just maybe, this was the final wake-up call I needed to straighten out my life.

"I've heard that before!" he shouted and tossed his hands up. "Why should I believe you this time?"

He was right, because I'd said it before. And I'd lied. But this time I meant it. "Grandpa, please. I'm so sorry."

"Sorry won't cut it this time. Action will cut it. You were entrusted to me after your parents passed, and they would be horrified to see what you've become... what I've *let* you become through faulty indulgence."

There it was, hanging in the air between us. That weight I'd gained two years ago when they died, the same one I'd shed last night for a while, came crashing back down on me and pummeled me into my chair. Hot tears burned behind my eyes hearing those words... *after your parents passed. They would be horrified to see what you've become.*

"NO tears! Not this time! Crocodile tears won't work on me now. You've shamed yourself and this family for the last time."

After bringing up my parent's death, I lost all will to argue back. I sat quietly in the chair while tears slid down my face. Poppy sensed my sorrow and licked my chin before pressing her head against my chest.

"I understand their loss was devastating to you, Cassandra. I do," he said, his voice softening. "It was devastating to me, too. You lost a father and mother. I lost a son and daughter-in-law. But you went from a straight-A Columbia grad student who lit the world with your light to...

to *this*." He gestured to the photo of me and I cringed again. "And I allowed it because I didn't know how to handle you in your grief. But enough is enough. You cannot continue like this."

"I know, Grandpa," I whispered, choking on the words as they slid over the lump in my throat.

"I gave your father Davenport Industries when I retired, and you were set to inherit it from him one day when he retired. But he died, and you weren't ready to take it on then. So, I came out of retirement to run it until you were ready. But you have done nothing to show me that you can take the reins of this company I worked so hard to build, and I wouldn't dare hand them to you anymore."

When I opened my mouth to speak, he raised his hand, and the temporary softness in his eyes disappeared.

"No. You don't get to defend yourself anymore, Cassandra. I'm tired. I want to retire. I was supposed to stay retired, but I didn't want someone else but my family running our *family* business. But I know now that isn't going to happen. It's time for me to sell the company because you can't be trusted to run it."

"Please, Grandpa!" I sat forward, nearly sending Poppy tumbling to the ground, but I caught her before she slid off my lap. "I can do this! I studied so hard to learn how to run the business! Dad spent years showing me the ropes and taking me to meetings with him so I would be ready. I can be ready. I am, Grandpa. I'm ready. All I need is a chance."

His head shook even while I spoke. "No, Cassandra. You're not ready. And I'm going to tell you why. Even if we ignore your recent behavior," he said, waving his hand over my photo again. I wanted to snatch it off the desk and toss it in the garbage. "You have turned into a spoiled, selfish woman. You treat others with no respect. And you have no concept of the real world or what it takes to live in it. My employees are my family and there is no doubt in my mind you don't have what it takes to understand their needs and see to it they are all protected and cared for. No. You are not ready, and I doubt you ever will be."

It felt like the world got picked up and turned upside down. Since I was a child, my father would tell me about the day I would take over the company from him. My proudest days involved sitting on his lap behind his desk while he told me all the things I would need to do someday when it was mine. I studied hard through high school so I could get into a good college and learn the skills I needed to not just take over the business but ensure its success. My whole life I'd planned to take the reins, but I was now being told I couldn't be trusted with them. "I swear, Grandpa. I can do this. Just give me a chance. Please don't sell the company."

"I don't want to see our family legacy sold off, Cassandra. But I need to ensure its survival and the jobs for my employees. It breaks my heart to see my dreams, and your father's dreams of having you take our place dashed into pieces, but I see no other way."

With a quivering chin, I struggled for the right thing to say. The right words to convince him, and myself, I could crawl out of this dark hole I'd fallen into. But the words stuck on my tongue while I tried to spit them out.

Because words fell short.

"This is my fault as much as it is yours," he said. "I spoiled you. Money... my money, spoiled you. You've never had to work for a thing in your life. You've never had a job, earned your way, or known hardship. When I was your age, I was dirt poor. I grew up never knowing where my next meal was coming from. But with hard work, and loyal employees, I created this empire. An empire that could ensure you, your children and their children will be well taken care of for many generations. But right now, it's money that's allowing you to throw your life away. So, starting today, things will be different. If it means saving your life, then I will do what is necessary."

"What are you saying, Grandpa?"

"I'm cutting you off."

"What?" The word came out harsher than I'd intended, and his eyebrows rose in a challenge.

"It's my money that has allowed you to live this way." His hand swiped over the photo again. Unable to stare at it any longer, I ripped it off the desk and crumbled it up before tossing it on the ground.

"What am I supposed to do?" Panic changed the tone of my voice to a pitch similar to a whining five-year-old. "Please don't do this. Don't sell the company. Don't cut me off. Just give me a chance to prove it to you. Please, Grandpa." I was begging now, but I didn't care. The darkness had stripped me of my desire to go after my dreams these past two years since my parents died, but knowing they were being ripped away had me grasping the air desperate to get them back.

"It's too late, Cassandra. I've lost faith in you. You're not capable."

"I am, Grandpa! I swear I'm capable!" Sucking back the tears I straightened back up. "I got off track. Yes, I admit it. But you taught my father everything you know, and he taught me everything he knows. I'm the best of both of you. Just let me prove it. Please don't do this."

He sucked his cheek between his teeth like he did often when giving a thought careful consideration. Sitting back in his chair, he rubbed a hand across his bald head. "You think you have what it takes?"

"I know I do." Raising my chin, I gave him my most confident stare, wishing there wasn't mascara dripping down my face and snarls in my hair to destroy the appearance of a woman capable of taking the reins of a billion-dollar company.

"Then you must prove it."

"Anything. I will do anything, Grandpa."

While he stroked his face, I stroked my dog, waiting for his decision. A decision that would alter my entire life.

"If you want to prove to me you have what it takes, then I want to see you out in the world on your own two feet. I want to see you succeed without your name or my money. I want you to get your hands dirty and rise from the ground like I did. To understand the strife of the people you consider below you... the type of people who will one day be your employees and count on you to make decisions that secure their jobs and their income. Their very *livelihoods*. I want you to live like the other half."

"Anything, Grandpa. Just tell me what to do."

Silence settled over us while I struggled to control my breathing and the minutes ticked by. Just when I couldn't take the suspense any longer, I saw a flash in his eyes and a smile lifted one corner of his lip.

"I know how you can prove it to me."

"How?"

"You are going to leave New York City and travel to a place where I'm certain no one will know you. You will find a job, pay your bills, and live with people who don't own private jets and travel in limos. You'll live amongst good people and hopefully you will come back here with an understanding of how the world really works and with a new appreciation for the life you can have. Should you choose to *work* for it instead of having it handed to you on a silver platter."

"I can do that, Grandpa! I swear I can!"

"Good. Then I will make arrangements and you can prove to me you have what it takes, and you aren't just a spoiled Park Avenue Princess."

I put my hand up as if taking an oath. "I will. I promise."

His eyes, a mirror of my own, narrowed into slits. "There will be rules."

"What kind of rules?"

"You can tell no one who you are." Leaning forward, he pressed his elbows into the desk and steepled his fingers. "No one. You will not use your name to get any favors. If I find out you told people your name to pave your own way and make things easier, the deal is off."

"Okay. I can do that."

"You will not tell your *friends* where you are and get them to help you. The only money you get is the money you earn on your own."

"Ok. Fine. No friends. No outside money."

"I mean it, Cassandra. I want you to live like the common man and woman so you might appreciate them more. Don't think Eleanor didn't tell me how you treated her. I won't have you treating people you feel are inferior to you that way again. No one is inferior to you. No one."

Cringing, I nodded.

"Do you agree to my terms?"

"I do."

"I'll be keeping tabs on you. If you so much as take a penny from someone to pay a bill, or call those wretched friends of yours, I'll know. Then the deal is off, and the company will be sold before you can come crying back with your latest sob story. And you will be cut off completely until you get your parent's trust when you turn thirty."

"It won't come to any of that. I promise I'll do better, Grandpa. I can do this."

"You inherited your mother's incredible looks and your father's incredible brains. And my eyes." He smiled at me for the first time and I nearly melted into a puddle seeing the kindness returning. For several agonizing minutes, I'd thought I lost the only person in this lonely world who still loved me. "I've had such big dreams for you and seeing you throw your life away is more painful for me than you realize. I know the loss of your parents sucked the wind out of your sails, but it's time to move on, to fill them back up and move forward. It's what they would want for you."

As I bit my lip I nodded, swallowing down the lump in my throat that formed anytime someone mentioned my parents. But he was right, they wouldn't want this life for me, and I needed to make them proud. "I will make you all proud, Grandpa. I promise."

"I will pray for your success. I'll let you know when I have everything organized for your journey."

"Thank you, Grandpa." When I tried to rise from my chair, I grimaced as the leather stuck to my bare legs. It peeled off, and I lifted my little brown bundle to my chest and tottered on my heels over to my grandpa. "I love you."

Leaning down, I kissed him on the head. He caught my hand in his and lifted it to his lips. "I love you more than you could ever know, child. Please know, with everything that I am and all the love that I have, I'm doing this for you."

"I won't let you down."

With a deep breath I left the room and closed the door behind me. Eleanor appraised me with an arched brow, and I pressed my lips into a sheepish smile. "I'm sorry, Eleanor. About everything. I will make it up to you all."

"We just want to see you succeed, Cassandra. That's all."

"I know." Without her permission I pulled her in for a hug and we squished Poppy between us. "I'm sorry, Eleanor," I whispered in her ear. After a moment I felt her soften and her arms wrapped around my bare shoulders.

"You're forgiven," she said, and the squeeze she gave me filled me with the resolve to straighten my life back out. It was time.

"Want to help me pack?" I asked, pulling back and arching a brow.

"Oh, Lord," she said, shaking her head. "How long are you going away for?"

"I don't know, Eleanor. Awhile, I think."

"Well then I better pull out the big bags. And the trunks. And we'd better get the new suitcase we picked up for Princess Poppy out as well!" She slung her arm around my waist, and we walked to my room together as I prepared to pack for my new journey. Hopefully, the journey that would take me toward a future that would make my parents proud.

CHAPTER TWO

Cassandra

The Australian voice from my phone's GPS chattered away at me. "Turn left."

"Damn it! Tell me sooner!" I shouted at my phone over the chugging of my Oldsmobile when I passed the turn on the map. Glancing at the phone propped in my lap, I saw the "redirecting" words appear on the screen again. I'd just passed County E and after a three-and-a-half-hour drive from the airport, I was more than ready to get to the summer house my grandpa had arranged for me to stay in. Missing my turns only meant it would take longer, and as a bonified city girl, I was already feeling uneasy driving on these winding country roads.

It had been years since I'd been in a car, much less driven one. Ever since my earliest memory, I'd spent all my time traveling in limos, helicopters and jets. When I'd kissed Grandpa goodbye last night, he'd shoved one hundred dollars in my purse, the only money I was allowed to start this journey. He'd reminded me to say goodbye to my old life and embrace the new changes. I was prepared to give up my limos, but this rusty twenty-five-year-old car, if you could even call it a car, was an even farther stretch from the life I thought would be waiting for me on the Door Peninsula in Wisconsin. If I saw it coming toward me on the street, I would run from it, certain a serial killer lurked inside.

When I had arrived at the Milwaukee airport this morning, a man holding a sign with my name had flagged me in. Expecting him to be my driver, I had hurried over to him and told him where he could find my bags. All he did was hand me a key and a piece of paper with the words "You're Welcome" and a parking spot number on it before turning away. Left standing at the baggage claim with enough suitcases to clothe a small Army, I had begged a security guard to help me. The two of us had pushed my bags and chests on luggage carts to the far end of the parking lot where this brown, rusted Oldsmobile sat waiting for me.

"You've got to be kidding me," I'd said, checking the piece of paper again.

Yep.

This was it.

This was the car my grandfather had procured for me so I could get around Door County since they didn't have any cabs. Not that I'd have the money for cabs anyway. I could almost hear him laughing all the way from the safety of his iron throne back in New York when I'd climbed in and started the engine. A puff of grey smoke surrounded me when it chugged back to life. To perk up my dormant driving skills, I spent the better part of an hour maneuvering the over-sized rust-bucket around the parking lot before I punched in the Baileys Harbor address on my GPS and started my travels to the small peninsula in Wisconsin called Door County.

Now I'd just passed my turn, and it meant being in this stinky metal box even longer. I looked down at Poppy who was curled up on the cashmere sweater I'd used to make a bed for her since I didn't want her sitting on the stained orange upholstery. Sensing my eyes on her, she blinked and looked up at me, then yawned and dropped her head with a snort. At least I had my little girl with me on this journey.

"Turn left," my phone said, and I looked up to see the road on my left disappearing behind me.

"Damn it!" I shouted again and slapped the wheel of my car. The road curved right, and I followed it along while my GPS started redirecting me again.

As I descended the winding hill, a view of the water opened up in front of me. The drive up here had been admittedly pretty with the novelty of all the trees and grass, but the scene in front of me stole the breath from my lungs. The late morning sun sparkled on the lake and a small boat cut through it with a water-skier flying behind them. As I followed the road more, I saw a beautiful sand beach stretched out along the waterfront and a stand-up paddle boarder drifting out into the endless blue water. Children ran down the beach and sunbathers peppered the sand. Maybe Grandpa didn't want me to suffer as much as I thought. Baileys Harbor was downright picturesque.

"Wow, Poppy. It's pretty here."

She inhaled a deep breath and returned to her soft snores, unaware of the beautiful scenery surrounding us. Continuing the drive, I entered a town that looked more like a Hallmark card than what I expected a small town in Wisconsin to look like. In fact, I felt more like I was on

Cape Cod than puttering around the Midwest. I passed a quaint gas station on my right where several pickup trucks sat at the pumps, and I caught another glimpse of the water as I drove by. I passed a beautiful church on my left, and a scattering of small restaurants and shops lined the streets of this beautiful little waterfront town. As I drove past a motel called the Beachfront Inn, I slowed down when I noticed an odd building across the street. It looked like it belonged in the Old West, and I furrowed my brow when I noticed the cutout of what looked like a big blue cartoon bull hanging over the doorway.

"Turn left," my phone said, and this time I grabbed the wheel and careened up the road, refusing to miss my turn.

The quick maneuver sent Poppy and my cashmere sweater sliding across the seat and she woke up, racing over to my lap to settle in again. "Sorry, Poppy." I stroked the smooth, short hair on her head while she curled back up again. A couple more almost missed turns, and a couple more quick maneuvers of this car that should have been in a junk yard a decade ago, and I saw the destination on my map up ahead. Knowing I was close now, I slowed down while I crossed over a small causeway situated between two stunning little lakes. My eyes darted back and forth between them and I tried not to get distracted by the beauty and swerve, taking out a few of the fisherman dotting the sides, each casting into the calm water while I drove between them all.

"Turn left," my phone said after we got off the causeway. Since I was driving slower now, I made the turn with ease, then I continued following the GPS for the last few turns around these back roads until it said, "Your destination is on the left." I stopped in front of the long, gravel driveway that disappeared into the woods and double checked the address on the old wooden mailbox that tipped like the Leaning Tower of Pisa, which I'd seen several times in my travels.

"This is it, Poppy. Home for now."

My car chugged when I pressed on the gas again and turned down the driveway. Grandpa wanted me to figure things out on my own, but since I had nothing in this world that truly belonged to me, he'd agreed to let me keep my phone, provide me with a car, and get me a place to stay. Apparently, our family owned property in this vacation town in Door County, Wisconsin called Baileys Harbor. None of them had been here in decades but he said we had a summer cabin on Kangaroo Lake I could stay in.

Since none of the locals would know me, and he was confident none of them read the tabloids around New York chronicling my lavish lifestyle, it would be the perfect place to try living amongst the other half. With the summer season in full swing, he was also confident I could find a job without too much trouble since the tourists were here in droves and apparently finding summer help was hard. Without a single job on my resume, I needed desperate employers willing to give me a chance.

The driveway wound through thick trees that stretched higher than my neck could crane. When I took the last turn, I slammed on the brakes, gravel grinding beneath my tires as dust plumed around me.

"This can't be right," I whispered while I stared at the dilapidated cabin sitting at the end of the turnaround.

No. *This must be the wrong address.* I checked my GPS again. The little dot had me sitting at the destination and my heart hammered when I looked up and saw the matching numbers hanging above the doorway. The six at the end had fallen and dangled over the doorframe resembling a nine, but that was definitely the address he'd given me.

"No. No, no, no, no, NO!" I shouted, banging my fists on the steering wheel. When Grandpa said we had a "cabin" in Door County, I thought he meant something akin to our cabin in Cape Cod. A few thousand square feet, renovated, and more Martha Stewart beach chic than a cabin I may have seen in a horror movie. The dark wood constructing the small box shaped house was faded and cracked. A ripped screen door sat askew on its hinges, and years of leaves and branches fallen in storms littered the yard and the small porch on the front.

Unable to believe this is where Grandpa would want his one and only granddaughter living, I picked up my phone and pressed his number.

"Hello, darling. Did you find the car and make it to Door County all right?"

I could hear the amusement in his voice, and it answered my question. Of course he knew the state of the car I currently sat in. He'd done this to me.

"Hi, Grandpa. I found it. Thank you for getting me a car," I said, trying to keep from shrieking about my mortification that I was driving around looking like that serial killer I'd have avoided. No. I needed to show him I was capable of living without the means and money I'd never been without. "I am here safe and sound. I think."

"You think? What do you mean?" Concern clouded his voice.

"I'm just double checking the address of the cabin I'm staying at. I *think* I'm here but it's... well, seen better days. I'm not sure if this is the right place and I don't want to break into someone's house by accident." I covered my true feelings which were prompting me to scream out a question like how in the hell he expected me to set foot in that place, let alone live there. Staying at a four-star hotel was a stretch for me, and this place looked like a comfy-cozy cabin for the Unabomber.

He rattled off the address, and I gulped when it confirmed the cabin in front of me.

"Yep. This is it."

"I was only there fishing a few times with your father decades ago, but I'm sure it will suffice. It was much nicer than the shack *I* grew up in. Is there a problem?" That amusement returned to his voice, verifying he was well-aware of its state. It seemed in this new life he wanted me looking and living like a serial killer.

Refusing to let him in on my internal horror, I inhaled a stilling breath. "No, it's great. This will work fine I'm sure. I just wanted to make sure I was at the right place."

"Good luck, sweetheart. I'm proud of you."

Proud. That wasn't something anyone had been of me since before my parents died and I went down the rabbit hole into the life that had landed me here. Hearing that word refilled my resolve to make this work and prove to him I could be a better person, one capable of continuing his legacy. "Thank you, Grandpa. I miss you already."

"I miss you, too."

We hung up, and I looked down at Poppy who stood on my lap, her bug-eyes scanning out the window into the woods... the first time she'd ever been in woods.

"Looks like we're home, Poppy." I turned off the car engine and it sounded like a gun went off when it backfired. My scream rivaled the sound of the boom still echoing through the quiet woods.

After calming down from my start, I joined Poppy in scanning the surroundings, searching for bears or anything that might gobble us up for lunch. The car door creaked when I pushed it open, then I hooked up Poppy's leash. I didn't dare let her off it for fear she might run straight into the jaws of one of the many predators I pictured lurking in the trees. She hopped out and shook her body, then pressed her flat nose to the ground and searched for the perfect spot to potty after our long drive. While she examined the ground, I examined the surroundings. The quiet was startling, and without so much as a breeze, the only sounds I heard were Poppy's feet crunching in the old leaves.

"You can do this," I mumbled to myself, starting toward the shack with Poppy in tow. After she'd finished her business, I scooped her up in my arms and held her tight while stepping onto the wooden porch step. It bent beneath my modest weight and I cringed as I took the next one. The same bow in the wood swayed beneath my feet and I hurried onto the small porch, hoping I didn't fall through. One cautious step after another, I made my way through the leaves to the door. Cringing while I reached out and touched the dirty handle, I pulled open the crooked screen door and then stuck my key in the lock. When I tried to turn it, nothing happened and I realized the door was already unlocked.

Worried that meant someone was already here, I carefully pressed the door open, calling into the dark cabin. "Hello?"

The moment I did it, I cursed at myself. I'd watched enough horror movies to know shouting 'hello' into the empty room only alerted the killer to your location and was swiftly followed by your own gruesome death scene. But when I started backing away, shielding Poppy from the upcoming attack, I looked back at my brown rusted car and realized that in this movie *I* was the serial killer. Or at least I felt that way.

"You'll be safe in Door County," I heard my grandfather's words in my head while I stood in the doorway. "There's no crime. No one locks their doors, and I feel confident it's the safest place in the world for you to be while you go out on your own."

He'd promised me there were no serial killers in Door County, and he'd also said no one locks the doors, so with his words driving me on, I stepped inside. The smell of must permeated my nostrils, and I waved away the dust that flew up when I stepped onto the old rug. Plaid curtains matching my brown and orange car hung from the windows and coordinated with the couch and single chair sitting in the center of the living room. A small dining table with two chairs sat beneath an inch of dust and the kitchen comprised an old stove, a green refrigerator and a sink covered with rust stains.

"Oh, God," I breathed, struggling to keep from racing back outside. Impossible. It was impossible to imagine staying in this room for one more minute, let alone an entire summer, or however long Grandpa insisted on leaving me fending for myself before I earned my way back into his good graces. Digging as deep as I could into my resolve, I remembered if I gave in and left, I would just be confirming my grandpa's suspicions. In his eyes, I was a spoiled socialite, undeserving of the family legacy. Since he'd grown up with meager means, he wanted me to experience his struggles.

I can do this.

Poppy sniffed the air and her already wrinkled face puckered even more when she sneezed out the dust still clouding around us as we moved toward the only two doors in the small room. Pushing one open I found a small bathroom with a toilet, shower stall, and sink in the same avocado color as the refrigerator. Gold sparkles embedded in the tiles on the floor caused me to cringe. *Whoever decorated this cabin must have been blind or had a very dark sense of humor*, I thought while I moved to the other door.

It was cracked open, and I peered inside to find a single bed pressed up against the lone window. The rough wooden logs constructing the frame looked right at home with the orange and brown plaid comforter draped over the mattress I assumed was about as comfortable as the back seat of the car. At the rate things were going, I wondered if sleeping in the car wouldn't be a better idea.

A thick layer of dust coated every available surface, and suddenly I missed Eleanor more than I expected. Even though she would want to see me suffer, she would faint if she saw the state of this place. Her feather duster would be wiggling a mile a minute while she whisked away the grime and dirt years of neglect had left in its wake. I imagined sitting at the salon getting my nails done and returning to find the cabin transformed into a clean, beautiful little getaway with new furniture, bedding, and even a new kitchen with granite counters and stainless-steel appliances. Okay, maybe I'd need more time than just a manicure to see all the changes I envisioned, but I knew she could work miracles in a short time.

But this is exactly what they expected of me, to call for help and go live my luxurious life while someone else took care of my problems. There would be no housekeeper rushing in to sweep the dust out from my path, no cook whipping up my favorite carb-free recipes in the kitchen, and no maintenance man putting the screen door back on straight. It was me. Just me. This was on my shoulders now and I lifted my chin, preparing myself for the work it would take to make this place habitable.

"Don't touch anything, Poppy," I said, holding her tighter and refusing to let her precious paws touch the filth surrounding us.

Movement by my foot drew my eyes and a long, slender shape slithered past me and the bedroom door. Grandpa could have heard my scream back in New York as I shrieked and bolted over it back out the front door. "Snake!" I screamed while I kicked open the screen door and it slammed open against the wall. With the slithering creature following behind me, I held Poppy tight while I bolted across the porch. When I took the first step it cracked beneath my weight and my foot slammed through the wood, down to the dirt.

"Poppy!" I screamed as she tumbled out of my arms and landed in a pile of leaves. Struggling to free my leg from the wooden stair trap, I watched her get up and shake herself off, unscathed by the fall.

Assured of Poppy's safety, my efforts turned back to my imprisoned leg, and I pulled at the wood, desperate to free myself. When I saw the snake sliding toward me, another scream ripped out of my throat. This one was loud enough that my friends who went to Paris for the weekend likely heard it.

"Oh, my GOD!" I shrieked as it loomed closer. My leg throbbed from the pain, but I pulled harder, desperate to get free and away from the grey and black creature moving across the porch. This is it. It wasn't a serial killer in the house that would be the end of me. It was a snake. A venomous, dangerous, vicious reptile! And I waited for it to wrap around my neck and squeeze the life out of me.

As I accepted my gruesome fate, Poppy yipped at it and bounced around me. But her bark changed tone, and she aimed it to the other side of me. Whipping my head around to see what could possibly be worse than a snake, another scream ripped out of my lungs when a large man covered in green and black shaggy camo hovered above me. Nope. *It was going to be a serial killer that ended me*, I thought while my scream continued shaking the world around us.

With speed to rival the snake, he reached out and snatched it by the neck. A quick toss and the long creature flew through the air and landed twenty feet away, pausing for a moment before slithering into the trees. My scream petered off as I ran out of oxygen and I looked up into the man's painted face. When my eyes locked with his, I saw iridescent blue irises peering out from behind the black paint surrounding them. Other than his eyes, camouflage or paint covered every inch of him.

Panic ripped through me from his scary getup and yet I couldn't help but wonder what he looked like beneath all that paint. Those eyes bore through me and I struggled to refill my lungs, the screams having depleted me of every last breath.

"Are you going to kill me?" I asked, freezing while his eyes perused me and landed on my trapped leg.

Without a word he leaned down and grabbed the jagged edge of the broken stair and pulled. It gave way easily to his brute strength, and the pressure around my leg released. He tossed the rotten board off in the same direction he'd sent the snake. When I turned back from watching it thump to the ground, his rigid back was already striding away. Poppy hopped into my arms and covered my face with kisses. Dodging her tongue and trying to see, I watched him disappear into the woods, a bow in one hand and a backpack in the other. It was incredible how quickly he disappeared into the brush, his scary shaggy suit helping him blend in in mere moments.

"We're alive," I breathed, and crumpled into a boneless pile. It seemed neither a snake nor the man resembling a sasquatch would be the end of me. At least not today.

CHAPTER THREE

Jake

"What the hell is she doing here?" I grumbled while I pushed through the woods, away from the cabin with the hysterical woman scared of a harmless pine snake. That place had been abandoned my whole life and now suddenly this woman appears? When I had heard her scream, I'd thought I'd find an injured fox or at least one mating. They sounded a hell of a lot like a screaming woman. After seeing an *actual* screaming woman, I'd felt about as shocked as she probably had when her snake friend had tried to shake her hand in welcome. Unlike her, at least my shock didn't end in me screeching so loud there likely wasn't a creature left in these woods.

Looking back over my shoulder to where I'd see the cabin if it weren't for the trees blocking the way, I shook my head. Great. My whole life I'd been able to roam free through these woods and now, just like that, they were no longer safe from the invasion of the outside world. I knew my feelings were irrational since I didn't own the property, so I didn't really have a say, but at twenty-eight years old and never having left this town, I'd never seen anyone here before. It felt like mine even if I didn't have the official deed... even though I wished I owned it. I loved this twenty-acre spread of land butted up against mine. Now there was a stranger on my turf, and I felt my hackles rise at having my territory invaded. It didn't even matter she was easy on the eyes, more than easy if I admitted it to myself, but I didn't care how good she looked. She didn't belong here.

VRBO. Had to be. I bet whoever owned this property tossed that God-forsaken shack up on the internet and advertised it as a "charming waterfront cabin" and charged an arm and a leg. Then the unsuspecting snake screamer had arrived and... surprise. The thought of her horrified expression realizing what "charming" really meant made me chuckle. From the looks of her, she wouldn't last an hour in a place without internet and a maid service. If I had to guess, she'd arrived today, and she'd be gone by afternoon. Then I could get back to the peace and quiet these woods always afforded me.

But then I realized if she'd found the place online others would as well. Soon my little stolen piece of paradise would be booked every week and I'd have people running amok on the property bordering my two acres. From the state of the abandoned cabin, they'd be knocking on my door in no time begging me for help when the electric went out, or the plumbing, or the roof caved in. I didn't have time to play handyman to a bunch of city folk and I certainly wouldn't do it for free.

While I wished for a million dollars to snatch up this land and make it my own, I looked around and listened for the panting that followed me everywhere I went. All I heard was a soft breeze brushing through the leaves above me, so I put my fingers in my mouth and blew. My high-pitched whistle broke the silence, and a moment later I heard the rustle of leaves and something that sounded more like a bull charging than a black lab. But out through the bushes burst my dog, Hank, and he galumphed across the forest floor and slid obediently to my side, panting hard.

"Did you find anything good out there, buddy?" When I scratched his head, his pink tongue dropped out farther and he closed his eyes. "Any signs of those coyotes?"

A pack had moved in and was picking off my new fawns. Hank and I had spent the past three days in the woods hunting them down, hoping to scare them off before I lost another one. The resident deer in my woods were more pet than prey, and they lounged around my back yard most afternoons. Even though I hunted each year for meat, none of these deer would ever find themselves in my scope. I went up north to snag my yearly buck and left them meandering about, safe within the confines of my woods. And even though I didn't own this property, as *her* presence reminded me today, I hoped this new development wouldn't impede my hunts and walks through these woods.

"Come on, Hank." With a pat on his head we started back to my house. After we walked a few more minutes, we wound down the worn path from our daily hikes and stepped into my yard. My small two-bedroom house on the lake was the only place I'd ever lived. When my parents moved to Arizona three years ago, I'd bought it from them for well under market value with the promise they could stay here anytime they wanted to visit. This property had been in our family for seventy-five years, since before the prices had skyrocketed when Door County became a vacation spot.

Inheritance was the only way anyone like us could afford waterfront property in Door County, so I had no intentions of giving it up. Even when the developers offered me a fortune for it, I'd still said no. This was my home and I wouldn't sell it for any amount of money. I had the lake for fishing out the back door and the woods surrounding me on three sides. It was peaceful here. Private.

Just how I liked it.

Hank beat me to the door and wagged his big black tail while he waited for me to open it. When I caught up with him, I pushed the door open and he raced inside to his water bowl. Big laps of his tongue sent water flying everywhere, and I laughed, wondering why he hadn't figured out how to drink without making such a mess. It was a good thing for that towel I kept under the bowl.

I walked over to my den and hung my bow up on the rack. One layer at a time I stripped off my ghillie suit and hung it back up in my closet. A quick spritz with de-scenting spray and I closed it behind the doors until the next time I needed to be incognito in the woods. After wiping off my face paint, I went back into the kitchen. Hank trotted up beside me. Those big brown eyes found mine, and I knew that look. He wore it often.

"It's not dinner time, Hank. You're like three hours early, buddy." But hearing the word dinner had his whole-body wagging, and I cursed myself for saying it. "You can have one bite. One."

As if he knew he'd worn me down, he raced over to the bowl and sat down like he'd been taught since I got him as an eight-week-old pup. Unable to resist his well-honed begging routine, I walked over to the cupboard and pulled out a handful of dog food. Drool slipped out of his mouth and onto the floor before I could toss it in the bowl.

"This will tide you over. You can have your full dinner later."

While he gobbled up the bites, I walked over to the over-sized window in my living room overlooking the lake out back. In another hour or two the fish would start biting, and even though I fished for a living on a commercial boat, I'd still spend my evening sitting on my dock casting into the water. Even after spending countless hours a week helping tourists haul in their own catches, I still enjoyed fishing. It was my therapy. But after what I'd been through this spring, there wasn't enough fishing in the world to ease all the pain.

A red blinking light flashing on the answering machine caught my attention. Odd since everyone I know would call me on my cell. I'd forgotten we even had a landline, but I never disconnected the damn thing and my Dad must still be paying the phone bill. Probably had it on autopay and never turned it off. Making a note to tell him, I walked over and looked at it, then found the 'play message' button and pressed it.

"Jake, it's me. You've blocked my number, but I remembered this one from high school, so I tried it. I just wanted to talk to you and—"

The sound of her voice filled me with unchecked rage. I grabbed the answering machine and tossed it against the wall. It shattered in an explosion of plastic parts and the sound sent Hank skidding into the other room.

"Fuck you, Nikki," I snarled at it. The remnants of the wreckage on my floor looked similar to how my heart looked after she'd stomped on it. Even though I'd blocked her number on my cell and told her to leave me the hell alone, she'd found one more way to wiggle back into my world. Of course, she would. She was too selfish to give me what I needed… a life without her. This time I meant it, but she still thought I'd forgive her. Again. She thought I'd let this sick cycle we'd been in since I met her in ninth grade continue. But this time I was done with her. All I wanted now was to be alone, and the fact she'd found a way to invade my home had the heat coursing back through my veins.

"Hank! Come on!" I called, and he peaked out around the corner. Storming to the porch door, I pushed it open and held it until he raced out in front of me. I grabbed my fishing pole and tackle box and headed down to the dock. The only thing that could calm me down now was a few casts into the lake.

CHAPTER FOUR

Cassandra

"What do you think, Poppy? Better?"

She sat on the pink eiderdown comforter I'd stuffed in my trunk before I left. It was my favorite blanket and after seeing the state of the bed in this cabin, I was glad I remembered to pilfer some of my most beloved linens for the trip. Pink satin covered the pillows and matching sheets hid away the mattress that had been covered in so much dust I nearly choked when I'd cleaned it.

After spending the entire day scrubbing up my shack, it was starting to look a little less like a hovel and more like something I could tolerate living in. Sure, I wouldn't be inviting Martha Stewart over anytime soon, but with a lot of cleaning using the supplies I'd found under the sink, and the personal touches I'd brought with me, I felt a little less like screaming every time I looked around. A little.

Poppy dug on the comforter, spinning in circles while she fluffed it how she liked it. With a grunt she flopped down.

"I'll take that as a yes. It's better."

Exhaustion drove me to her side, and I collapsed beside her. The day had been an emotional rollercoaster. I spent as much time sobbing as I did scrubbing and I'd picked up my phone to call Grandpa and beg him to reconsider more times than I wanted to admit. After the discovery of a desiccated mouse on the floor sent me screaming outside to collapse in a leaf pile, I'd wailed about my misfortunes to the birds squawking above me and decided to end my misery.

This was too much.

Then I remembered the look in Grandpa's eyes that day he'd called me into his office and the disappointment he wore so plainly on his face. The memory of him pointing to the picture of my crotch sporting a censored tag confirmed I needed to do this. I needed to earn his respect, and if it meant roughing it in this dilapidated shack in the woods for a couple months, then I would make the best of it. With more unchecked screams, I'd used an old newspaper to pick up the mouse and tossed it out into the grass in the direction that stranger had tossed the snake.

A flash of the man's terrifying appearance filled my mind again, and I worried he was out sitting in my bushes in his strange suit watching my numerous meltdowns. Plotting. Planning. But then I remembered the brief glance I'd gotten into those blue eyes, his azure orbs lacking malice. Even though he'd been dressed like something straight out of a horror movie, his eyes didn't hold a hint of venom. Unlike the snake he'd tossed as if it were nothing. In fact, they were some of the prettiest eyes I'd ever seen.

While I lay next to Poppy, I thought I'd never be able to fall asleep in this creepy cabin, but my aching body begged for sleep. It turned out cleaning was much harder work than I'd expected. Everything hurt, and I was too tired to get undressed, so I rolled under the covers and pulled them up tight. It was so dark out here without the lights of the city I couldn't convince myself to turn off my disturbing bedside lamp shaped like a creepy owl. My belly grumbled its displeasure that I hadn't eaten all day, and it accentuated the absence of my cook. Normally, if I was in bed feeling hungry, a quick lift of my bedside phone produced anything I wanted delivered to my bedroom in under an hour. But there was no cook to whip me up poached eggs, and no housekeeper to keep the fridge stocked. Now that my cabin was clean enough, and I could sleep without suffocating on the dust, going to the grocery store tomorrow would be the next step in my new self-sufficient life.

Trying harder this time to listen to my GPS, I steered my big brown boat of a car through Baileys Harbor. The loud engine drew the eyes of the people strolling down the streets and heat flushed my cheeks while I slunk a little lower in the seat.

"This is so embarrassing, Poppy. Everyone is staring at my hideous car! If I saw anyone I know, I would die... DIE of embarrassment!"

Ignoring my mortification, she stood on her back legs stretching as tall as she could to see out the window. The GPS told me the nearest grocery store was fifteen minutes away in Sister Bay. It shocked me I'd have to drive that far just for groceries. In New York there was a grocery store on almost every corner. Though I'd never actually gone shopping in one, I'd seen them at least.

The drive to Sister Bay was as beautiful as the drive through Baileys Harbor. Rolling hills and blue skies stretched out in every direction. I passed a small farm and nearly swerved off the road staring at the cows grazing in the pasture. Between my drive up yesterday and my travels today, I'd seen more trees here than I had in my whole life combined. While I continued taking in the breathtaking scenery, once I reached Sister Bay the little voice on my phone chirped and told me to turn onto the little winding road leading to the only grocery store in this part of the county. The Piggly Wiggly. *What the hell kind of a store is called the Piggly Wiggly*? I wondered while I steered my car into the parking lot.

Opening my purse, I looked inside at the one-hundred-dollar bill that remained unspent. It was the only money I had until I found a job. Luckily my car had been filled with gas when I picked it up at the airport and I still had a quarter tank left. But not knowing how long it would take to find a job, I knew I needed to make this money count. Twenty-five dollars should get me plenty of groceries, and I'd save the rest for gas to get around town and hunt down jobs.

I opened Poppy's pink Prada carrier, and she hopped inside and got situated. Pulling her and my purse out of the car I walked across the parking lot and paused at the entrance to the Piggly Wiggly. Shopping carts were stacked to my left, and the big sliding glass doors looked more intimidating than I expected. What would it be like in there? Realizing how pathetic it was I'd never been in a grocery store at the age of twenty-eight, I grabbed a shopping cart and pushed it inside.

"We've got this, Poppy."

Rows of fruit and vegetables glowed under the bright lights. I started in the produce section since my normal morning breakfast consisted of an array of fruits. Since I didn't eat gluten, carbs, or sugar, and I didn't have a cook, I figured fruits and vegetables would be a large source of my diet until I could learn how to use the stove. That was if it even worked.

"Blueberries. Perfect," I said while I reached forward to grab a plastic container. "$4.99?" I shrieked to myself and dropped them like they were made of lava. That was a quarter of my twenty-five-dollar grocery budget. When the hell did fruit get so expensive? With a groan I started down the fruits and vegetable aisle searching for the lowest prices. *Is this how other people have to shop?* I wondered while I continued with an inward groan each time I saw something I wanted but it was out of my price range. When I finished in the produce section, I had a head of iceberg lettuce, celery, and one banana.

Moving my cart through the aisles, sticker shock met me at every turn. Did Grandpa not realize how much food cost when he handed me one hundred dollars to live off? No, he knew, I realized and took a deep breath. This was part of my challenge. I just needed enough to get by for a few days while I found a job. When I found all the items I could afford were filled with sugar and carbs, I nearly dropped to the floor in another sobbing fit. One week of living on a budget and I'd be putting on twenty pounds. I needed a job. Now.

After finding a dismal assortment of healthy foods that wouldn't push me over my twenty-five-dollar budget, I pushed the cart Poppy sat in toward the checkout lady. Feeling grateful I'd brought Poppy's food after seeing the dog food selections available, I noted that Grandpa would have to make an exception and ship in her specialty food to me. It was one thing for me to suffer with nothing good to eat, but Poppy shouldn't have to pay for my terrible choices. She deserved nothing but the finest gourmet kibble on the planet, and I had hers custom made from a little company out of New York. Heck, at this rate maybe I'd have to start eating her food too. It was nothing but high-quality human-grade meats, vegetables and grains.

My face puckered as I realized I'd just considered eating dog food, and I glanced down at my cart. Nope. This would have to do. I wouldn't be eating the Wagyu beef and organic vegetables I'd grown accustomed to, but I would make do with my simple selections.

Mimicking the woman in front of me, I put my banana, lettuce, celery, cans of tuna, peanut butter, and mustard up on the little black conveyor thing.

"How are you doing today?" she asked with more enthusiasm and cheer than any store clerk I'd ever seen in New York.

"Fine, thank you."

"Good! Another beautiful summer day, eh?"

"It is," I answered, still taken aback by this friendly stranger.

"That will be $22.46."

Pleased I'd stayed under budget the first time in my life I had a budget, I handed her my one-hundred-dollar bill. When she passed back the change, I felt a swell of panic surge inside me. Staring at the meager money in my trembling hand, my stomach flipped over. These bills and this change represented survival. Swallowing hard, I looked up at her.

"Do you know anywhere hiring?"

With a snort, she nodded. "*Everywhere* is hiring. It's tourist season. We have more jobs than employees!"

Letting out an external sigh I shoved the money back in my purse. "Do you know where I can look?"

She pointed toward the door. "There's a corkboard over there with jobs. Take a look. Have a wonderful day!"

"Thank you," I answered, then pushed my cart over to the board nailed to the wall. Dozens of flyers with the words "Hiring" were stuck on with thumb tacks. I perused over them all. *Server Wanted, Hostess Wanted, Busser Wanted...* the jobs seemed endless. And then I realized that even with my Columbia MBA, I had absolutely no freaking experience for any of them. Panic crept up inside me while my eyes flipped through them, discounting each one because I hadn't even the faintest idea how to do the job. Then I saw that big blue cartoon bull caricature at the top of the bottom flyer on the right. I knew that bull. It was the same one on that western-looking building I passed near my house in Baileys Harbor.

Bartender Wanted at the Blue Ox. Great money. Great people. No experience necessary. Will train.

No experience necessary! That was me! And even though I had no experience as a bartender, I had a *lot* of experience at bars. I drank at them, danced on them, and had ordered countless drinks at them. As embarrassed as I was to admit it, my limited skillset made the job as a bartender the most logical choice. And it was close to home. Considering my gas was dwindling down, the job's proximity to my cabin would help with this newfound need to budget my money.

I scooped Poppy and my grocery bag out of the cart and pushed it back into the return rack. With a skip in my step I returned to my car and fired it up before chugging back to Baileys Harbor to the Blue Ox to apply for a job.

After sitting in my car parked out front for a few moments, I tried to muster up the courage to walk inside. How does one apply for a job? Should I have a resume or something? Just walk inside? This lack of confidence that plagued me every second of my new life here unsettled me. Normally, I was confident and brave. But everything here was new and with no one to guide me I felt lost and overwhelmed. The truth of my grandpa's words settled over me again. I really did have zero life skills. With one look into my purse at the only crumpled up bills I had to avoid starvation, I decided to march inside and ask about a job.

Leaving Poppy sleeping on my sweater, I climbed out and scooted through the cars across the street. When I arrived at the front of the building, I paused on the giant blue shoe prints painted on the sidewalk leading to the building. The big blue bull looked down at me between the words "Blue Ox" and I looked across the rickety porch where two chairs and a wooden bench and a table sat. It looked more like the type of porch where I'd see people sitting out blowing on jugs than the porch of a bar in a tourist town. Antique signs covered the door and neon lights flashed from the windows. "Go Pack Go" glowed yellow just below the Miller Lite sign. This was no New York City club, and I started to lose my gumption.

The door swung open and a normal looking couple stepped out. They weren't wearing overalls and chewing on straw like I now imagined I'd find inside but looked like a couple of regular people. The woman, wearing a big grin and an oversized summer hat, stepped out while the man in khakis and a button-down held open the door.

"Coming in?" he asked while he continued holding the door.

Nodding my head, I bit my lip and started up the steps. "Yes, thank you."

He waited until I stepped inside before letting go of the door. It slammed behind me and I jumped at the sound. Frozen in place, I stood with wide eyes while I tried to take in the overwhelming atmosphere. Only two patrons sat on the round bar stools lined up along the rough wooden bar. Antique decorations and signs covered every inch of the plank wood walls. They hung over my head, and I looked up at the giant American flag suspended above me. It was surprising this old building hadn't collapsed under the weight of the countless trinkets clinging to every inch of it.

When I looked to my right, I saw a man in a black fedora hat slumped back in a chair in front of the window. One look at his distorted face and the scream started gurgling up in my throat, but it stopped when I realized it wasn't a real man.

It was a life-sized mannequin of sorts, and he sat unmoving beside me.

"It's Captain Bailey. Don't let him scare you," a woman's voice called, and I spun to the sound. A cute little brunette in jeans and a tight tank top with the words "I Got Oxidized at the Blue Ox" across her chest stood behind the bar wiping a glass. She stared at me while I remained frozen like my feet were glued to the brown carpet. "Can I help you?"

With a long gulp sliding down my throat, I nodded my head. "Yes. Hi. I, uh, I'm looking for a job. I think." I managed to say while I forced my feet to move toward her.

"You think?"

I shook my head. "No. I am. I *am* looking for a job." It was the first time in my life I'd uttered those words.

"Have a seat," she said, gesturing to a barber chair at the end of the bar.

What the hell is this? I thought while I tried to climb in it. After shifting around to get as comfortable as I could in the odd chair, she came up and leaned forward on the bar. Chocolate colored eyes the same color as her hair raked me up and down.

"I'm Jo," she said, sticking out her hand. Even though she wore little makeup and her hair was pulled back in a messy ponytail, she was as beautiful as the women I normally rolled with in the city. With some makeup, high heels, and a cocktail gown she could have fit right in with us.

"Cass—" I stopped myself. I couldn't use my real name. Even though these people didn't read New York papers, my name had gone national on more than one occasion. Remembering Grandpa's warning I couldn't use my name or risk losing the company, I pulled one out from thin air. "Cassie Sinclair," I spit out without thought. Saying the name sent a familiar wave of grief surging inside me and I immediately regretted not choosing something that wouldn't remind me of my parents every time I said it. My father used to call me Cassie when I was young, before I grew up and demanded everyone call me Cassandra because it sounded more elegant. Visions of him saying the name while I curled up in his lap and got a kiss on the head flooded me with sorrow. And Sinclair was my mother's maiden name. Struggling to keep from dissolving into a puddle of tears, I swallowed them down while I reached out and shook her hand.

"Nice to meet you, Cassie. So, you've bartended?"

I thought there was no experience necessary? "Um, yes," I lied. Though was it really a lie? Pouring shots into people's mouths while standing on the bar and spraying them with champagne counts as bartending, right?

"Good. We're desperate. I'm working doubles every day trying to keep up and Friday and Saturday nights I'm here by myself and I could use a second. Tips are great. We've got lots of locals and they're pretty easy. How often are you available?"

"Anytime, I guess."

"Anytime? Really? You don't have a bunch of other jobs I need to schedule around?"

I shook my head.

"Then you're hired."

"What?" I nearly choked out the words. This was all it took to get a job in the real world? With great tips?

Thoughts of organic blueberries and full tanks of gas danced through my head.

"Seasons about to hit full swing and I need a body. Let's try you and see how you do. As long as you can tap a beer and take money, I can use you."

"Okay," I answered, but wondered if I *could* tap a beer. Taking money? Now that I knew I could handle. Making a note to Google *tapping a beer*, I took a deep breath. "I'll take the job."

"Can you start tomorrow?" Her dark brows rose, and she pursed her full lips into a thin line while she waited.

"Sure, why not."

"Awesome!" A smile lit up her face. "Then get here at three. It will give us a little time to train you before the locals come in for happy hour at five."

"Great. I'll be here. Do I need anything?"

"Just bring your ID and I'll have you fill out the forms then you can start."

An ID? Shit. I'd given her a fake name. "Perfect. I'll see you then."

Struggling to get out of the odd chair, I smiled at her and finally made it to the ground. Another look around the bar and I wondered what I'd gotten myself into. But a glance at my purse and knowing how little money was in there, I knew this was what I needed to do.

I climbed back into my car and Poppy was still snoring away. Even though I didn't want to break the rules and call Grandpa for help, there was one thing I knew I couldn't fix this fast. Pressing his number on the phone, I sat back against the torn orange fabric of my seat.

"Hi Grandpa, it's me."

"Giving up already?" he asked, condemnation thick in his voice.

"No. The opposite in fact. I got a job."

"You did?" Pride swelled in his voice and it flooded me with the resolution to keep going down this path.

"I did, but I do need something from you."

"Oh," he said, the condemnation returning. "What is it?"

"I need an ID. You told me I couldn't use my real name, so I lied when I took the job, but they need an ID tomorrow. Can you help me?"

There was a moment of pause and then he answered, the judgement now absent. "Of course, Cassandra. I hadn't thought of that. I'll have one delivered to you tomorrow morning. Do you need anything else?"

Even though I wanted to scream out a list of things I wanted, I knew it was a test. "No Grandpa, just the ID. Then I promise I'm on my own."

"I'm proud of you, Cassandra."

Pride swelled inside me to hear those words. "Thank you, Grandpa. I'm learning a lot."

"Good. Now, what name do you need for the fake ID?"

Pausing to fight the lump returning to my throat, I took a breath. "Cassie Sinclair."

Silence hung in the air and then I heard a soft sigh on the other side. "Your parents would be proud."

"Thanks, Grandpa. I'm trying."

"I love you, Cassie."

"I love you, too."

We hung up, and I sat in silence for a moment before turning the key and listening to the engine chug back to life. With his money and connections, I had no doubt I'd have an ID by morning. Now I needed to go home and sit on my phone googling drink recipes and how to tap a beer. Tomorrow I started my new job.

CHAPTER FIVE

Cassie

"Hey, Cassie!" Jo called when I stepped inside the Blue Ox. "Perfect timing. There's no one here so I can show you around."

"Hey, Jo. I'm excited to get started. Here's my ID." When I held it out, my mind drifted back to when I was seventeen and used a fake to get into a club for the first time. My heart had hammered in my chest while the bouncer gave it a once over, much like it hammered now when Jo took it from me.

"Awesome. I'll make a copy and you can fill out your W-4."

W-4? What the hell is that? "Great."

"So, this is the place. It's looked the same since I used to come here with my uncle when I was a little kid. Though, the saddle stools are newer." She pointed to one of the bar stools crafted out of a western saddle. "And they made a little loft not long ago. But other than that, nothing changes, except we add a few more trinkets to the walls every year."

I wondered how that was possible since there was barely an inch not covered with some strange memorabilia. As she took me around giving me the rundown of the history and nuances, I noticed even the bar had stuff in it. Underneath a thick coat of lacquer were historical photos from Baileys

Harbor with captions retelling the history. License plates lined the walls just below the ceiling, and when I turned around, I clutched my chest in surprise when I came face to face with a creepy white rabbit mask hanging off a nail.

"You get used to it all." Jo had noticed my frozen face and continued on the tour. Even though it was still light out, the bar was aglow not from the sunlight but from the video games and gambling machines scattered around the corners. It helped while I tried to read all the bumper stickers, and I realized by the end of my time here, whenever that was, I probably still wouldn't have seen everything in this bar.

"It's haunted, but nothing bad will happen. Just weird stuff sometimes."

"What?" That little tidbit of info had me ready to run out the door.

"Nothing to be scared of, but sometimes things get moved when you're here alone. Just last week I heard a clatter in the kitchen and found things scattered all over. I was here by myself."

Swallowing hard, I tried to keep from letting my bulging eyeballs pop out of my head.

"There's a haunted trolley tour that comes through a couple nights a week and you get to hear all our haunted history. It gets really busy really fast, so I won't put you on those shifts until you're ready."

"A haunted trolley tour?" The hair on the back of my neck stood up, and I felt like eyes were peering out of the knots in the few spots I could see in the wooden walls.

"Really good money, though."

"Mmmhmm." I swallowed, remembering that money was why I was here. *You need this job, Cassandra,* I thought while I kept myself from bolting past Captain Bailey and out the front door, picturing ghosts hot on my trail. Then I pictured him coming to life, turning his creepy head to look at me and a shiver snaked down my side.

"And this is bimini." She pointed to the bull's head with a hook on its nose mounted to the wall. "You grab this string with the metal ring and try to swing it and catch it on the hook." Grabbing the string dangling from the ceiling she stood back, pulling it tight, then let it loose. The little silver hook dipped low while it swung and then rose and landed on the bull's nose.

"Whoa," I said, impressed with her skill.

"I've been here for six years. Lots of practice." With a grin she took me behind the bar. "Tap beers are here, bottles in the coolers, cold shots in this one, and we've got the booze here, here and here."

Following her pointing finger, I tried to make sense of everything and keep up.

"Cash register is easy. No computers here. Price list is there." She pointed to a yellow sheet of paper with some prices jotted down beside the alcohol names. "Just take their money, hit these buttons to total everything up, then this one when you're done." When she pushed the last button, the drawer popped open.

"Menu's easy, too. Just burgers, cheese curds, onion rings, and stuff. No need to memorize fancy specials at the Ox."

Cheese curds? What the hell is a cheese curd?

It hadn't occurred to me I'd be serving food. I hoped my years of ordering at restaurants would give me enough of an idea of how to play the part of the person taking the order instead of the one giving it.

The door swung open and an older man wearing a flannel, torn jeans and a Packers hat sauntered in and slid into a stool at the end.

"Hey, Larry," Jo said, and he greeted her with a grunt. "Grab him a draft of Bud Light, would ya?"

I thought back to the tutorial I'd watched last night on pouring beers and saw the handles sticking out of the counter. Grabbing a glass from the mat in front of me, I lifted it to the spout.

"What are you doing?" Jo asked, and I turned to face her. "That's a rocks glass. Beer goes in pint glasses." Her arched eyebrow made me feel about two inches tall.

"Right. I did know that. It's just my friends like their beer in these glasses," I lied. My friends would never drink beer. "Sorry."

"No worries. Just grab one from there." She pointed to the taller glasses, and I grabbed one then put it under the tap spout. Finding the blue handle marked Bud Light, I slid it over and pulled. Golden liquid poured out and landed in the bottom of the glass. Instantly white foam started creeping up and soon it was ready to overflow with the bubbles.

"You need to tip the glass," Jo said, and I turned to see her and Larry exchange a look.

Tip the glass! Damn it! I knew that! It was part of the lesson I'd watched on YouTube last night and already forgotten.

"Oh, yeah. Sorry, been awhile," I said and heard Larry snort.

"Gotta break the new 'un in, eh, Jo?"

"Apparently I do," Jo grumbled, and I could hear the irritation slip into her voice.

Dumping out the foam and starting over, I angled the glass like they showed me in the video and tried again. The beer slid down the side this time, and instead of white foam, the golden liquid rose toward the top. When it got as high as it could without spilling, I brought it straight up and pushed the tap handle back. A perfect glass of beer.

"I did it!" I cheered, stopping just short of jumping up and down so I didn't spill the beer.

With a huge grin celebrating my accomplishment stretched across my face I turned to Jo and Larry and held it in the air like a prized trophy.

"Congratulations?" Jo said, and I realized the experienced bartender I told her I was wouldn't think tapping a beer was worthy of a celebration akin to climbing Mount Everest. Trying to stifle my excitement, I carried it over with care and set it in front of Larry. "Here you go. That'll be four dollars."

Grey bushy brows snapped together, and he shot Jo a look. "Seriously?"

"Sorry, I didn't tell her yet. Locals don't pay as they go. You start them a tab and they pay when they're done."

"Oh, sorry," I said, my excitement deflating beneath Larry's stare.

"She just started fifteen minutes ago, Larry. Give her a break."

"What the hell's the fun of breaking in the new help if I can't give 'em a hard time!" The anger in his eyes subsided and mirth replaced it. "I'm just shitting you, kid. Welcome to the family."

"Oh," I breathed, then smiled. "Thanks."

"Jo here's a good shit. She'll teach ya right."

"Thanks, Larry. Wish I could say the same for him, but he'll never stop giving you a hard time."

A gruff laugh filled the empty bar then dissolved into a coughing fit.

"Quit smoking, Larry," Jo chided.

"Quit yapping at me like you're my wife," he snarled back. They both smiled, and I realized their banter was playful. "I'm goin' out for one. Save my seat."

"Will do, Larry," Jo answered.

When he carried his beer outside, Jo turned to me and cocked her head. "You've never bartended, have you?"

Biting my lip, I shook my head. "No. I'm sorry. I'm so sorry but I really need this job. I promise I can learn."

With a huff she tossed up her hands. "It's fine. But you'd better learn fast. Pretty soon this place will fill up and I won't have time to hold your hand. I wish you would have told me, and I would have had you come in earlier to train you more."

"I'm sorry, Jo. I didn't think you'd hire me."

"It's fine. I need the help. *Any* help. Just pay attention."

For the next hour she gave me a basic rundown of how to count the alcohol while I poured, how to work the soda gun and the other basics I would need to know. Some of it I knew from my crash YouTube studying, but letting her in on my secret helped shed some of the stress I felt starting my very first job. At least now the only thing I would need to keep from her was my identity.

Sweat beaded on my brow while I struggled to keep up with the orders getting called over the bar. Jo was right. The bar went from empty to packed in under an hour. Locals bellied up to the bar and tourists flocked in, each oohing and aahing over the same décor I'd been gawking at earlier. The ring continued flying through the air while bimini games caused laughter and good-natured taunting between friends. Pool balls clanked together, and the gambling games chirped in the corner, adding to the music pouring out of the old jukebox. It wasn't like any club I'd been in, but the same energy pulsed through this old bar.

"Another Bud Light, Cassie!" Jo called. Since I had no experience mixing drinks, she'd put me on beer duty while she did the heavy lifting. Moving faster now that I was learning where things were, I grabbed a bottle from the cooler and slid it into the bottle opener nailed to the side of the bar. With the flick of my wrist the top popped off. I was still struggling not to cheer and clap for myself every time I accomplished the smallest thing.

"Here you go!" I said, setting it in front of her while she shoveled ice into glasses.

The door swung open again, and I groaned when I saw more bodies pushing in. We were already so busy. There was no way Jo could keep up on her own and I felt guilty for lying to her and putting her in this position. Money waved at us while everyone vied for our attention, each desperate to be the next served.

"I can make drinks, too, Jo."

"You sure?"

"Yes. I've got this." Remembering I had an MBA before I got sidetracked, I knew I could figure this out.

"Who's next?" I shouted, and the money flapped harder.

"Spotted Cow!" A woman called, and I laughed. My first official order and I was back to tapping beer.

Once I'd filled it and rang up her money, I turned around to the next person who'd just sat down. A camouflage baseball cap was tipped over his face, and he stared at the bar, elbows resting on the jagged wood.

"What do you need?"

Slowly his head rose, and a pair of icy blue eyes appeared underneath the brim of his cap. When they clapped onto mine, the intensity inside them forced me to step back, and I bumped the rack of glasses behind me, sending one to the floor. With a gasp I turned and watched it bounce across the floor, exhaling a deep breath when it rolled to a stop unbroken. Snatching it up off the floor, I fumbled while I set it by the dishwasher. When it was safely in place, I looked back up to see those translucent blues still watching me.

Those eyes. Not only were they beautiful, they were familiar. Something in them resonated with me, but the face surrounding them wasn't one I'd seen before, and definitely one I'd never forget. That rugged jawline and those firm lips would have been the envy of every photographer in New

York. With his broad shoulders, straight nose, and those piercing eyes situated beneath contrasting dark eyebrows, all I'd need to do is strip him of his camouflage outfit, toss him in a suit and he could own any runway at Fashion Week.

"Uh, hi," I stammered. "I, uh, I... Can I get you a drink? Rusty nail? Bay Breeze? Alabama Slammer? Greyhound?" I started nervously rattling off the four drinks I'd memorized last night after searching "Drink recipes every bartender should know."

Those eyes impaled me while he studied my face. The muscles around his jaw tightened momentarily, and I waited for him to speak.

"Whiskey coke," he said, his coarse voice caressing the simple words. With a face and a voice like that, maybe movie star made more sense than a fashion model. How a man with features like that was sitting at a bar in Wisconsin and not at a swanky club in New York was a question I didn't think I'd ever find an answer to.

"Sure, yeah. Coming right up." I started away then paused, lifting a finger to my chin. "Wait, what's all in that? Just whiskey and coke?"

One of his dark eyebrows rose. "Yep."

"Oh, yeah. Makes sense." *Come on, Cassie!* Flustered from the way he looked at me, I felt my face heat to boiling. It wasn't that he looked at me like most men did, like someone they wanted to take home and screw. There wasn't lust inside those eyes watching me, but a sadness that permeated the air around him. It settled around him like a cloak and I could see the sorrow brewing in those eyes before he dropped them back to the bar. It seemed as if it pained him to look at anything. Especially me. When the brim of his hat covered his face, part of me wanted to reach out and take it off. I hadn't quite had my fill of the show.

Grabbing a tub, I filled it with ice and worked my way down the rail until I found the whiskey. Counting to three like Jo taught me, I poured it over the ice then picked up the soda gun and aimed it into the glass. Pressing the button marked "C" I watched red liquid shoot out.

Cranberry juice. Damn it! C is for cranberry not Coke, I remembered too late. Looking over, I saw him peek out from under his cap just in time to see me mess up his drink. With cheeks flushing even hotter from embarrassment, I dumped it out and got a new glass, repeating the process and this time pressing "P" for Pepsi. After I'd successfully made my first drink, I carried it toward him, moving behind Jo while she finished up her own drinks. She spun around fast and collided into me, sending his drink pouring down the Blue Ox tank top she'd given me to wear.

"Shit!" she called out, covered in some of her own drinks. "You've got to say 'behind' anytime you move behind me, remember?"

"I'm so sorry!" I said, remembering those instructions that must have flown out of my head that was bursting with new information.

The man at the bar stared at me again and then at the mostly empty glass I still clutched in my hands. When our gazes locked again, flashes of the unique eyes belonging to the mystery man in the funny suit hovering over me invaded my mind. Those were *his* eyes that had stared at me when he saved me from the snake. Even though his face had been covered with paint and his body covered in camouflage fur, I knew those were the same eyes now. My savior. I knew him from the snake incident, and that's why I didn't remember his face. It had been covered in black and green paint. Recognizing him sent me backward a step again, and I bumped into the glasses. Again. Two tumbled to the ground, and I cringed when I heard them shatter.

"Seriously?" Jo shouted over her shoulder and I cringed a little more.

"Sorry!" I said, but my eyes moved back to his. The heat that had already been building in my cheeks rose to unbearable levels. I worried my skin would slough off at any moment.

"Brooms by the register!" Jo shouted.

"Sorry," I whispered to him while I raced by and grabbed the broom. But his eyes were already back on the bar, his shoulders slumped while he sat in silence.

Hurrying to clean up my mess, I swept the glass into the pan and dumped it in the garbage. When I was done, I made him a new drink and carried it across the bar with the same care I would as if it were a bomb ready to detonate at any moment. After I set it down in front of him, he glanced up and gave me a gratuitous nod before sliding it into the camouflage cocoon his body made over the bar with the way he hunched.

As much as I wanted to keep drinking in my fill of those eyes and that face, I was grateful he'd stopped watching me now that I had to start taking more orders. After several more messed up drinks and a few more irritated groans from the customers, and I was still struggling to make sense of this whole bartending thing. It was a *lot* harder than I'd anticipated and I had a whole new respect for the bartenders who'd kept up with me and my friends all those years. After one more glance at the solemn man at the bar, I pulled my eyes away and took my next order.

CHAPTER SIX

Jake

Of all the things I expected to see at the Ox tonight, the woman from the cabin working behind the bar wasn't one of them. It seemed she wasn't some weekend tourist after all. If she'd gotten a job here, that probably meant she was staying. I wasn't sure if that was a good thing or a bad thing. On one hand, at least it meant there wouldn't be a steady stream of strangers next door each weekend. On the other, it meant my summer solitude had just gone up in a puff of spilled beer and broken glasses. Taking a swig of my whiskey and coke, I peeked up to watch her again.

I may have sworn off women completely, but I'd be a liar if I didn't admit how good she looked fumbling back there behind the bar. Those jeans hugged every curve of her slender legs, and when she'd bend over to fill the glasses with ice, that low scooped tank top gave me a peek of the breasts that filled it out damn well. The long, blonde hair that had cascaded down her back when I'd arrived was now pulled into a ponytail after she'd gotten frustrated fighting it a few minutes ago. Even though she didn't look as out of place as she had stuck in that step, she still didn't look like the kind of girl I'd see behind the bar at the Ox. And from the way she struggled to make drinks, it looked like she'd never been behind a bar in her life.

"What's all in a gin and tonic?" I heard her ask Jo.

Pursing my lips together, I tried to stifle my smile waiting for Jo's response. Ever since we were kids, Jo had a mouth on her and when I saw her face drop at the question, I held my breath for the incoming storm of words.

"Seriously? What's in a gin and tonic? Um... gin and tonic! Come on, Cassie! Have you ever even *had* a drink?"

Cassie. So that was her name. When Jo snapped at her, those green eyes of hers shot to me rather than to Jo. A pink hue rose in her cheeks and she dropped her eyes back to the ground.

"Sorry, Jo. Stupid question."

"Yes. It was a stupid question. He told you the ingredients. Remember? Gin and tonic is gin and tonic. Captain and coke is Captain and coke. Whiskey and coke is—"

"Whiskey and coke," Cassie answered like a scolded child.

"Good!" Jo chided, and I felt a little sorry for the poor girl. Jo always meant well, but she was all business and when the bar was overflowing with thirsty customers, she didn't have the patience to hold the hand of the new girl.

The ice in my glass clinked against my teeth when I slid the last of my drink out. After I set it back on the bar, I slid it forward toward the rail. Cassie appeared in front of me, and I looked back up from the spot on the bar I spent most nights staring past my pain.

"Another?" she asked, and those emerald eyes locked onto mine. The feeling that surged through me when our eyes met filled me with as much anger as it did some other feeling I was having trouble identifying. It was the same one I'd felt when I first saw her behind the bar tonight. The anger came from the fact I didn't want to be having pesky feelings about some girl. The last time I had feelings about a girl ended up the reason I was sitting here drinking pissed off and alone, and intending to keep it that way.

I gave her a quick nod, and she picked up my glass and turned to fill it. Before she made it a step away, she spun back around. Uncertainly filled her eyes while she chewed on her lower lip.

"Sorry. What was it again?"

"Whiskey coke."

"Oh, yeah!"

"That's whiskey and coke mixed together," I added, unable to stop myself from a little good-natured jab.

A soft smile lifted her full red lips and her chuckle induced a small one in me. It startled me to hear myself laugh. It'd been awhile. Struggling to suppress my smile, I lowered my eyes back to the stain on the bar I stared at every evening I came in for my two drinks after work.

Even though I tried not to look, I couldn't help peeking up to watch her fill up my drink. Something about her stirred something in me, and I grumbled again at myself for allowing myself to feel it. Miserable and alone. That's how I planned on spending my remaining days. Well, hopefully the misery would pass sooner or later, but the alone I fully intended on hanging on to.

When she returned with my drink and set it down, I gave her another nod and forced my gaze to stay on the bar. Nothing good could come of looking into those eyes. Nothing good at all.

After standing in front of me for a moment, she moved on to the next customer and I exhaled a deep breath. If she'd stood there any longer, I'd have been tempted to look back up at her. And if I looked back up at her that damned feeling would invade my misery again. I wasn't ready to stop feeling miserable, so I did my best to ignore her.

"Hey, Jake," Jo said while she blew by.

"Hey, Jo."

"Those guys bought you a drink." I looked up to the end of the bar where she pointed while she tapped a beer. I'd taken those two guys out on a fishing trip earlier. They both waved and still wore the same grins they'd had stretched across their faces since they each pulled in the two biggest salmon of their lives.

With a nod and a lift of my glass, I thanked them for the drink. The hundred-dollar tip they'd given me was more than sufficient, but I'd take another drink as well.

"Thanks, Captain Jake!" They lifted their beers toward me, and I heard them start recounting the tale of their trip to the men gathered around them. *Free advertising*, I thought when all eyes turned toward me. Not that I needed it this time of the year. My charters were booked up weeks in advance.

When I looked away, my eyes drifted back to the blonde behind the bar. Damn those jeans were making looking away more difficult that it should be.

"What's up?" I heard Aaron's voice and turned to my left. He pushed into the space between the stools and leaned up along the bar beside me.

"Hey, man. Not much. Finishing up and heading home."

"Catch anything today?"

"Oh, yeah. We had a good run."

"We got skunked."

I sucked the air through my teeth. "Damn. Hate when that happens." Aaron ran his own charter as well, and we'd been buds since middle school.

"Yeah, it does. But still sucks."

"I got skunked a few trips ago. Happens to the best of us."

"You saying you're the best?" He raised a blond brow in a challenge, but his blue eyes could never hide his humor.

"Damn straight." I took a swig of my drink and he burst into laughter.

"Whoa," he said, his laughter stalling in his throat as his gaze stared behind the bar. "Who's the hottie?"

A surge of jealousy rose inside me when I saw his eyes fixated on Cassie. Surprised by the sudden emotion, I cleared my throat. "New girl. Just started today. I think she's my neighbor."

Wide eyes stopped devouring every inch of her figure and he spun back toward me. His mouth, situated between his scraggly strawberry-blond beard, was open when he looked at me. "Seriously? She's your neighbor? Dude! I'm coming over! And bringing binoculars!"

"You're such a perv." I rolled my eyes, but it reared its ugly head again. Jealousy.

"Dude! Look at her! How in the hell does a girl that looks like that end up here?"

"Hey!" Jo said, catching the end of our conversation. "I'm a looker, too. And don't you forget it."

He scoffed. "You're like our sister. We're not allowed to ogle your goods."

"Even if you can't ogle 'em, doesn't mean I don't have 'em." She smiled and shook her ass.

Aaron slammed his eyes shut and tossed his head back like she'd smacked him in the mouth. "Knock it off! That's like incest!"

Jo waggled her brows and went back to work. The men on all sides of us didn't seem to mind her impromptu show.

"Who's got dibs on the new girl? I don't want to fight you for her. I mean, I know not many women can resist this face of mine," he said, waving his hand over the face so covered in hair I barely remembered what he looked like under there, "but let's be honest. If she's anything like every other woman around, she'll be throwing herself at you in no time."

Snorting, I almost spit out my drink. "I don't think so, man."

"Really? Are you trying to say women *don't* throw themselves at you?"

"Not really."

He rolled his eyes. "Whatever you say, man. Hey, Jo!" he called. "Beer me!"

"Hold your horses, Aaron! I'm busy!"

The door opened, and a gaggle of girls dressed in hot-pink wigs and white sashes stumbled inside.

"Dude! A hot new bartender and now a bachelorette party? Can my night get any better?" Aaron spun around and gave them his best smile.

"Lucky you."

"Lucky *us!* There's like six of them."

"All yours," I said, turning my attention back to what I came here for.

Whiskey.

Loneliness among friends.

Pain cloaking me like pleasure.

"Come on, man." His voice softened, and he turned back to me. "You gotta snap out of it. It's been months. It's time to get back on the horse."

"No horse. No more riding for this guy."

"Jake. Get on the fucking horse. Like six of them just walked in and I bet you could ride any one you wanted!"

"Dude, you're disgusting."

The pack of wasted women moved through the Ox, turning the heads of every man they passed. I made the mistake of looking at one, and the whole group turned toward me like a school of fish. "Fuck."

"What's that about you not having women throw themselves at you?" he said while they came at me.

"Shut up, Aaron."

"Hi!" The one wearing the maid-of-honor sash said when she stumbled up to me. "You're hot!"

"As I was saying?" Aaron whispered, but I shrugged him off.

"What's your name?" she asked, but I turned my back to her and focused on my whiskey. When she tapped me on the shoulder, I tried to shrug it off, but looked up to see Cassie staring at me. Not wanting her to think I went for every cheap piece of ass, then wondering why I cared what she thought, I plucked the woman's hand off my shoulder and brushed it aside.

"Oh, come on!" she said, pressing her breasts into my back while she leaned into my ear. "We just need a pair of underwear for our scavenger hunt." A hiccup broke up the last word.

"You can have mine!" Aaron said, squishing in between us.

"We want his," she whined, but I continued ignoring her and caught Cassie's quick glance with my own.

"Dude, I gotta go." I slammed the rest of my drink and set it down. "Jo, I'll tip you later. I'm outta here."

"You got it. See you later," she called over the crowd.

Rising from my stool, I tried to push through the group of women surrounding us while Aaron flirted with each one of them. As I turned toward the door it opened, and the face I never wanted to see again appeared. Rage rose inside me like an inferno burning away all my good senses. This was *my* bar, and he knew it. The Cornerstone was his, and this one was mine. Just because it'd been months since it happened, didn't mean he could pretend away his betrayal and waltz back in here like we were still best friends.

"Oh, shit," Aaron mumbled when he saw Matt in the doorway, and he moved in front of me. "Jake. Dude. Jake, look at me."

I couldn't look at him. When my gaze locked with Matt's, red swirled before my eyes. I didn't care that I saw remorse mirrored back at me. I didn't care that he'd tried to call and apologize a hundred times. To care, I'd have to give two shits. This was the first time I'd seen him since it happened and the emotions I'd felt back when I found out flooded back into every cell with the force of a hurricane. Before Aaron could get ahold of my shirt, I flew across the room.

"Jake!" I heard Jo shout, but it didn't slow my charge.

"Jake, I'm sorry. Jake!" Matt said just before I collided with him. We tumbled onto chairs by the window and landed on Captain Bailey, the stuffed mannequin taking up the middle one. Patrons launched out of the way as I let my rage rip out of me. My fist connected with his face three times before I felt someone stop my arm from making it four. Hands gripped me, and I struggled against them until too many arms wrapped around me and dragged me off him.

"Jake! Stop!" Jo yelled, though it was hard to hear her with the ringing in my ears. "Get him out of here!"

"Jake, come on!" Aaron was part of the group of men wrangling me to the door. I gave up my fight against them, but my glare found its way back to Matt's bloodied face once more before they got me outside onto the sidewalk.

"I'm fine!" I shouted, shrugging off the hands still pushing me along. With rage still radiating off me, I stormed away. As I reached the Beachfront Inn across the street, I spun back around, my gaze fixated on the Blue Ox while I contemplated racing back inside to finish what I'd started. If looks could kill that building would be enveloped in flames, a fiery inferno that still wouldn't compare to the fury inside me.

"Jake, Jake, JAKE!" Aaron clapped his hands in front of me to get me to refocus. "Dude! Calm down!"

Deep, quick breaths lifted my shoulders while I huffed, feeling the adrenaline still coursing through me. When he grabbed my shoulder, I shoved it off and practically snarled.

"Whoa. Jake. Come on, man. What the fuck? This isn't you."

"He had it coming," I growled.

"I know he did. And I feel for you, I do. But you can't just launch across the bar and kick his ass every time you see him. He's a douche, but he's allowed to live."

"It was the *first* time I saw him. He had it coming." How we'd made it this many months in a small town without running into each other was a wonder, but from what I'd heard he'd been avoiding me like the plague. Which was probably a good thing since I still wanted to kick his ass months later. If I'd seen him right after it happened, I'd probably have killed him.

"Okay. You saw him. You kicked his ass. Now it's time to move on, man. I'm worried about you. We're *all* worried about you."

"I'm fine." The adrenaline subsided, and my hand throbbed from the punches.

"You're not fine. I mean, you've always been a broody son of a bitch, but you're downright depressed. And I get it. I do. But it's time to get on with your life, Jake. And you both live here. You're going to run into him. You can't beat the shit out of him every time you see him or I'm going to be bailing you out of jail. Okay?"

He was right, and I knew it, but I just stared back at the bar that housed Matt inside.

"Okay?" he asked again.

"Okay," I finally answered.

"No more kicking the shit out of Matt. No more moping. Deal."

It had felt good to punch that asshole, but it didn't erase all the pain he'd caused. Deflating like a balloon, I felt the remaining rage seep out of my system now and even though I never wanted to see him again, I knew I could control the urge to pound his face in the next time I did.

"Fine."

"Good. Want to go to the Coyote Roadhouse? Cool off?"

"No. I just want to be alone," I answered and started off down the street.

"You going home?"

"Nope." I headed toward the docks to sit on my boat and calm down.

CHAPTER SEVEN

Cassie

"What the hell was that?" I asked Jo while we stared at the door they'd dragged him through.

"That was Jake Alton."

Jake. So that's his name.

"That guy screwed his fiancée." She pointed to the guy with the brown hair and brown eyes leaning on Captain Bailey.

"Shut up," I breathed.

"Yep. This spring. And that guy, Matt, the one who screwed his fiancée, was his best friend since they were in diapers. They were like brothers."

I looked again at him while he wiped a drip of blood from his nose. He would have been handsome if it weren't for the blood splattered across his already bruising face. Even though the two weren't brothers, they easily could have been mistaken for them. "Holy shit. That's awful."

"Yeah, it's really messed up. Matt's been hiding from him since it happened, and it's kind of an unspoken rule that this is Jake's bar, so he avoided it. Apparently, he thought it was safe to see Jake. It seems he thought wrong."

Very wrong, I thought remembering the way he'd launched across the room and the sound of his fist colliding with that guy's face.

"Where's the girl?" I asked, the thought of Jake with another woman not sitting well with me.

"Left. It wasn't the first time it'd happened, and everyone really loves Jake. We kind of drove her out of town."

"It wasn't the first time?"

"Nope. They'd been together since high school. She cheated on him senior year with some college dude and he forgave her. Then she went to college and dumped him, but she snagged him back every summer she came home. When she flunked out, of course Jake was there to take care of her, then she cheated on him again. It was a never-ending cycle."

"Seriously? Who is this bitch?" Anger seethed through me on his behalf. I had been cheated on before and knew how awful it felt. I couldn't imagine how hurtful it must have been having it happen again and again.

"Just some dumb girl he happened to fall in love with. I've never understood what was so special about her. She's gorgeous, but that's about all she has going for her. Even though you wouldn't know it from tonight, Jake's a sweet guy, and as loyal as they come. So, he forgave her when she popped up again last year, and this time slapped a ring on her finger. Then she went and banged his best friend."

"Wow."

"Yeah. Messed up."

"So, you ran her out of town?"

"Basically. We'd all had enough of her shit, so we made her life a living hell until she tucked tail and ran. Good riddance. Hopefully she stays gone. Lives in Chicago now from what I hear. Jake doesn't need to go through that shit again. But this time, since it was with his best friend, it really messed him up."

"I can't even imagine. Poor guy."

"Poor guy is right. They don't come any better than Jake Alton. I grew up with Matt, too. He, Jake, and I were best friends since before we could walk, but after what he did to Jake, I'm not even going to bother tossing him a clean rag for his nose. Asshole."

Matt took the hand of a man who pulled him up. Silence still settled over the once-lively bar and he started toward the door.

"I wouldn't do that, Matt," Jo said, shaking her head. "Jake's still out there." She looked out the window, and I followed suit, then saw Jake storming away.

Matt dabbed the blood on his split lip. "Sorry about that, Jo. I didn't think that was going to happen."

"You didn't think what would happen? That Jake would kick the shit out of you the first time he saw you after you screwed Nikki? Wow. Shocker." Jo rolled her eyes.

"I didn't—never mind." He sighed, and his eyes heavy with sorrow dropped to the floor.

Jo peeked out the window again. "He's gone. Now get the hell out of here and don't come back. You dug your grave, now get inside and stay there, dick."

Even though I knew what he did and found it despicable, the sadness pulling the corners of his eyes down almost had me feeling sorry for him.

"Sorry, Jo," he said on a sigh while he moved to the door.

"Whatever, Matt. Just don't come back. This is Jake's bar."

Nodding his head, he ducked out the door. I saw him pause, likely checking to make sure the coast was clear. Who could blame him? When I'd seen Jake stand up, the size of those biceps was unmistakable even underneath his camouflage pullover. Standing well over six feet tall, he'd towered over Matt just before tackling him. Matt hadn't stood a chance against Jake's size, strength, and the rage that nearly blew apart the bar.

"Dick," Jo added when the door closed behind him.

"So, you're friends with Jake?" I asked, hoping I didn't seem too interested.

"Yep. We've been best buds since we were kids. He's a great guy. One of the good ones. Figure that means he gets his heart stomped on."

"Jo!" A guy with an bushy orange beard said when he came back into the bar. I recognized him as the guy who'd been talking to Jake before the fight.

"Is he okay, Aaron?" she asked when he arrived at the bar.

"Yeah, he's fine. Physically at least."

"Poor Jake."

"I'm worried about him, Jo."

"Me, too. But we'll get him through this."

They both noticed me standing and listening, and two sets of eyes turned toward me.

"Aaron, Cassie. Cassie, Aaron." Jo introduced us.

"Hi," I answered.

"Hey, there." A familiar smile lifted his lips. *There*. That was the look most guys gave me when they saw me. The "take me home and screw me" look. It was the look that was strangely absent from Jake's face when he'd watched me tonight.

"Can you go clean up the mess they made?" Jo asked me, and I nodded.

Grabbing a bar rag off the counter, I walked through the Ox. Most of the tourists bolted after the fight, leaving only a couple dozen stragglers behind. After straightening up Captain Bailey, I wiped the spilled drinks off the chairs and picked up the bottle of beer that hadn't survived the fight. Looking out the big window over-looking the street, I saw Matt standing alone on the sidewalk. Once again, I felt sorry for him, but then remembered what he'd done to Jake and shook my head, returning to the bar to go screw up some more drinks.

"Listen, it's pretty slow now. Why don't you head home for tonight and we'll pick up where we left off tomorrow?" Jo said.

Hearing those words nearly sent me crumbling to the ground in a puddle of relief. Everything hurt. My feet swelled within my Prada shoes, my thighs burned from squatting up and down to open the coolers, my back screamed for Eloise, my masseuse, and my fingers were red and swollen from opening cans of beer all night. Even though I worked out daily in New York with Alex, my trainer, I'd never been this sore in my life. Bartending was exhausting, and I wondered how many nights I could do this before my body just gave out and Jo found me unconscious on the floor.

"Are you sure?" I asked, holding my breath and hoping she didn't change her mind. The bar had never recovered after the fight, and now that it was eleven o'clock, I figured she was right and it probably wouldn't pick up again, but I wanted to be sure. I'd already pissed her off enough times tonight, I didn't need to do it again.

"Yes. It's kind of a weird night with the fight, so why don't you go home, and I'll close up. I don't want to overwhelm you on your first night. Especially since you've never bartended before." A dark eyebrow rose, and I shrunk a little beneath her accusatory stare.

"Okay, Jo. And I'm really sorry I lied. I was desperate."

With a playful roll of her eyes, she shook her head. "It's fine. I get it. And all things considered, you didn't do *too* horrible. Although I never thought anyone in the world actually thought we put real rocks in a glass when someone asked for something 'on the rocks.'" A smile punctuated the sentence.

Bursting into laughter at the memory of me asking her where she kept the rocks, I shook my head. "I promise I'm not an idiot, contrary to what it may have looked like tonight. I won't let you down, Jo."

"I know. Glad to have you on board."

Limping my way out of the bar, I climbed into the big brown beast I'd parked on the side street after I'd run home to let Poppy out during my break earlier. The engine sputtered when I turned the key and for a moment, I didn't think it would start. I tried again, and the engine roared back to life. Whispering a silent thank you, I put it in drive and started up the hill toward home.

As I drove across the causeway, my headlights flickered and went out. A moment later the car lost power, and I screamed while I slammed on the brakes and steered toward the side of the road. When I puttered to a stop, I put it in park and tried starting it again. Nothing happened when I turned the key and panic rose in me while I tried again.

"No, no, no, no, NO!" I cried out then gave up my fight to get the old girl going again. "Shit."

Looking around and trying to remain calm, I searched the soft glow of the streetlights illuminating the causeway. It was pitch black everywhere those lights didn't touch, and I pulled out my phone to call for help. Dead. Of course it was. I remembered I'd forgotten to charge it before I left for work and it died halfway through my shift.

Feeling like I was back in that horror movie I'd starred in when I arrived at my cabin, I sat for a moment debating what to do. With no phone to call for help, a car that wouldn't start, and my cabin a good mile-walk away, I thought about hunkering down here until daylight. Unless, of course, a serial killer's face popped up in my window just before he stabbed me to death. Once that visual got in my head, my heart raced while my gaze darted to all my windows, each time thinking a sinister face would meet my eyes even though he hadn't been there a second ago.

With panic guiding me, I whipped open the door and started out of the car to run home. Then I remembered my swollen feet and realized how painful every step home would be. If walking home on swollen feet wasn't enough to stop me, picturing a car pulling up beside me and dragging me inside to transport me to the dungeon in their basement did the trick. With that new visual in my head, I slammed the door shut and ducked back inside my car. *Stay here and get slaughtered*, I thought while I peeked in the rearview expecting to see a murderer's face or run home and get kidnapped on the way. A frustrated squeal squeezed past my closed lips as I pondered each future, but then I remembered Poppy.

Worry that a bear or some other predator would break into the house and eat her while I was gone, I'd locked her in the bathroom with no windows and set her up on a big bed of cashmere sweaters with a bowl of food and water. It'd been four hours since I'd been home, and I knew she probably needed to go out. Without Lily to let her out, I knew she was depending on me. Taking a deep breath, I grabbed the door handle and opened the door. Poppy needed me, and I would have to take my chances with getting kidnapped to get home to her.

Stepping out, I winced when my swollen feet touched the ground. Making a note to order shoes like Jo's as soon as I got a paycheck, I started one painful step after another toward my cabin where Poppy waited. The still air and chirping of some creatures near the water were the only sounds filling the night while I walked. Part of me found it peaceful to be out here all alone without the constant buzz of traffic and voices that echoed through the streets of New York. The other part of me was near paralyzed from the feeling of being truly alone. That and the fear that the car carrying my kidnapper would come down the road at any moment.

Just as I made it off the causeway, I saw a set of headlights coming up behind me. *The kidnapper.* Of course. My heart hammered in my chest while I ran in frantic circles under the streetlight trying to figure out where to hide. A tuft of weeds on the side of the road caught my eye, and as the headlights got closer, I dove into them. With a grunt I landed in the dirt, and curled up into a ball, covering my head with the long weeds as the vehicle came by. The engine slowed, and I heard the tires grind to a halt on some loose stones.

I'm spotted! Reaching into my purse, I fumbled around and got ahold of the mace I carried on my key chain. When I heard the door open and footsteps start up, I flicked the lid off my mace and held my finger on the button. With fear coursing through my veins, I crouched low, ready to attack and hoping those self-defense classes I'd taken with Liza had stuck.

"Are you okay?" a deep voice called, and I crouched lower. Not wanting to give away my location, I remained silent. "Hello? Cassie? Is that you?"

He knows my name? A shiver snaked up my spine. I was being stalked. By a gritty voiced psycho kidnapper rapist killer stalker. Whoever he was probably messed with my car so it would die. I've seen Dateline NBC. With visions of horror movies flying through my mind, I held my breath and prepared for a fight. I wasn't going down easy.

Never, ever let them take you to a second location.

"It's Jake. From the Ox. The whiskey and coke guy. Are you in the weeds? Cassie? I saw you."

Jake? Now recognizing his voice, I peered out from my vegetation fortress and saw him standing beside a giant black truck. The headlights illuminated him, and he shielded his eyes while he stared at me.

"Jake?"

"You okay?"

"Um, yeah," I answered, standing and smoothing the dirt from my knees.

"Is that your car?" He pointed down the causeway to the hunk of junk dead on the side of the road.

Even though I didn't want to admit it was mine, I nodded. "Yeah. It's mine. It just stopped."

"I'm surprised it ever started." He snorted and eyed the broken metal heap with disdain.

Horrified at his observation of the state of my beast, I cracked a shy smile. "Yeah, it's not in the best shape."

"Why are you in the weeds?"

I started out of them, climbing up the small incline back onto the road. "I thought you were a kidnapper or a serial killer, so I hid."

"A serial killer? In Door County?" He chuckled, shaking his head.

"You never know," I argued, finally making it back onto the road. "Haven't you seen any horror movies?"

"It's Door County. I *do* know." The laughter hovered just under his words. "There's no serial killer here."

"Well I didn't know that. I'm from the city."

"Well, I'm from a small town. When people in small towns stop to offer you a ride, they aren't serial killers. They're just, you know, nice people."

Feeling embarrassed for my irrational thinking, I shrugged. His eyes dropped to the little pink cylinder in my hand. My thumb still hovered over the button at the top.

"Were you going to mace me?" he asked, and a smile played on his lips.

"Sorry." I gave him a close-lipped grin while I snapped it shut and put it back in my purse. The smile starting on his lips faded, and he shook his head.

"Come on, I'll give you a ride." With the nod of his head, he gestured to the passenger side of his shiny black truck.

"Are you sure? I don't want to be a bother."

"We're neighbors. It's fine."

Neighbors? I thought while I walked to the truck. That would explain why he was in my yard. Opening the door to the truck, I paused for a moment while I tried to figure out how to get in. It was so high off the ground the seat came up to my boobs. Jake hopped in with ease and looked over to see me hanging on the seat trying to pull myself up.

"There's a step-side you can stand on."

Looking down I saw the metal bar that had been banging my shin while I tried to scramble up. I stepped on it and grabbed ahold of the handle above the door and pulled myself in. Landing with a grunt, I blew out an exasperated breath while I settled and took in the contents of the truck. Piles of camouflage clothing, tackle boxes, and a giant plastic deer head littered the black upholstered back seats. "This thing is huge!"

"Yep," he answered as he put it in drive.

"It's nice," I kept on.

"Yep."

"You okay after that fight? It was pretty crazy."

Silence was his only answer and the sullen look that seemed to be his permanent expression only deepened. *Not a man of many words*, I thought to myself when he started driving. I realized I shouldn't have asked about the fight, so changed the subject. "So, we're neighbors?"

"Yep."

"How long have you lived here?"

"My whole life."

"Oh yeah? I just moved here."

"I figured," he said, and I saw his lip quiver like he wanted to smile but it stiffened again. Betrayal had stolen his smiles. That thought sent a ripple of sadness through me.

"Yeah, I suppose you would have noticed having a neighbor sooner." I had to stop myself from slapping my forehead. It had been a long time since a man had me so unglued and I was unraveling by the second while we drove down the road. "You're Jake, right?"

"Yep."

He'd already said that when he got out of the truck and I felt even dumber. "I'm Cassie." It wasn't so much a lie, since my nickname *was* Cassie, but it felt wrong introducing myself to him with a name I hadn't used in a decade.

"I know," he answered, and I fought my inward groan. Of course, he did. He'd said that when he pulled up as well.

"I'm up for the summer just trying to make some money. Jo gave me the job at the Ox. It was my first time bartending."

"I figured," he said, and that lip lifted just a hair again. But no smile formed while we turned onto my road.

The more I talked, the quieter he got, which made me nervous, so I talked more. "You said we're neighbors? Where do you live? Like right next door?"

"Yep."

"Cool. It's pretty on the lake. My cabin leaves a lot to be desired, but I'm trying to fix it up. Hey, thanks for the save from the snake and the porch, by the way. That was you, wasn't it?"

"Yep."

"Well, thanks. If you hadn't come, I was sure it was going to strangle me while I was stuck in that step."

He snorted. "It was a pine snake, not a boa constrictor. It was just trying to get out. You weren't in any danger."

"Oh," I answered, and wished that I could say *something* right. Why was he so intimidating? I mean he was hot, like stupid hot, but I'd spent a lot of time with celebrities, models, and other hot guys and none of them had gotten me this flustered. However, none of them had been mutes, so there was that.

He turned the truck down my driveway, and we wound through the trees until his lights shined on my little cabin.

"I really appreciate the ride. My feet hurt, but I really had to get home to Poppy, so I was walking."

"Poppy?"

"My dog. You saw her the other day."

He snorted again and something resembling a chuckle slipped out. "I don't think you can call that thing a dog. It looks more like a squirrel mated with a bat."

"Hey!" I laughed and crossed my arms as we pulled to a stop. "She's beautiful! I tell her that every day."

"Looks more like Musky bait than a dog."

"Musky bait? What's that?"

"A Musky is a fish and some people use small animals as bait to catch them. She looks like she'd be the perfect size."

My mouth dropped open, and I struggled to respond. But then I saw a glimmer of mirth flashing in those blue eyes lit up from the dashboard lights. "You're a dick. She's *not* Musky bait! And what kind of person fishes with live animals? Disgusting!"

"I'm teasing. I never would, and I think it's just an old wives' tale that people do, but she certainly would fit the bill."

"That's beyond awful."

"Yep."

After getting a few full sentences out of him we were back to one syllable again. Damn it. I found I enjoyed multiple-syllable Jake much better.

"Well, thanks again for the ride. I appreciate it. Now I need to figure out what to do with my car tomorrow. I don't even know how this works. I've never had a car break down before."

"Never?" His brows snapped together.

"No. What do I do?"

"Kiehnau's in Baileys Harbor can probably grab it for you. Otherwise call Kenny at Sister Bay Automotive. They're both honest and no one will rip you off. Just tell them you're on the Kangaroo Lake causeway and they'll grab you with the tow truck and give you an estimate to fix it."

An estimate to fix it? As he said it, I realized I didn't have any money to pay for a tow truck *or* the repair. I'd made almost a hundred dollars in tips tonight, but that probably wasn't enough to get much fixed, and I needed to buy more food. "Do you think it will be a lot? I don't have much money right now." I chewed on my lip.

"I'm not sure. They won't rip you off, though."

"Okay," I answered, but even if they didn't rip me off, I still had no money to pay. "Well, thanks again for the ride."

"Yep."

I opened the door to the truck and looked at the sizeable drop to the ground. Trying to maneuver my feet to the step, I hung on the handle above my head. When I let go and stepped on the metal sidestep, the pain in my feet from the pressure hit me like a bolt of lightning. I shrieked as I tumbled out of the truck, landing with a grunt.

"Ouch." I groaned as I pulled myself up out of the gravel and used the open door to haul myself to standing.

"Are you okay?" he asked when I made it into view.

"Oops," I said with a bashful shrug of my shoulders. I prayed it was dark enough he couldn't see the crimson blazing heat across my cheeks.

After a moment of staring at me his lips twitched, but this time, instead of stiffing into a frown again, they drew into a huge grin. He did have teeth. Nice ones, too, I noticed while he flashed a smile so charming, I could almost feel my panties drop. The smile widened as he burst into laughter.

It started as a soft chuckle just shaking his shoulders and then grew into a deep belly laugh that shook his whole body. Palming my face, I couldn't help but join in on his contagious laughter. The brooding, quiet man had a laugh that made me dissolve into hysterics.

"That was so embarrassing!" I said between laughs.

"Not as embarrassing as asking what's in a whiskey and coke!" he added, his own laughter rumbling as loud as his big truck's engine.

"Shut up, Jake!" I said and laughed even harder.

"Or getting stuck in your porch when you thought a harmless pine snake was going to kill you!"

The shroud of sadness that had been wrapped around him slipped down even further. I stood in the truck's doorway struggling to breathe while we laughed together, memories of all the embarrassing things he'd already witnessed me do flooding back into me and fueling the laughter. "I'm just gonna go inside and die of embarrassment now if you don't mind."

"Try not to get stuck in your stairs," he added, then choked on his laughter.

"Good night!" I laughed and slammed the door, sealing him and his laughter inside.

While I hobbled to my cabin on painful feet, he idled in the driveway and kept his lights on until I made it safely over my broken stair into the front door. After opening the door, I turned around and gave a wave into the bright lights. I couldn't see him in there, but I imagined he was still laughing at me. As soon as I closed the door, I heard the truck drive off and I peeked out between the plaid curtains and watched his taillights disappear around the trees.

Poppy barked, and I ran over and opened the bathroom door I'd sealed her behind.

"Hi, Princess Poppy! Mommy worked a *job* tonight! Can you believe it?"

She launched into my arms and covered me with kisses. While I enjoyed her kisses immensely, I wondered what kind of kisses could come from the man with a smile that still had my stomach doing cartwheels.

CHAPTER EIGHT

Jake

I maneuvered Cassie's car into her driveway and stopped before I got to the cabin.

"What the hell am I doing?" I asked myself while I sat there with the engine rumbling louder than my truck. Considering I had special pipes put in for sound, that was saying something. It had taken a little more than an hour to get the thing running again, but now that I'd done it, I wondered why I had.

"You're just being nice, Jake. Doesn't mean anything," I reminded myself, remembering the worry in her eyes when she'd said she didn't have any money to fix it. After getting up early and taking a drive to the causeway, I'd popped the hood to see if I could fix it and save her a few bucks.

But now that I sat here in her car, my lies to myself that it meant nothing, and I'd have done it for anyone wore thin. Everyone didn't have eyes like that. Everyone couldn't make me laugh for the first time in months. Everyone didn't have a smile that flooded me with a warmth I never thought I'd feel again or had felt that intensely before for that matter.

She certainly wasn't just anyone, but it's what I kept telling myself and intended to keep doing so.

Because lying to yourself is safe.

When I pulled in after fixing her car, she was going to think I was nuts. Probably rip out her city girl mace again. Who drops everything to help a stranger? Considering backing out of the driveway and leaving it where I found it miraculously fixed, I decided to just drop the car in the driveway and hike back to my truck on the causeway. She'd find it here and just think some good Samaritan had brought it to her. *Perfect*, I thought while I started forward.

The loud engine shook, and I cringed, letting off on the gas while trying to keep it quiet so I didn't wake her. It was only seven in the morning, and if I wanted to get out of here undetected, I'd need to quiet this death-mobile down. But even at a crawl, the engine was probably waking the entire neighborhood. Hell, at least this thing would scare all those damn coyotes off.

Pulling up around the corner, I saw her little shack ahead. Still trying to keep my approach a secret, I rolled to a stop and put it in park. When I turned off the key a loud backfire exploded and echoed through the woods.

"Shit." I closed my eyes, hoping it would make me and this hideous car disappear. When I opened them again, I saw her face appear in the window. *Busted.*

The front door opened, and she stepped out. Pink satin pajamas hung loose off her figure, but even from here I could see she wasn't wearing a bra. The sight of her in a messy ponytail and cute outfit brought back that infuriating feeling that shot my racing pulse out of the starting gate.

"Jake?" she asked from the doorway, folding her arms across her chest and covering her breasts.

There wasn't any escaping unnoticed now. With a deep sigh I opened the door and stepped out. "Hey, Cassie. Sorry I woke you. I was just going to drop this off."

"Did you fix my car?" she asked while she stepped onto the porch and started down the stairs, careful this time not to fall through.

"Um, yeah," I said, sliding my hand behind my neck. Was I sweating? If it weren't for the dew still on the cold ground, I would have tried harder to pretend it was the heat causing me to perspire.

"Oh, my God. I can't believe you fixed it."

"Oh, it's not a big deal. I just figured I'd take a look."

"Not a big deal? Are you serious? You fixed my car! You're my hero!" She launched herself forward and threw her arms around my neck.

The feeling of her body against mine startled me, and I froze while she pressed into me. That racing pulse she induced took off like there was a Formula One car flying through my veins. With my breath trapped in my lungs, I stood unmoving while she squeezed me tight.

"Thank you. Thank you so much," she said, and her breath brushed across my neck. Goosebumps pricked on my skin and I closed my eyes while a surge moved through my whole body. For a moment I let myself sink into her embrace and my arms started closing around her without my permission. But then my brain turned back on and I dropped them to my sides and pulled back out of her arms.

"It's nothing. No biggie. Easy fix."

She stared at me and I saw the hurt flash in her eyes. Damn it, I hadn't meant to make her feel bad.

"Sorry. I just got excited."

"No, it's fine. I just... not a big hugger."

"Of course. My bad. Didn't mean to attack you." A sweet smile tugged up her lips.

"Don't apologize. It's me. And I'm covered in grease." I lifted my hands, blackened from working on her car, grateful for the extra excuse why I didn't dare hug her back. We stood together in the awkward silence until I shrugged. "Should be working now. Spark plugs and battery needed a little work. I wouldn't go too long without getting into a mechanic for new ones, but this should tide you over for a while."

"Thank you, Jake. Seriously. You're a lifesaver. You have no idea."

"No problem. I'll see you around." I turned and started down the driveway.

"Are you walking back?"

"Yeah. My trucks on the causeway."

"No way. You are *not* walking after fixing my car! Let me grab Poppy and I'll drive you back."

"It's fine. I like walking." Really, I just didn't want to be near her any longer. It was getting harder by the second to keep those feelings she elicited at bay.

"I'm driving. Stay. Put. Give me one second!"

Before I could argue she spun around and ran up the stairs. The way her ass looked in those pajamas had me biting my lip and tugging at my hair while I spun in circles debating running off down the driveway. But not wanting to look like even more of an asshole than I already did after hug-gate, I waited. A minute later she popped back out still wearing her pink pajamas and holding a dog in her arms. She'd added fuzzy brown boots to her wardrobe, and I was disappointed when I noticed she'd also added a bra. Didn't matter, I reminded myself. I wasn't interested in her that way, no matter how good she looked both in and out of that bra.

"Come on!" Her cheery voice called from the car before she climbed in the driver seat.

With a deep breath I walked around it and climbed inside. A little brown dog, smaller than most cats, trotted across the bench seat and climbed into my lap. Giant googly eyes stared up at me, and erect ears folded at the top stood a little taller while she examined my face.

"That's Princess Poppy."

"Well good morning, Muskybait," I said to the strange little creature staring me down.

"She's not Musky bait!" Cassie scolded then laughed. "She's a princess. Aren't you, Poppy?"

Hearing her name had the little dog wiggling in my lap. "What happened to her face? She looks like she ran into a wall at full tilt."

"It's supposed to look like that!" she said while she started the car. "She's a smooth-coated Brussels Griffon. That's what they look like. And I think she's beautiful. Aren't you, Poppy?"

The engine roared, and I exhaled a breath that my repairs still held steady. "I still think it looks like a bat and a squirrel had a baby."

Poppy did a little circle then curled up on my lap. Furrowing my brows, I looked down at her then over to Cassie, who appraised the sight of us with a wide grin.

"She likes you."

"It would seem she does," I answered, then gave Poppy a little scratch behind the ears.

Cassie drove the car around the turnaround, and we started back down the driveway.

"Your truck is on the causeway?"

"Yeah."

"I really can't believe you did this. You've got a knack for saving me. You must think I'm such a mess."

"It's fine. I'm honestly surprised I got this thing working again. Where in the hell did you even get it?"

There was a moment of hesitation, then she answered. "My grandpa."

"Did he get it when he was a teenager then hand it down to you?"

"It's not *that* old. At least I think it's not." She laughed, and I joined her. The same shock I felt when I'd laughed last night hit me again. How was it she could inspire laugher in me with such ease after so many months of not even being able to smile?

One look at Cassie and I was spitting out smiles like a malfunctioning ATM.

"This interior is... wow." I ran a hand over the orange velour.

"Shut up, I know!" She laughed harder and my own smile grew with hers. "It's so ugly!"

"It is *not* the kind of car I would picture someone like you driving."

"Someone like me?" she asked, glancing over.

"Um, yeah, you know..." *Hot. Gorgeous. Stunning.* "A woman," I lied.

"A woman?" Her dark-blonde brow rose in a challenge. "You think because I'm a *woman* I can't handle this massive machine?"

Ugh. I'd just dug myself a grave I didn't know how to get out of. "No. Not that you can't *handle* it, but that you wouldn't *want* to drive it. I figured women care more about their cars than men. This looks like something my buddy Aaron would drive. Hell, the interior matches his beard."

"I met him last night!" she said, and I was grateful she let go of the subject so quickly. "Nice guy."

"Yeah. He is. We've been buddies for years."

"That's what Jo said. You all grew up together?"

They'd talked about me? I wondered now how much they'd told her. I hoped not everything. Being cheated on was embarrassing enough and having the hot new girl view me as a pathetic loser wasn't a pleasant thought.

"Yeah, we did. We all went to Gibraltar from kindergarten straight through high school. Jo's like a sister to me, and Aaron... well, he's like the weird uncle no one invites to Thanksgiving."

Laughter erupted from her and it coaxed it out of me again. God it felt good to laugh again. I'd almost forgotten how mine sounded.

When we reached the causeway, I saw my Tundra parked on the side of the road. A couple fisherman had taken up posts on either side and they cast into the still water. I was going fishing today, but it involved taking a group of four guys out on a charter. I wished I could spend the day on the causeway just snagging fish solo and enjoying the solitude like these lucky bastards. But that wouldn't pay the bills and I still had a mortgage and a few truck payments left before it all belonged to me. At least a charter on the lake looked a hell of a lot better than sitting in an office in the city all day. The thought of living in a congested city overflowing with people made my skin crawl, and I counted my blessings a hard day at work for me involved fresh air, a boat, and fishing.

Cassie pulled to the side of the road opposite my truck and put the car in park. "Do I owe you anything for fixing it?"

I snorted. "No. Of course not. I wanted to."

"Well, then you need to come into the Ox tonight and at least let me buy you a couple drinks. It's the least I can do."

"Considering I stop there every day on my way home from work, I guess I'll be taking you up on that."

"Okay," she said, and that sweet smile sent my stomach plummeting to my feet again.

Damn it.

"Okay."

"I'll see you tonight then?"

"Yep." With a quick nod I started out of the car but then remembered the nearly weightless dog on my lap. If Hank sat in my lap, all one-hundred pounds of him would have crushed my femurs. "Oops. Sorry, Muskybait."

Lifting the little ball of fur off my lap, I handed her to Cassie. When she took her from me, our fingers brushed, and it felt like a sledgehammer slammed into my stomach. From the look on her face I could see she felt it, too. Desperate to get out of this car and away from this woman, I spun away and whipped open the door. Moving so fast, I almost tumbled out myself, but unlike her performance last night, I managed to stay upright. Without a word I slammed the door and hurried over to my truck. I could see her watching me until I made it into the driver's seat. When I gave her a quick nod, she drove away, and a black plume of smoke kicked out behind her car. The sight of that beautiful woman in her pink pajamas driving off in the ugliest car I'd seen in my life brought another unwanted smile to my face.

Damn it.

CHAPTER NINE

Cassie

"What do you think, Poppy? Too much?"

Her little head tipped to the side while I did a spin around in the outfit I'd picked out to bartend in tonight. Jo had given me a couple Blue Ox tank tops to wear but said I could wear whatever I wanted. Knowing Jake was coming in tonight, I wanted to wear something to make him sit up and take notice, so I'd torn through my suitcases to find just the right outfit.

"I can't believe he fixed my car," I said to her then flopped on the pink chenille blanket I'd used to cover the hideous couch. A little hop had her in my lap and I scratched under her chin. "Can you believe it?"

When I'd heard incoming fire this morning, I'd run to the window expecting to see another one of those non-existent Door County serial killers standing in my yard. But instead of the masked man sporting an arsenal of weapons I'd envisioned, my car had greeted my eyes instead. And Jake.

He'd emerged from the mud-colored monstrosity, flipping my stomach around when I'd seen him, and sending my heart racing like the first plunge down a rollercoaster. But what did it mean that he'd fixed my car? Was it really something he'd have done for anyone, or did it mean something more?

Unsure how to read the intent behind those brooding eyes, I decided that it *had* to mean something. He'd gotten up early and spent his time and energy fixing my car. Maybe it was just a small-town thing, but in New York if a man did something as chivalrous as fixing my car, it meant he was definitely interested. Although, honestly, no man I knew in New York could fix a car, and I didn't own one, but regardless I felt confident it meant *something*.

Or did it? My head spun again while I remembered how he wouldn't hug me back and how he'd shot out of my car like he couldn't get away from me fast enough. Maybe it was just me who'd felt something when we touched, and it was just me who came unglued every time our eyes met. Ugh. *He's so hot.*

Since I had no idea what was going on in his mind, I decided to pull out my big guns... the outfit that turned every head in New York when I went out in it. At the very least, it couldn't do any harm at feeling out his intentions... or perhaps swaying them to the side of wanting to kiss me. With only a few minutes left to get ready for work, I decided my outfit would be just the thing to get Jake to start looking at me like I was used to other men doing. At least I hoped it would.

After getting Poppy situated in her predator-proof bathroom fortress, I buckled the straps of my stilettos around my ankles then cringed when I stood up. The pain searing through my still-sore feet sent me tumbling back down onto the couch.

"Ouch," I breathed while I blew through the pain and stood again. *Fashion first*, I reminded myself and remembered the many times I'd chosen fashion over comfort. *It's worth it*, I thought while examining how good they looked with my outfit and how stellar my legs looked when they were perched on top of four-inch heels. Next week I'd get some of those comfortable black shoes Jo swore by. But tonight, I was going to get Jake's attention, and unless he was blind, this outfit would do it.

Trying not to limp, and forcing my body to accept my painful decision, I climbed into my car and drove to the Ox. When I walked in, a half dozen locals were already belly up to the bar and Jo leaned up against it chatting with them. The door closed behind me and every head turned toward me. One by one jaws went slack as the men at the bar raked me up and down. Jo's mouth dropped along with theirs, and the shock on her face had me reconsidering this decision.

A long, slow whistle broke the silence. "Is it a bachelor party? Are you the stripper?" A man I hadn't met yet, but who looked a lot like every other man at the bar in a faded t-shirt, jeans, and baseball cap said, wiping his brow. "I've got money!"

A stripper? Now I really questioned my red mini-dress while I stood in the rustic bar. Sure, I would have fit in at any club in New York, Paris, or Milan, but the way they were looking at me had me ready to turn and bolt back home to change.

"Wow," Jo said, shaking her head. "Are you planning on working in *that?*"

Biting my lip, I nodded. "Um, yeah. I guess maybe it's a little much?"

"A little *much*? It's a little... *little!*" She snorted.

Trying to force the blush from my cheeks I stood while they drank in every inch of the view this tight dress and plunging neckline offered them.

"Should I go change?" I asked, my confidence faltering to zero. Dressing like a runway model for a locals' bar was such a stupid idea. I'd have to add it to the list of my previous stupid ideas topped by that time I almost got arrested in Tijuana last year.

"No time. Happy hour starts in five. Just try not to break a heel. Or a leg." Jo gestured to my stilettos.

Feeling only an inch tall, even though I soared above her in these shoes, I walked behind the bar with her. Another slow graze over my outfit and she shook her head.

"You're something else," she said with a chuckle. "At least we'll make great tips. I may have to reconsider my own choice of footwear."

The door opened, and more locals filed in. One by one they slid to a stop when they saw me. A couple came in together and the woman took one look at me, then at her gawking husband, and dragged him out by the arm. Even though I'd felt like I could own any club in the world when I'd left my cabin, I now wanted to crawl into the beer cooler and stay there until my shift ended.

With no time to feel sorry for myself, I jumped into action as quickly as my heels would let me go. Jo called out the beer she needed, and I realized in an instant how difficult tonight would be trying to keep my ass covered while I pulled beer out of the below knee level coolers. This dress was made for standing and being appreciated, not a night spent bending and squatting. Cursing myself for not thinking this through, I tried to squat down while tugging at the bottom of my skirt with one hand and pulling out a beer with the other. As I looked behind me, I saw the neck of every man at the bar craning and their wide eyes staring at my ass. Each one looked ready to fall over the bar they were trying so hard to vie for a better look.

When I stood up without revealing the ass cheeks my lace thong would reveal, a long-conjoined groan rumbled through them.

"It's going to be a long night," Jo said while she blew past to deliver another drink.

After an hour of teetering on my too-tall heels and trying not to flash the bar every time I bent down into the coolers, the bar was still packed, but Jo and I had caught up. While she chatted up the locals, I slid a wet rag down the bar and wiped up the rings left behind by glasses. The door opened, and I looked up. Even beneath his hat with his head dipped low, I saw a flash of those blue eyes.

Jake.

He made his way through the small crowd and up to the bar. Only one stool remained open, the same one he'd been in last night. When he slid onto it, I wondered if he'd lain an unspoken claim to that particular stool, since there was an unspoken rule this was *his* bar.

"Hey, Jake," Jo said, and I wondered how the hell she could act so calm around him. Granted they'd known each other since they were kids, but I didn't think any woman could ever get used to being in a room with him without turning into a puddle of mush.

"Hey, Jo," he answered, then his eyes moved to me. His eyebrows shot to his hairline when he saw me, then he dropped his gaze back to the bar. "Hey, Cassie."

The confidence I thought this outfit would help me project came out as a whisper. "Hi, Jake. Whiskey and coke?"

"Yep." His eyes seemed to burn through the bar while he kept them forced down, when every cell in my body demanded that he look up.

That he *see* me.

Closing my eyes and wishing I could click my heels three times and go home, I waltzed my Manolo's over to the ice bin and filled up his drink. When I delivered it to him, he didn't even peek through the fringe of his eyelashes.

"This one's on me. Thanks again for fixing my car. I really appreciate it."

"Yep." His eyes remained glued to the dark stain beside his glass.

"You fixed her car?" Jo asked, as she dropped a drink to the man beside him.

"Uh, yeah," he answered.

"It broke down last night on my way home. Jake gave me a ride then fixed it this morning for me."

"He did, did he?" Jo arched a brow and smiled, her gaze darting between us.

"Yeah. It was really amazing of him."

"It sure was. What a guy. Pretty nice thing you did for her, huh, Jake?"

His hunched shoulders lifted with a sigh and I saw a smile tug on his lip. "It was nothing."

"Mmmhmm," Jo said, and her closed lip smile grew.

Scrunching my brow, I wondered what she was getting at. Jake's face slid further behind his cap while he lowered his head even more.

"How was work?" I asked, noting everyone at the bar had a drink so I had a few minutes to spare.

"Fine."

One-word answers again. Trying not to lose what little confidence I had left, I pressed on. "What do you do, anyway?"

"Fish."

"Fish? For a job?"

Another sigh lifted his shoulders and then his eyes rose. When they locked with mine, I reached out and grabbed the bar for support. Between my throbbing feet, these heels, and the way those eyes unraveled me, I was certain I was going down.

"I charter fish."

Three words! Progress! "What's that?"

He took a sip of his drink. "People pay me to take them out on my boat and fish."

"People actually get paid to fish?"

"Yep."

Damn it. One word again. "How long have you been doing it?"

He shifted on his stool and his gaze skipped to the side, like he searched for an escape. But instead of bolting out the door, he took a deep breath and his face softened, just like it had when he'd been laughing in his truck last night.

"Well, my dad used to take me fishing as a kid. He taught me everything I know. When I was a teenager, I was pretty good at it, so I got a job on a charter boat one summer. I worked with them every summer through high school, then full time after I graduated. Five years ago, the owner retired, so I bought his boat, got my Captain's license, and went out on my own."

That was like... I couldn't even count all the words. The mute man faded, and I saw a glimpse of the charming one I'd met for a moment last night.

"That's amazing. So, you own your own business?"

"Yep."

Not wanting to let him crawl back into his camouflage cubby and curl up over the bar again, I kept on.

"I've never been fishing."

"Never?" His eyes widened.

"Nope. Never."

"Not even as a kid?"

"Not even as a kid," I said. I didn't think there was a lot of fishing in New York, and it never even occurred to me to try.

"I've been fishing since before I could walk. Rarely make it a day without reeling in a fish. Or at least trying." One side of his lips lifted, and I watched to see if the other side would follow suit and give me a full smile. Even though they stopped just short, his half-smirk still had me grinning.

"Is it fun?"

"I think so. Relaxing at least."

"You should take her," Jo said as she passed by.

Both sets of our eyes shot over to her, and I saw the two of them exchange a glance, like a silent conversation was happening between them.

"I don't think so," he said, shaking his head.

"Why not? You fish every day. She's never been. You'll love it, Cassie, and you're off tomorrow night. I bet Jake is, too. Aren't you, Jake?" A sinister smile curved her lips.

"Jo," he warned, but she ignored him.

"You two will have so much fun! Pick her up around six?"

Daggers shot from his eyes and impaled her, but she kept grinning. They both looked at me and he shook his head, exhaling the breath he'd been holding. "Fine. I'll pick you up at six."

My eyes widened. Was this a date?

"Unless you don't want to," he grumbled.

I nodded my head. "Yeah. I want to. Why not? But only if you agree not to use my dog as bait." This little hiatus from my life *was* about trying new things, wasn't it? And getting to spend an evening alone with Jake had my heart racing even if the thought of touching a fish made my skin crawl.

"Then it's settled." A triumphant grin flashed across Jo's face and she gave him a playful glare before she walked down the bar.

"What should I wear?" I asked, noting I had no idea what one would wear out fishing.

"Not that," he answered with a snort and gestured to my dress with his drink.

"Shut up!" I retorted with a blush that heated my cheeks. "So maybe it wasn't the best outfit choice I've ever made."

"I'm surprised Jo let you work like that." He chuckled, but his gaze shot fire before he could mask it.

"I look that bad?" I asked, my prior shame crashing back into me.

"Uh, no. Not bad. Not at all, it's just... it's not... it's fine, I guess." His tumble over his words while his eyes locked onto my impressively lifted breasts refilled me with the confidence I'd been lacking. He *did* think I looked good.

"Well, at least I'm not wearing camo," I retorted and arched a brow.

"At least my outfit serves a purpose," he said with a brow that rose to challenge my own.

"And what purpose is that? I mean, it's not like you're in the woods. Though I do suppose you blend in pretty well here." I gestured to the line of men sitting at the bar also wearing camo from head to toe. "I'm surprised I can even see you, you stealth thing, you. Jake? Jake? Where are you?" I shielded my eyes and looked all around him.

His mouth opened, but no words came out. Then a chuckle shook his chest before another one of those contagious belly laughs I'd heard in the truck last night started up. Giving me a conceding nod, he lifted his glass. "Well played," he said between laughs.

While we laughed together, I glanced over to see Jo leaning against the bar, those dark eyes of hers watching us while a smirk played on her lips.

"Can I get a beer?" A man approached the bar, his "I Love Door County" shirt giving away his tourist status.

"Besides, my outfit serves a purpose as well," I said to Jake with a wink before sauntering away. Leaning against the bar, I gave the tourist a good, long look at my barely concealed breasts while I twirled a piece of my long hair. "What can I get you?"

"Um, a bottle of Spotted Cow." Drool practically slid down his chin while he swallowed hard.

Giving Jake a glance, I saw him watching me while I strutted across the bar. With a well-thought-out bend into the beer cooler, I arched my back while I pulled out a bottle. Slowly rising, I emphasized every asset while I slid back to standing, every eye in the bar caressed my figure. Jake sat with mouth agape while I delivered the beer and leaned over the bar again, biting my lip at my captivated customer. "That'll be four dollars."

After fumbling through his wallet, the man pulled out a twenty-dollar-bill. "Here. Uh, thanks. Yeah. Keep the change. Thanks."

"Thank you," I cooed, sliding the money off the bar.

When I walked away, I locked eyes with Jake and waggled my brows. The jealousy I could swear burned behind his eyes simmered down, and soon another laugh ripped out of him.

"See. My outfit serves a purpose. Making money."

"Indeed, it does." He shook his head as I strutted by. "Well played, again."

"Damn girl, you'd better wear that thing every night!" Jo laughed while she walked by. "We'll be retired in no time!"

"But not tomorrow night," Jake said, smiling. "You'll break an ankle fishing in those things." He pointed to my stilettos.

"I'll try to rustle up some camo."

With a deepening laugh, I saw him glance over to Jo. His face dropped and his laughter petered off when they locked eyes. I looked over to see hers still burning with satisfaction and then saw his cheeks turn a dark crimson. *Is he blushing?*

"Can I get you another?" I asked him, pausing while I watched her stare him down like a mother who knows damn well her son stole the cookies.

Standing abruptly, he shook his head. "No. I'm good. Gotta go."

"Good night, Jake," she crooned, as another knowing smile tipped her lips.

"Night," he mumbled then turned to me. "Thanks for the drink."

"Thanks for fixing my car."

"Don't forget to pick her up at six," Jo called after him as he headed toward the door. A quick nod of his head acknowledged her then he bolted outside.

I stared at the closed door for a moment after he left, then turned to Jo who stepped up beside me. "What the hell was that about?"

"He likes you." She smiled.

"He does?" My eyes bulged, and I struggled to suppress my own smile. "You think so?"

"Oh yeah. I know so."

Elated I'd made progress with my small-town hottie, my smile grew before faltering. "Wait a minute. If he likes me, then what's the problem? Why did he leave?"

"For Jake, it's a *big* problem. You're threatening to ruin his vow to be miserable and alone for all of eternity." She snorted and gave an exaggerated eye roll.

"Is that a bad thing?" I asked her, still unsure what had all transpired.

"No, Cassie. It's a good thing. That was the first time I've heard him laugh in months. You're good for him. It's a good thing."

"Oh," I whispered.

"Just don't break his heart, got it?" She turned to me and that playful glimmer that was in her eyes while she'd watched us had faded. That dark gaze bore into me while she stared me down. "He's a good guy. He's been dicked-around with enough, and he deserves someone who will treat him right. Break his heart, I break your face."

The power of her words sent me back a step, and I gulped while nodding. "Got it."

"Good." The playfulness in her eyes returned, and she exhaled a breath. "And seriously, don't wear those fishing tomorrow night," she said, pointing to my shoes.

"Okay," I said on a sigh, grateful she didn't look ready to kill me anymore.

I was going fishing with Jake. And I really had no idea what to wear.

CHAPTER TEN

Jake

After slamming my truck door, I pulled out my phone, clicked on Jo's contact and typed a text.

I am going to kill you.

When I looked back up into the window of the Ox, I saw her smiling out at me before she looked down. A moment later her response popped up.

Get over it. Time to get back in the saddle. You'll thank me later.

What the hell was everyone's obsession with getting me "back in the saddle?" My horse had bucked me off. Hard. Sometimes people got bucked off horses, realized it was stupid to do something that could get them killed, and never got back on again. Maybe I wanted to be one of those people. Those *smart* people. But when I looked back up into the window, I saw Cassie walk past in that dress and my stomach dropped to my feet again, just like it had when I saw her.

Sure, she looked out of place at the Ox in that slinky red getup, but I was certain my heart wasn't going to restart when I'd clapped eyes on her. Every incredible curve of her body was on full display and all I could think about was what she would look like without it. Even though I'd tried with every damn fiber of my being to ignore those feelings brewing inside me, her persistence and the way those eyes looked straight through me were like an icepick tapping away at my hardened heart. As quickly as I could patch an exposed hole, she made another.

Pick.

Pick.

Pick.

I still hate you. I typed back to Jo then started my car.

The kissy-face emoticon popped up just before I pulled out. Tomorrow I was taking Cassie fishing, and I already regretted my decision. Sitting across from her in a car or at the bar was hard enough. Spending an evening with her alone? Even my solemn vow to avoid women at all costs risked faltering under those emerald eyes.

The next night I tossed my extra rods in the car and whistled for Hank. He galloped up to the truck and launched himself inside when I opened the door.

"This is such a bad idea," I said to him while I closed him inside. "Can you believe I let a woman talk me into a date with a... woman?"

Hank gave me a slobber of solidarity. After climbing into the driver seat, I looked at the glowing clock on the dash. Five fifty-five. I was less than one minute down the road from her, but I didn't want to be late. But just before I tossed my truck in drive I paused. Being early wasn't a good idea either. Not only did I not want her to think I was eager, but Nikki always bitched me out when I was early. She always needed more time to get ready.

Nikki. Just having a flash of her face invade my mind had me ready to storm back in the house and forget this whole damn thing. It wasn't even that I was still in love with her. Hell, I didn't know if I'd ever really *been* in love with her. We'd just been together so long. Pretty much my whole adult life was spent in a relationship with Nikki, except for the half a dozen women I'd dated between Nikki's disappearances and abrupt returns to my life. I knew I was her fallback, the security blanket that covered her up anytime things went bad. When she'd flunked out of college, when her boyfriend had cheated on her, that time she'd gotten fired from her first job. Each failure sent her flying back into my arms.

And I'd been too stupid to keep them closed.

Each time she came back crying, my resolve to avoid her for eternity would weaken and I'd forgive her, unable to be the cause of her tears. And this last time, I thought maybe, just maybe, if I married her, we could stop the Ferris wheel of hell that had been our relationship. Up, down, on, off. I'd hoped that diamond ring would strap her in, and we could settle down and start the family I'd always wanted.

I'd known better. I did. But I proposed to her anyway. Then I got the call she'd hooked up with Matt. At first, I didn't believe it. Not because I didn't think *she* was capable of it, but because I never believed *he* would betray me. I shook it off, had a chuckle, and looked forward to meeting him for a beer so we could laugh about it. Small town rumors could often be entertaining, and this one was going to have me in stiches all night.

And then Nikki had showed up at the bar, big crocodile tears streaming down her face as she'd begged me to forgive her. Told me she and Matt had made a mistake and she was sorry. I didn't even let her get another word out. I'd just stood up and stormed out leaving her sobbing behind me. This time those tears weren't going to change my mind. As of that moment, we were officially done.

My entire world had shattered when she'd confirmed the rumor. It wasn't just the cheating from Nikki, again. This time she'd stolen something irreplaceable from me. My best friend. My brother. As much as I'd wanted to drive over and beat his ass that night, it was too hard for me to even see him again. I couldn't. My already decimated heart couldn't handle the regret I knew would be in his eyes. I didn't want her apologies or his. I didn't want him to say the right thing and make me forgive him. I just wanted to forget they ever existed. So that's what I did. Ignored the calls, deleted the messages, and put the word out that they needed to stay the hell out of my way, vowing I'd never put myself back out there again... open myself up to go through that kind of pain again. Yet here I was about to take Cassie fishing and unintentionally throwing myself back out there once more.

Putting my heart on the line right along with my bait on the hook.

The clock struck five fifty-eight, and I knew it was now or never. Even though she looked good... damn good... I hoped maybe we could be just friends. Jo was an attractive woman, and I'd never had feelings for her, so maybe, just maybe, I could think of Cassie like I did Jo.

"This is it, Hank. If I start looking interested in her, bite me. In the balls."

Hank clamped his mouth shut and tipped his head, his big ears lifting while he tried to interpret my words.

Tossing the truck in gear, I pulled down my winding driveway, turned left, then drove the twenty seconds to her gravel drive. When I made it to the end, I saw her big beast of a car parked in front of the house. It still made me chuckle every time I thought of her driving around in it. She must have been quite a sight last night in her fancy dress rumbling through Baileys Harbor in that car.

The front door popped open while I put it in park and Cassie stepped out. A relieved sigh slipped past my lips she wasn't wearing that dress that could unravel every strand of my resistance. But those tight jeans and t-shirt still had her looking so good I almost backed straight down the drive.

Go to the door and get her. I heard my father's voice scolding me and even though this wasn't a date, manners dictated I go up to the door.

A little wave greeted me while I climbed out of my truck. Hank hopped out behind me and his big, awkward strides sent him galumphing toward her.

"Oh my! He's huge! Is this your dog?" Cassie said while he bounced circles around her.

"Yeah, that's Hank." I stepped onto the porch.

The little creature she called a dog raced out of the house between her legs and yapped at Hank.

"Poppy! Oh, my God! Poppy!" Her panic was palpable as she tried to snatch her up. "Don't hurt her, Hank! Poppy!"

"He won't hurt her," I calmly stated, furrowing my brow at the panic sending her in circles after the little dog.

"She's not on a leash! And she's never even been to a dog park! Don't eat her, Hank! Poppy!"

"He's fine, Cassie. Just let them meet. Hank. Sit." Hank sat down and cocked his head while Poppy pounced around him. Mimicking his calm demeanor, I stood at his side while her dog settled down. The only one still frantic was Cassie.

"No, Poppy! No!" she screeched when Poppy leaned forward, a tentative touch bringing her nose to nose with Hank.

"Cassie." I laughed. "He's not going to eat her. Calm down."

Poppy dodged Cassie's next attempt at picking her up and her nervous barks transformed into playful yips. Hank looked at me for permission and I released him with a nod. Leaping up from his stay, he dropped onto his front legs and pushed his butt in the air. Startled by the sudden movement, Poppy skirted away, but then turned and faced him. His big tail wagged back and forth, and soon Poppy dropped down in front, mimicking his play bow.

"See, they're fine. Just let them be." I stepped to her side. Biting her fingers, she watched the two dogs frozen in a state of anticipation, each waiting for the other to make the first move.

"Are you sure he won't hurt her?"

"Positive. He's got lots of dog friends. Although, none of them are bat-squirrel crossbreeds."

A sideways glare met my eyes and even though it was only a second, and without the full weight of her gaze, I almost toppled off the porch. Damn. This was going to be a long night trying to resist the feelings those eyes induced.

Hank popped up and took off racing through the yard. Poppy shot after him and soon a game of tag ensued, each dog taking their turn tearing across the yard after the other. Little barks of happiness came out of Poppy's smooshed face, and Hank returned them with a big, loud *ruff*. The sound made Poppy turn and flee in fear, racing between Cassie's legs.

"Are you hurt? Is she hurt?" Cassie picked her up and turned her in all directions, looking for injuries that didn't exist.

"She's fine. Aren't you, Muskybait?" I scratched the little dog on the head.

"Her name is *Poppy*," she corrected with a playful glare.

"Hasn't *Poppy* ever played with another dog before?" Cassie shook her head, and I reared back in surprise. "Never?"

"No. I was too worried she'd get hurt."

"Wow. Hank loves playing with other dogs. I've even thought about getting a second one just so he could have a buddy."

Poppy wiggled in her arms, the shock from the big sound Hank made long forgotten.

"Poppy, hold still!" Cassie said, trying to restrain her.

"Just let them play for a minute. They were having fun."

Worry furrowed her brow, then she gave in and set Poppy down. The little dog took off after Hank and the game of tag resumed.

"You've really never let her play with other dogs?"

"No. I was too scared. I've never even had her off leash outside. I'm trying not to freak out."

"You gotta let her be a dog and have some fun, you know."

"She's not a dog. She's a princess." Her soft smile lifted those lips and when she looked at me, I felt her ice pick tapping away at my shell again.

Tappity – tap – tap. I wanted to take that damn pick and drive it so far into the ground the earth's molten core would incinerate it.

"You ready to go fishing?" I asked, dropping my gaze to my feet.

"I think so. Am I dressed all right?"

"You're not in stilettos like I was expecting, so I think we're good."

"Dick," she teased, and I chuckled.

"You want to bring Poppy? Hank loves coming along. He eats the guts."

Pulling a face, she shook her head. "God, no! I'll be worried enough about myself. I don't need to be worrying about Poppy falling in, too."

"That would be bad. You know, with the Muskies and all. Since she's—"

"Don't say it," she warned, fighting a smile.

"I'm just saying."

"Well, don't. Come on, Poppy!"

Her little dog ignored her and continued chasing Hank in circles. When she called again and got ignored, I snickered. "Hank, come." After skidding to a stop, he spun around the returned to my side. Expectant eyes stared up into mine waiting for the next command. Poppy followed him onto the porch and Cassie was able to snatch her up.

"We've never really worked on the whole commands thing." Cassie shrugged. "I like her to feel like she has freedom of choice."

Pinching my brow, I shook my head. "I like him to stay alive and having solid commands he listens to does just that."

"I suppose." She sighed. "Let me just lock her up."

"Lock her up? Does she destroy stuff?" I asked, wondering how much damage a dog that size could do. When Hank was a year old, he'd eaten a hole through my wall and most of a couch. What could Poppy really do? Nick a shoe?

"I lock her in the bathroom with a big fluffy bed since it doesn't have any windows. That way if a bear or a wolf or something breaks in, they can't get to her."

A lone eyebrow rose while I choked on my laughter. "What?"

She nodded, but I could see her losing her confidence in the decision under my stunned stare.

"You do know that's insane, right? And we don't have any bears or wolves for that matter. The only thing around here, besides Musky, that might take her are coyotes or maybe a hawk."

"See! *That's* why I lock her up!"

"In the history of Door County, no coyote or hawk has ever broken into a house and stolen a tiny dog." I snorted.

"Really? You're sure?" Those eyes searched mine and the child-like innocence inside them hammered away a little harder at my walls.

"I'm positive. She's safe loose in your house. Where the hell are you from, anyway?"

Silence settled between us for a moment.

"Um, Chicago," she answered then turned on her heel and went into the house. "Here you go, Poppy. You can be free in the house. Don't get eaten. I love you."

Peeking around the corner into her cabin, I watched her shower her dog with kisses. The state of the cabin surprised me as I looked around. Pink accents clashed with the brown and orange I imagined were there long before she moved in. The mismatched fabrics and colors made it look like she'd attempted to redecorate as best she could, and it only made her more endearing. Glancing to my right, I saw the open door to her bedroom and got a glimpse of the bed covered in soft pink blankets. While I wondered what she slept in, naked or maybe those cute pajamas I'd seen her in, the creepy owl lamp beside the bed made my eyes bulge.

"Ready!" she said, and I shook my head.

"How in the hell do you sleep next to that thing?" I jutted a finger at the owl lamp.

Sucking the air through her teeth, she shrugged. "Yeah. It's the creepiest lamp in the history of the world. But it's the only one in there and I don't have the money to get a new one. So, every night I have to sleep with that hideous thing lording over me."

"I'm a dude, and even *I* couldn't sleep with that thing nearby."

"It's rough." She laughed.

Trying to force the image of the distorted owl lamp from my mind, I helped her over to my truck. When I opened the door, Hank jumped in and settled into his spot in the middle. Cassie grabbed the handle above her head, and this time got in with less struggling. I was prepared to catch her in the event she tumbled out again.

"You in?" I asked before closing the door.

She smiled and nodded, so I closed the door and walked behind my truck.

"She's just a friend. Like Jo," I mumbled to myself before I made it to the driver's side.

But when I opened the door and she brushed a long, golden strand of hair from her face, an inward groan forced my eyes shut. That wasn't Jo sitting beside Hank in the truck.

Don't get on the horse, Jake. Don't get on the horse!

CHAPTER ELEVEN

Jake

"So, this is where we fish?" she asked after climbing out of my truck and meeting me on the causeway.

"It's one of the places I like to go."

Usually I fished Kangaroo Lake from my house just a little further up the lake. But the thought of bringing Cassie to my house had me thinking of bringing Cassie to my bed upstairs, so I opted to take her fishing on neutral territory. The fish biting from my dock would be the same fish that would bite over here. And over here there wasn't a bed.

"Remember when I thought you were a serial killer and I hid in those bushes?" she asked, bursting into laughter while she pointed to the bushes just down the road.

"I remember it well." I chuckled while I pulled the fishing poles out of the back of my truck. Man, she'd looked cuter than I wanted to admit climbing out of the ditch that night.

"You can use this pole. It's a little shorter so it will be easier for you to cast."

With Hank panting at my side, I handed her the pole.

"What do I do with it?" Nervous eyes looked at me as she held it away from her body, scanning it like it was the strangest thing she'd ever seen.

"Come here. I'll show you."

We stepped down the small embankment to the rocks jutting out along with causeway. After a quick assessment, I found the spot looking prime to snag a few walleyes.

"First, you can watch me. Then I'll help you. Okay?"

Nodding, she watched me unclip my lure from the eye of the rod. The tension in the line disappeared, and I cranked my reel until the line was the right length. Before casting, I looked to make sure she was a safe distance away and saw her scratching Hank's head. The way he stared up at her with stars in his eyes reminded me not to let myself stare at her that way.

She's just a friend.

Trying not to lose my concentration and attempting to extinguish the stars that sparkled momentarily in my own eyes while she scratched my big dog, I focused back on the lake.

"First, you're going to reel until you have about six inches of line hanging from the tip, just like mine."

She nodded while I gestured to the rod.

"Then you're going to place your index finger on the line right here and hold it tight. When you've got it secure, you're going to flip the bail. That's this thing."

Astute eyes followed my movements while I went through the motions I could do in my sleep.

"Now, keeping your finger on the line, you're going to look around you and make sure there's no one nearby you can snag. Me and Hank included." I smiled, and it prompted a giggle from her. "When the coast is clear, you bring the rod back to vertical, and in one smooth motion use your wrist and your elbow and cast it forward, letting go with your index finger when you're about half-way down."

"That sounds insanely complicated."

"It sounds complicated, but it's pretty easy once you figure it out. Just like this." With one swift move, I sent my lure sailing into the lake. The sound of the reel whirring was like music to my ears. That same sound soothed my soul and set my world back upright when life knocked it down. The plunk of the lure in the water sent ripples of waves extending out around it. I turned the crank, and it snapped the bail back into place. Another melody providing the soundtrack to my life.

Turning the crank, I brought my lure in a little faster than I normally would. This cast wasn't about catching the fish. I wanted to show her one more time.

I heard her crank spinning and turned to see her fumbling with her lure in a pile of line on the ground. Looking up at me, she sucked the air through her teeth.

"Oops."

"What happened to waiting for me to show you?" Laughing, I hooked my lure to the eye and set my rod aside. "You forgot to put your finger against the line to stop it from dropping."

"Well, shit," she said, and the swear word sounded cuter than it should coming out of her mouth.

I unraveled the line piled on the rocks and helped her set up the rod again.

"Put your finger here." I reached for her hand to guide it but froze when I thought about touching her skin. "There." I pointed instead, and she looked up at me.

"There?"

"Yep."

"Now, let me get Hank out of the way, then we can practice the motion of casting. Hank. Truck," I said. Hank hopped up from where he lay by her feet and leapt onto the open tailgate of my truck. It was a launch for him, and he scrambled to keep from sliding back down. "Good boy."

"He really listens well."

"He's a damn good dog. Now, let's see how well you can listen." I smiled.

"I'm all ears. Show me how to wield this thing."

While I talked her through it again, she hung on every word and practiced bringing the rod back to position and casting.

"Am I ready?"

"Only one way to find out."

Exchanging a nervous glance, I stepped out of the way. Since I taught people to fish for a living, I'd been on the receiving end of those hooks on more than one occasion and didn't feel like digging one out tonight.

"Here I go!" Grinning wide, she got into position. The rod came back and with the flick of her wrist it flew forward, but instead of a long, smooth cast, the lure snapped in the air and remained hanging from the tip.

"You forgot to release your finger," I said when she looked at me with confusion flooding her eyes.

"Oh, yeah!"

This time she drew back, but before she could cast, she released her finger too early and the lure dropped to the rocks behind her.

"Oh, no!" Laughter peppered her words while she looked at the mess behind her.

"It's okay. It takes a few times to get the hang of it."

"I'm never going to get it." A big pout pushed out her bottom lip.

Damn it. I knew what I had to do, but it made my stomach twist in a lethal combination of fear and excitement.

"I'll show you," I said on a sigh while I took her rod and cranked it back up. After getting the line the right length, I stepped up behind her. Trying not to brush up against her, I positioned myself with my arms along her sides and held the rod out in front of her. This next part was going to hurt.

"Wrap your hand around mine and put your index finger over mine. I want you to feel the moment I release."

While I held that rod for dear life with my arms around her waist, her hands found their way on top of mine. When her small fingers settled on mine, a surge of electricity traveled down my spine. A shudder followed, and I hoped she hadn't felt it.

Yep. This is downright torture.

As if I wasn't in enough agony feeling the soft skin of her hands caressing mine, she leaned back against me and our bodies snapped together like the last piece of a jigsaw puzzle. The top of her head rested just under my chin and her back pressed into my chest. Without my permission, my arms tightened around her body and she leaned in harder.

Oh, God.

Swallowing hard, I struggled to regain my composure. A soft breeze blew and the floral scents from her hair drifted into my nose and made me dizzy with desire. With sweaty palms, I struggled with my grip on the rod.

"Like this?" she asked while she slipped her index finger on top of mine. With a curious peek up from below me, our eyes locked. When I looked into them, I felt a strong current pull at me. Even though I fought against it, it sucked me under, and I got lost beneath the weight of her stare. And this time I didn't want to come up for air.

"Yes, like that." Her finger stretched as long as it could but only went half the length of mine.

"Now just keep your body relaxed and soft and move with mine."

I drew back the pole as she softened into my embrace, together we moved it back and forth until I felt like she had the motion down.

"Can you feel it?"

"I think so."

"Now, I'm going to cast, and I want you to pay attention to when I release my finger. Just keep yours soft and it will move with mine."

"Okay."

Together we cast out the line, and her finger released with mine. The lure dropped into the water and disappeared beneath the ripples.

"We did it!" she shrieked, turning her head up and beaming at me. That smile almost sent me tumbling in after my favorite lure.

"We did." I smiled back.

"Now what?"

"Now we crank. Put your other hand on the handle here."

Holding the pole tight, I braced while she turned the handle.

"Like this?"

"Perfect. Now it's all in the pace. Slow then fast. Keeping it changing, pause sometimes. You never know when a fish may be down there chasing it."

"Sounds like sex." She laughed.

Like I need any more reminders of sex right now.

"Yep." I swallowed hard. The tip of the rod wiggled. "We got a nibble! Keep it slow and steady now."

"A fish? There's a fish?" she squealed.

"Slow and steady." I cupped my hand over hers and together we turned the crank. "Get ready."

The tip dipped low, and I popped up the rod. The reel whirred as the fish ran and that sound normally got my heart racing. This time having Cassie in my arms had it pumping at full tilt before that fish even bit. It wasn't possible for it to hammer any harder unless I planned on dropping dead on the side of the road.

"We got one!" she screamed while she bounced in my arms.

"The key now is the tension. You need to keep the tension just right. Too much and you'll break the line. Too little and he'll slip free. When he runs, we let him. When he tires, we crank."

"Okay. This is *way* more fun than I was expecting!"

"Just help me keep the tension."

Something told me she and I would have no trouble keeping the perfect tension... as much as I tried to ignore it, God knows we had it in real life.

The minutes ticked by while we fought the fish. Together we held the pole and Cassie reeled it in.

"What kind is it?" she asked as the line got closer and closer.

"Probably a walleye. But could be a pike. And there's at least one huge sturgeon in here. Though if it was a sturgeon we would know. I caught it once. Son of a bitch gave me a serious run for my money."

With the sun setting and the darkness settling in, I wished I had my headlamp to shine on the water and get a glimpse of the struggling fish. As much as I was dying to see what was on the other end of our line, I didn't want to catch it and have Cassie's sounds of joy stop. Every time the fish ran, she squealed with excitement while I coaxed her into pausing her reeling and letting the fish get tired. The pitch of her squeals rose when the fish gave up and we started cranking again. As much as I enjoyed fishing alone, I had to admit, it was pretty fun reeling this one in with Cassie wrapped up in my arms.

There's a moment in every battle against a fish when I could feel it surrender. When I felt this one succumb to his situation, regret plucked at my heart that soon I'd have to release her from my embrace. Just as I predicted, the fish came in without any more of a fight. Taking a deep breath and one more inhale of her hair, I released my grip on the rod.

"Hold it steady while I bring him in."

"This is so crazy!" She laughed as I reluctantly backed away.

With the longing to press back up against her slowing me down, I moved to the edge of the water and grabbed ahold of the line. After a couple slow pulls, I saw the walleye rise to the top, and he put up no fight when I pulled him out of the water.

"Well done, Cassie! You caught your first fish!"

"Oh, my God! I did it! We did it!" She squealed again and the sounds of her excitement had me wondering what she'd sound like in bed.

Trying to force the recurring vision from my head of her writhing in my sheets, I lifted the fish triumphantly out of the water.

"What kind is it?" Wide eyes stared at the silver fish I held suspended by the gills.

"Walleye. A nice one, too! One of the bigger ones. Easily a five pounder. Atta girl!"

"It's a big one?" she asked, stepping closer to examine the fish.

"It's a really nice fish. It's going to be great for dinner."

"Dinner?" Her voice jumped several octaves.

"Yeah. Dinner. You know... to eat?" I set the fish down on the rocks and it flapped its tail.

"Wait! We can't *eat* it!" she shrieked, her eyes darting to the fish lying by my feet.

"Seriously? You don't want to eat your first fish?"

"No! Help it! Is it dead? Did I kill it?" Tears welled in her eyes and it felt like she had her hand wrapped around my heart instead of that rod.

"No. It's fine. Just resting."

"Put it back. Please! I don't want to kill it!"

Raising my hands, I nodded. "Okay, okay. Calm down. I'll put it back."

"Oh, my God." She bit her nails while I picked up the exhausted fish and plucked my hook from its mouth. "It looks dead. I killed it. I'm a monster."

With a deep chuckle, I shook my head. "You're not a monster. He's fine. He just needed a rest. It was a long battle on both ends of that line."

Holding the walleye gently, I lowered him into the water and held him upright.

"He's not moving!" She nibbled her nails faster.

"Just give him a minute," I said, giving her a reassuring look. Rocking the fish back and forth, I waited for the moment I knew was coming. Right on cue, the tail flicked, then his whole body exploded in movement sending water spraying. Releasing my grip, the fish darted out of my hands and disappeared beneath the surface.

"It's alive!" Jumping up and down, she clapped her hands.

When I turned to see her, the single tear sliding down her cheek dried before it made it off her chin. "I can't believe you made me let that fish go. That was a nice fish and would have made an excellent dinner."

"I just couldn't. After I looked into its eyes, I knew there was no way I could kill it. I've never killed a living thing before."

"You'd have slaughtered that snake if given the chance." I snorted.

"That was different! It would have been self-defense!"

"It was no more harm to you than that fish."

Furrowing her brow, she crossed her arms.

"So, it's going to be catch and release with you when we go fishing?"

"Yeah. There's no way I can kill a fish."

"That's too bad, because they are great eating."

"It's cruel!"

"Do you eat meat?" I arched a brow.

"Well, yeah," she said, losing some of her determination.

"So, you're not opposed to eating animals that spend their whole lives in captivity and are slaughtered, but eating a naturally caught fish or free-range animals that lived a good life is immoral?"

Her mouth opened, but she struggled to form words. Being a fisherman and a hunter, I'd been on this end of the argument enough times I was confident I'd win it.

"I love animals. I also enjoy harvesting them naturally rather than going to the store and buying a filet of fish from one raised in a glorified tank. Both my father and grandfather taught me how to humanely hunt and help with conservation. It's what I was taught, and I never saw anything wrong with it. I toss back any young fish, allowing them to grow and reproduce, I never shoot does, only aged bucks. And every fall, I take enough ducks and turkeys to keep Hank and I supplied all winter along with our venison and fish. So, unless you're a vegetarian, I think we can safely argue that eating a fish caught after a long, happy life in Kangaroo Lake is a lot more humane than eating one that had a life jammed into a container barely able to move, swimming in its own filth, fed an unnatural diet and loaded with antibiotics."

I waited for the argument I knew would never come. In all my years of having it, no one other than vegetarians had a leg to stand on. Arching a brow, I smiled. "Maybe you should let me cook you a wild-caught fresh fish and let me know what you think. You don't even need to see me catch it."

The minute the words came out of my mouth I froze, wishing I could shove them back in. Did I just invite her to dinner?

"You'll catch it and kill it humanely?"

I was nodding. Why was I nodding? *Stop it, Jake! Stop inviting her to dinner!*

"And I don't have to see it looking like, you know, a fish with eyes and stuff?"

"No faces. I'll have it fileted before you get there." I couldn't stop myself. The words that meant I'd be having dinner with Cassie at my house kept pouring out like I'd broken the faucet and the handle was stuck open.

"Okay. Deal." She smiled, and it sent my stomach tumbling into the abyss again. "I'm sorry I made you toss back dinner."

Laughing, I shrugged. "It's fine. I've got a frozen pizza at home."

"Frozen pizza?" Her nose crinkled up. "Now I *really* feel bad. Let me buy you dinner and a drink. A thank you for taking me fishing and an apology for making you put it back."

"You don't need to do that." My head was shaking back and forth, and I was grateful this time it did my bidding instead of nodding like I knew it wanted to.

"Please? I owe you. And honestly, I'm starving and have no food at my house."

Great. Now I would seem like a total dick if I said no. There it went, my head nodded before I'd given it the go-ahead. "Fine. We can run to the Pen Pub."

Her smile lit up the dark now surrounding us. "Okay."

With a heavy sigh, I gathered up our fishing rods and tossed them in the back of the truck. Hank hopped down and got in, situating himself in the center before Cassie jumped in beside him. After I closed her in, I grumbled at my loss of sanity while I made my way to the driver's side. Remembering this was all Jo's fault, I made a mental note.

Kill Jo after dinner.

CHAPTER TWELVE

Cassie

Jake jumped in the driver's seat and I tried to steal another look at him, but Hank's big head blocked the way. His long pink tongue lolled out while he panted, little drops of drool landing in a puddle at his feet.

"Where is this place?" I asked, craning my head around the big dog so I could see Jake's face situated underneath his camo cap.

"Just a mile up the road." Those blue eyes locked with mine for only a second, but it was all it took to send me back into a free-fall of desire. If you had told me a week ago I'd be lusting over a guy in relaxed fit jeans and flannel shirts, I'd have asked what kind of drugs you'd taken. But here I was, hot and bothered once again by the big guy in the big truck. Donovan wouldn't have been caught dead in a truck, preferring the limo or, on the rare occasion when he felt like driving, the Lamborghini.

Donovan. I'd barely thought of him since my talk with Grandpa. Knowing he was bad for me, along with the rest of my friends, I'd sent them all a message I'd be going away for a while, and out of touch. I'd ignored the few messages they'd sent asking me where, and eventually they'd disappeared. Even though I hadn't officially broken up with him, I hoped he'd gotten the hint. And knowing him, he already had a gaggle of girls crawling across his lap while he sat on his yacht somewhere in the Caribbean. Considering I never really cared about him, or any of my "friends" for that matter, it didn't bother me at all thinking he'd already replaced me. Now that I had some distance from them and a little clarity, I saw what my grandpa had pointed out. I saw how toxic they were to me, and how lonely I was even when they were with me. They weren't real friends, and I knew that now.

The truck started down the road and it rumbled through me, mimicking the vibrations that had traveled down my spine when Jake had wrapped his arms around me to help me fish. Being enveloped in his arms flooded me with a sense of security I hadn't felt since before I could remember. Safety lingered in his arms, a powerful protection paired with a chemistry I knew he couldn't deny. All I wanted was for that fish to fight me all night long so I could stay there just a little longer.

"What kind of cuisine do they have there?" I asked, peeking around Hank.

"Cuisine?" Jake arched a brow and stifled a smirk. "It's a bar. It's got great bar food, but it's not *cuisine*."

"Oh," I answered, feeling silly I'd asked.

"Where did you say you were from again?"

Shit. I knew eventually this would come up. Not wanting to lie, but also not having a choice, I stuck to the story I'd told him and Jo. "Chicago."

"Figures." He laughed. "That explains the aversion to nature, the dress, and the fact you're searching for *cuisine*."

"Shut up," I retorted, glad he didn't press it and ask for more information. This was one of those times I was glad he was the strong silent type.

We pulled into a bar and Jake hopped out. Unsure if I should wait for him to open my door, I fumbled to find the handle. Before I could get it open, he appeared in my window. My door swung open and he stepped aside while I climbed out.

A gentleman.

"Don't fall." That smile lit up his face.

"Shut up!" I laughed and landed safely on the ground.

"Hank, we'll be back soon, buddy."

Hank wagged his tail while Jake closed him in. Together we walked up to the bar situated in the middle of a field at a deserted countryside intersection.

"Welcome to the Pub," Jake said, opening the door.

A long bar with stools filled with patrons stretched across the large single room we walked into.

"Hey, Jake!" the bartender said with a wave. His eyes fell to me, then back to Jake and bulged.

"Hey, Kyle," Jake said, shaking his head against the silent accusation.

With a sly nod, Kyle ducked his head of shaggy brown hair and turned back to the customers he'd been chatting with.

"Bar okay?" Jake asked, and I nodded.

We found the last two open stools and slid into them. Jake's hand brushed my thigh while we got situated and both our eyes shot together before dropping back to the coasters Kyle slid in front of us.

"Whiskey coke?" he asked Jake, and a nod confirmed it. "And for you?"

"Grey goose martini, straight up, extra cold, extra dry, extra dirty with two olives please."

Their furrowed brows mirrored one another while they turned to look at me.

"A martini? Seriously?" Jake snorted.

"Why? What's wrong with that?" I shrunk in my seat.

"Nothing at all. Coming right up," Kyle answered after blowing out a puff of air that tousled his shaggy brown hair.

"Do you even know how to make a martini, Kyle?" Jake teased, and I wasn't sure which one of us it was directed at.

"I think I remember. Just need to find a glass."

"Is that stupid? Should I order something else?" I asked, embarrassed by my drink choice for the first time in my life. Now that I thought about it, at the Ox I'd never been asked to make anything other than basic mixed drinks, and those brandy old-fashioneds everyone seemed to drink up here.

"It's not stupid. It's just not something you see in Baileys Harbor all that often."

"Wait! Kyle, was it?"

He looked up from where he was rummaging through random glasses looking for a martini glass.

"Yeah, what's up?"

"Can I have an old fashioned? I've made them at the Ox, but I've never tried one."

"Oh! That's who you are! You're the new bartender at the Ox I've heard about." A big grin stretched his stubbled cheeks.

"Hopefully good things?" I asked.

"Great things. And something about a red dress?" His dark eyebrow rose, and a smirk lifted his lip.

"Oh, God," I whispered, shrinking lower in my seat. Jake's laugh only threw salt on the wound. "Not my best wardrobe choice."

"I heard it was an excellent choice. Hell, I've been hearing about it all day!"

"Small town," Jake said between chuckles. "Word travels fast here."

"I can see that." Palming my face, I dissolved into laughter. "Note to self... wear nothing but jeans and t-shirts when in Door County."

"Well it's nice to put a face to the woman I keep hearing about. I'm Kyle. I own this place with my wife, and I'm slinging drinks tonight because Sam called in sick."

I gripped his extended hand and shook it. "Hi, Kyle. I'm Cassie."

His dark brown eyes examined my face, and he tipped his head. "It's so weird. I feel like I know you from somewhere, but I can't figure out where."

Hearing my grandfather's warning in my head while trying not to come undone, I shrugged. "I've got one of those faces I guess." He likely had seen me before. In my lavish lifestyle, I ended up in magazines and on TV at times. I doubted he watched Access Hollywood or E! News, but the way he looked at me had me ready to bolt out the door.

"Hmm. I guess." A quizzical look tipped his head before he stopped his intense inspection of my face. "Brandy old fashioned? Your first, you said?"

"Mmmhmm." Trying not to let out an obvious exhale of the relieved breath I held, I nodded my head.

"It will be an honor to serve you your first one! Menus?"

"Menus would be great. This one made me throw back my dinner."

Sucking air through my teeth, I smiled. "Sorry about that."

Jake smiled back. "I'm just teasing. It's fine."

As horrified as I was about the thought of killing the creature, he had a point. A lot of points, actually. Who was I to judge him for fishing and hunting? I loved meat. And the way he got it was a lot more humane than I gave him credit for. It didn't mean I was going to run out and buy a gun and join him in the woods, but I could at least climb off my PETA pedestal and give him some kudos for his conservationist attitude.

"What's the burger of the day?" Jake called to Kyle while he muddled the cherry and orange with the bitters in my glass. It was a new skill I was learning since these Door County people couldn't get enough of their old fashioneds.

"You want it," Kyle called back with certainty. "Burger, BBQ, bacon, onion rings, cheese curds, and cheddar."

"You're right. I want it!" Jake laughed.

"Wait. Is that all on the burger?"

"Oh, yeah." A goofy grin deepened Jake's dimples.

"You're kidding!"

"They have ridiculous burgers here. Every day a new one with some really bizarre, but delicious, things piled on them. You'll love it."

"I'm not having one!" I scoffed. "I'll just get a salad or something."

With the shake of his head, he let out a sigh. "Please tell me you're not one of those girls."

"Those girls? What do you mean?"

"The 'I'll just have a salad, no carbs, no gluten, gotta watch my figure' girls."

Heat flushed my cheeks. I was exactly that kind of girl since that's exactly what I would say about ordering food.

When my answer stalled out, he rolled his eyes. "You are one of those girls!"

"Well, I do have to watch my figure!" I defended.

"So, you live on salads? Sounds enjoyable."

"Well, I eat other stuff."

"You need to try a burger. Seriously, Cassie. You haven't lived until you've tried to fit your mouth around a Pub burger."

"I can't! It's a burger! With cheese!" The thought of eating something dripping with grease sent a shiver down my spine. "I can't even remember the last time I ate a burger."

"Well after tonight you will. You can tell people the last time you ate a burger was that time you were with Jake at the Pen Pub. Kyle, we'll take two burgers of the day. And an order of cheese curds."

"Cheese curds? What the hell is a cheese curd?"

"You'll love it. It's breaded deep-fried cheese."

"Deep fried?" The way my voice shot up even startled me.

"Yes. Deep fried. You'll love them."

"Honestly. I can't! It's gluten. Carbs. Deep fried. I literally can't!"

"You girls and your fucking carbs. I eat carbs all the time. Are you saying I look fat?"

Taunting eyes met mine, then I raked him with a gaze. There wasn't an ounce of fat on that body I was certain bulged with muscles beneath his blue flannel shirt.

"No." I sighed.

"Good. Eat the carbs, Cassie. Eat the carbs."

Groaning, I set down the menu. "I'm going to have to do like ten thousand hours of yoga to make up for this."

"Totally worth it." He grinned and winked at me.

Kyle appeared and set the old fashioned in front of me. "One old fashioned, on the rocks, extra cold, extra wet, extra brandy. Two cherries."

I laughed at the good-natured jab and took the drink. They both watched with bated breath while I took a sip.

"Well?" Kyle asked, leaning on the bar.

"It's delicious!" I took another sip of the sweet and strong drink.

"Old fashioneds kick the crap out of martinis any day of the week. Boom!"

He pounded Jake with a fist bump then strode away wearing a triumphant grin.

"Look at you go. Drinking sugar and everything!" Jake teased, and I shot him a glare. Admittedly, I'd forgotten we muddled a sugar cube in with the orange and cherry and if I'd have remembered, I'd never have ordered it. But not wanting to be "that girl" I shut my mouth and kept on drinking. And now that I had ordered one, I didn't know how I was ever going back to my martinis.

"Big night for you, huh, city-girl?" Jake said. "Fishing, old fashioneds, and soon... cheese curds and burgers."

"You may be laughing now, but when I'm five hundred pounds, I'm forcing you to push me around in a wheelchair when I can't walk anymore."

"With pleasure." He smiled and something popped inside me.

I don't know if it was the smile, the admission he'd take care of me, or the deeper meaning that meant he'd still be around down the road, but those two words, even said in jest, nearly sent me tumbling off my bar stool. While my stunned expression transformed into a grin, I struggled for my comeback. But before I could answer, the door burst open and a sea of green and gold spilled in.

This time it wasn't the Packers colors I was so accustomed to seeing at the Ox. It was men in baseball uniforms cheering while they came in single file.

"Haaaaabaaaaa!" They cheered, drawing out the word.

"Haaabaaa?" I asked Jake while we watched them pour in.

"It's the Baileys Harbor baseball team. Harbor. Haabaa." He smiled and shrugged. "It's a locals thing."

The bar exploded in applause for them when they entered.

"Looks like they won today."

"Haabaaaa!" They roared again when they made it to the bar. Kyle moved fast and started handing Bud Lights to all of them.

"So, this is like, a thing?" I asked, trying not to laugh.

"Yep. Each town in Door County has a team and they go to war every Sunday. Today they played Egg Harbor. It's a grudge match."

"This small-town thing really is a world of its own, isn't it?"

"That we are. And us Haabaa boys don't like to lose."

"Am I a Haabaa girl now, too?"

"Depends."

"Depends on what?"

"There are levels to being a local. There's not a hard and fast rule, but the general guidelines for calling yourself a local are all pretty similar. First, there's the native, who was born here. That's me. The local is someone who's lived here year-round for at least five years. Leaving in the winter for more than a vacation removes the honor and they need to start over. Then there are transplants, who moved up here and stay here the majority of the year but spend part of the winter elsewhere. Then there are summer people, who only come up during the season. In order to be a Haabaa girl, you'd need to be a Baileys Harbor local, meaning you stay at least five years. So, I guess that depends on you. Are you just here for the summer?"

The weight of his stare pushed me down into my stool. Swallowing hard, I struggled to come up with an answer. He was searching and I knew it, but the reality was I didn't know. I didn't know how long Grandpa would make me stay here, and now, after meeting Jake, I didn't know how long I'd want to stay here. Suddenly the gravity of this small town seemed to suck me to the ground. Did I want to leave anymore? Would I race home the minute Grandpa told me I had redeemed myself? A few days ago I would have bolted back in an instant, but the way those blue eyes stared through me had me wondering what I'd do when the call came.

"I guess we'll have to wait and see," I said, trying to keep it vague.

"Oh," Jake answered, then turned away and took a sip of his drink. Did he want me to stay?

"Here you go!" Kyle said, arriving with a basket of some little brown deep-fried balls. I was grateful for the interruption and hoped we wouldn't have to have this conversation again. At least until I could figure out what Jake's intentions were. He was still a closed book I hadn't even begun to pry open. One minute he treated me like a leper, and the next I felt like we were on a date. It was giving me emotional whiplash.

"It's her first time," Jake said to Kyle when he set them down.

"Ever?" Kyle's eyes saucered. "You've never had a cheese curd, either?"

I shook my head.

"Carbs." Jake rolled his eyes.

Kyle returned the roll and shook his head. "Women."

I stared at the basket of cheese curds while two sets of eyes bore through me. "Do I just like, eat it?"

"Dip it in the ranch dressing first, then eat it." Kyle pushed them toward me.

While they stared at me, I tentatively picked up the crunchy ball of cheese and dipped it in the white sauce.

After taking a deep breath, I popped it into my mouth. An explosion of flavor forced my eyes shut as I moaned. "Mmm... it's so good!"

Their mirrored smiles met mine while I reached for another one.

"Told you it was worth it," Jake said.

"Atta girl," Kyle added before scurrying away to another customer.

"These are amazing. Like... AMAZING!" I ate another. I'd forgotten how much I loved carbs, and these fried balls of cheese might have been the best thing I'd ever eaten. They were even better than the Kobe beef tenderloin I loved back at my favorite steakhouse in New York.

Jake popped one in his mouth and I savored another. Kyle appeared again holding two plates with burgers stacked so tall with stuff they looked ready to topple over.

"No," I breathed while my eyes swelled wide open.

"Yes," Jake whispered back as Kyle set one in front of each of us.

"How? How do you even eat it?" I spun the plate, knowing there was no way I could fit my mouth around it.

"Keep both hands on your burger until the ride is over!" Kyle smiled.

Jake picked his up and squished it down, brown BBQ sauce poured over the edges while he shoved it in his mouth. Staring at mine like I was ready to scale Mount Everest, I blew out a breath.

"There are cheese curds in there," Jake said with his mouth bursting full of food.

"Cheese curds?" I quirked a brow. At this moment in time, anything with cheese curds sounded delicious. Following Jake's lead, I pressed the burger down as flat as it could go and opened wide. Even as wide as my mouth could go, I could only get half the height of the burger inside. When I bit down, the flavors exploded, and my eyes closed again. Heaven.

"Hmmm?" Jake asked with baited eyes we chewed.

"So good," I managed to mumble over the impressive numbers of foods in my mouth all at once.

"Told you." His close-lipped smile held his burger inside those impossibly perfect lips.

Unable to speak, I devoured my burger until nothing remained on the plate but the remnants of some sauce. Groaning my discomfort, I leaned back and blew out a breath. It had been years since I'd eaten until I was full. That sense of satisfaction that came after a big meal was something I'd never forgotten but hadn't indulged in since high school.

"I'm so full." I moaned. "Like... I might pop full."

"I'm hurting over here, too," Jake admitted. "But good, right?"

"So good. So, so good. You really may end up pushing me around in a wheelchair when I'm too fat to walk."

"If we keep this up, I may be wheeling myself around beside you." He chuckled. When I started laughing, I stopped as the pain in my stomach from the movement threatened to send my burger back up.

"You guys want another round?" Kyle asked.

"I can't fit anything else in my mouth tonight."

When I said it, Kyle's eyes darted to Jake. I saw the scolding stare Jake shot him before Kyle turned around snickering. "I'll get your check."

Flushed with embarrassment, I avoided his eyes when they darted to mine. Even though there were many, many things I thought about doing to Jake with my mouth, tonight would not be the night. With onion breath and a stomach pressing against my jeans, I'd never felt less sexy in my life.

"Here you go," Kyle said, dropping the check in front of us. Jake and I reached for it at the same time, freezing when our fingers touched.

"I've got it, Jake. I said I'd buy you dinner after I made you throw yours back."

"No, I've got it, Cassie."

Was this a date? I still hadn't figured it out. On dates, the man always paid in my world. So, if I let him pay would that make this a date? Hoping he felt the same way, I nodded. "Thanks, Jake. It was really good."

"You're welcome."

After he paid, we made our way through the sea of green and gold covered baseball players. Every eye clapped onto my ass when we walked through. It didn't go unnoticed, and I saw a scowl come over Jake's face when he stepped between us, his glare sending their eyes darting to anywhere but me.

He's protective. Definitely a date.

Feeling like I'd made progress tonight, I fought to contain my smile while we drove the mile home. When he pulled up in front of my cabin, I turned and leaned around

Hank's enormous head. "Thank you for a great night, Jake. That was a lot of fun."

"Yeah. It was," he said, but this time he didn't look at me. His eyes bore through his steering wheel while he wrung his hands around the wheel like a lifeline.

Silence settled over us only broken when I cleared my throat. "Well, I guess good night."

No kiss. I shouldn't have been surprised, and though part of me was grateful I wouldn't be kissing him with onion breath, the other part longed to taste those lips every second more I spent with him.

"Good night, Cassie."

I reached for the door and heard his sigh even over Hank's panting.

"Do you want to come over for dinner tomorrow and I'll make you fish?"

Glad I was turned away so he couldn't see the elated expression on my face, I bit my lip. "Yeah. I'm off Sundays and Mondays, so I'm free. That sounds really fun."

"Okay," he said, and the insecurity that peppered his tones when he asked remained.

"Should I bring anything?"

"Um, maybe wine or something you like drinking? I only have whiskey."

"Okay. I'll get us a bottle of wine." I smiled, but he couldn't see it with Hank in the way.

"So, I'll see you tomorrow. Like six-thirty?"

"Perfect. I'm looking forward to it." Trying to keep my heart from leaping out of my chest, I opened the door. The dome-light illuminated the truck and just before I climbed out, I looked over and saw him staring at me.

"Don't fall," he said. The anxiety in his voice was absent now and that familiar grin lifted his lips.

"Shut up, Jake." I grinned back.

"Night, Cassie."

Hopping out, I jogged back to my cabin. Just like last time, he kept the lights shining on me until I got safely inside. I waved at him from the door and the truck started up and pulled out. Poppy leapt up off the couch when she saw me, and I caught her in my arms.

"Poppy! I've got a date! I've got a date with Jake!" I spun her in circles, kissing her face while I wondered what it would be like to kiss his.

CHAPTER THIRTEEN

Jake

After I finished filleting the walleye I'd snagged off the dock an hour ago, I tossed the rest to Hank, who was licking his chops below me.

"I shouldn't give you this. You don't deserve it. You had one job, Hank. One job. Bite me in the balls if I started staring at her with stars in my eyes. And what did you do when I did? Nothing. Absolutely nothing, Hank. Where were you on that one? Nice wingman you turned out to be."

Ignoring my taunts, Hank ate the remains of the de-boned fish and looked up at me hoping for more.

"That's all, buddy."

Taking the fillets inside, I popped them in the fridge before going to the sink to scrub my hands. I never cared if my hands smelled like fish, like they often did, but knowing Cassie would be here soon had me sweating to get everything just right. While I put on the third round of soap, I looked at the clock. Six twenty-five. I scrubbed harder. I'd already shaved and put on my best white t-shirt. After several back-and-forths debating about cologne, I'd opted against it, but slapped some aftershave on my skin instead.

Five minutes.

In five minutes, Cassie was coming to my house.

What the hell did you do, Jake?

Saddle meet horse.

But it was too late now. Not only was it too late to call off tonight, it was too late to shove the feelings that had grown for her back inside. That damn icepick of hers had done too much damage. There wasn't enough duct tape in the world to patch up all the cracks she'd made in my carefully constructed armor. Every look. Every laugh. Every accidental touch. Each one tore apart my resolve, begging me to toss away my inhibitions and swing my leg over the horse one more time.

The sound of her car chugging down my driveway sped my heart up to speeds reminiscent of that time I went to Great America with Matt and rode the roller-coaster.

Matt. Just thinking about him put one more patch over the armor Cassie had chiseled away. Thinking about Matt made me think about Nikki, and soon I slipped into a downward spiral fueled by fear and regret. Trying to stop myself before I hit bottom, I took a deep breath and looked out the window. That beautiful blonde climbing out of her car wasn't Nikki. Not every woman in the world was a cheater and a liar. At least I hoped not because the way she looked tonight in that little tank top and those jean shorts would make not kissing her even harder than it'd been last night. And last night was downright torture.

Hank barked when he heard her knock.

"Coming!" I called, trying to hold myself in position a few seconds longer so I didn't look too eager.

"She's not Nikki," I whispered before I pushed off to the door.

"Hi." She smiled when I opened it.

"Hi," I answered back.

Hank exploded out the door and jumped around her, his excitement mirroring how I felt, even though I kept my emotions locked tightly inside.

"Hey, Hank!" She knelt down and scratched his head. Like a boneless lump, he collapsed at her feet and rolled onto his back.

"Come on in."

"Come on, Hank." With one last pat on his stomach, she stood and waved him in.

"Did you bring Muskybait?"

A playful glare met me while she brushed by into the house. "No, I didn't bring *Poppy*. Should I have?"

"Well, you could have. She had fun playing with Hank yesterday."

"Maybe next time." The words hit me like a mac truck. *Next time.* Yesterday I was avoiding this at all costs. Now I was excited hearing she was already planning a next time. "This is a really nice place." She strolled through my house, looking at photos and examining the main rooms.

"What were you expecting? A palace like yours?"

"Shut up." She laughed. "More camo. And definitely more dead animals on the walls."

"In here." I waggled my brows and opened the door to the den. When she looked inside, she nodded.

"Yep. Like that."

Deer and fish mounts lined the walls. My various camouflage hunting coats and suits hung on hooks. Wooden racks displayed a massive assortment of guns and bows that would make any hunter green with envy.

She turned back to where I stood leaning on the doorframe. "It's a bonified man cave. I guess I figured the whole place would look like this."

"My mother didn't have a problem with my dad hunting, but she hated the mounts. So, they had a deal that my dad could do whatever he wanted in this room. He just had to keep the door closed."

"Valid."

We laughed while I walked to the big sixteen-point buck head overlooking the room. "Even though I bought the house from them and don't have a wife to bark at me to keep it in one room, I guess I just kept up the tradition. My grandmother had the same rule with my grandfather, as well. The men in my family get one room, and the women get the rest of the house."

"Also, valid."

Our laughs deepened when she flashed me a knowing look.

"Are these all yours?"

"Oh no. These are my grandfather's." I gestured to the east wall. "And those are my father's. And that wall is mine."

"As much as I hate the dead animals, I love that you have a family tradition and have your grandfather's and father's stuff up here. I think that's awesome."

"Yeah. It's pretty cool seeing a deer my grandpa shot decades ago." I gestured to the big buck. "He and my dad taught me everything I know about hunting and fishing, so I always feel like he's still with me when I'm out there in the quiet. My dad still hunts and fishes with me when they come up to visit a couple times a year."

"That's awesome."

"What about your parents? Do you still see them?"

It felt like the air got sucked out of the room. A heavy weight settled over her shoulders as her eyes dropped to the ground. "No. They died."

Shit. Way to go, Jake.

"I'm so sorry, Cassie. I didn't know."

"No, don't apologize. You couldn't have known."

"What happened?"

Silence settled between us and I instantly regretted the question. Pain saturated the depths of her eyes and I wanted to reach out and pull her into my arms.

"I can't really talk about it. I'm sorry."

"No, don't be sorry. I am. I shouldn't have asked. I'm sorry, Cassie."

Pursing her lips, she forced a smile. We both shifted, and my eyes dropped to the wine bottle she clutched in her hand. It didn't go unnoticed, and she hoisted it up in the air.

"Wine?"

"God, yes." I laughed, blowing out the breath I'd been holding. "Opener's in the kitchen."

We walked in together and I uncorked the bottle.

"I don't have wine glasses. I just realized that."

"No worries. These will work." She gestured to the coffee mugs upside down on the drying towel beside the sink. Grabbing each by the handle, she flipped them up and held them out. I poured the red wine into the cups, stopping when they were nearly full. When she turned them around, her eyebrows shot to her hairline when she read the fishing quotes on them. Each cup had a man holding a fishing rod, and each had a different saying.

"Which one do you want? 'I'm a Hooker' or 'I fish so I don't choke people'?"

"I'll take 'I fish so I don't choke people.' It's funny cuz it's true."

Bursting into laughter, she handed me the mug. When she lifted the "I'm a Hooker" mug to her lips I nearly doubled over in laughter.

"At least the fish is pink on this one." She gestured to the pink fish dangling beside the word 'hooker.' "I like pink."

"I noticed. Your cabin looks like a bubblegum machine exploded in there."

She glared. "It's better than camo."

"You know they make pink camo, right? Maybe we could try that out."

She pulled a face. "The only way I'm wearing pink camo is if someone dresses me in it after I'm dead."

"Well now I'm definitely getting you pink camo." My grin widened, and her glare narrowed. "You hungry? Ready to try some fresh-caught fish?"

"I am."

"Come on, I've got the grill going outside."

We walked together with Hank leading the way out onto the porch. The smoke from the grill drifted up into the amber sky.

"Wow. It's gorgeous out here, Jake!"

"I got pretty lucky."

"Seriously! You're right on the water! The lake is so beautiful and looks so clean. Can you swim in it?"

"Oh yeah. People swim in it all the time, and there's a little public beach area just up the way. Nothing better than a dip in the lake on a hot summer day."

"I need to try it sometime. But I have to hike a minute through the woods down to my water and I'm too scared to get eaten by a coyote."

"You're not going to get eaten." I laughed.

We stood staring at my freshly mowed backyard. It stretched down to the small wooden dock jutting out into the lake. A few shade trees dotted my yard, and my mother's vegetable garden off to the side had fresh plants since I'd been trying to keep it up.

"This place is amazing."

"It's been in the family for years. There's no way we could afford waterfront property in Door County if it hadn't been. Fucking rich people just keep gobbling it all up."

Her gaze dropped to the ground. "Yeah. That sucks."

"Developers keep offering me more and more for it, but there isn't a dollar sign in the world that will make me give it up. I love it here."

"I can see why."

"Whose place is that next door, anyway? If you look on the land map, it's just registered to some trust somewhere, but we've never seen the owners. Do you know who owns it?"

"Huh?" she asked.

"Your place. Does your family own it or are you renting it?"

"Oh. Um. My grandpa set me up there."

"Is it his?"

"Huh?"

Scrunching my brow, I watched her shift her eyes to everywhere but mine.

"Does your grandpa own the land? I've always wondered who owns it."

"I, uh, don't know. He just told me I could stay here. Hank! Whatcha doing?" Cassie turned to where Hank was rolling around the yard with a ball. Hearing his name, he perked up and grabbed the ball in his mouth. "Come on, Hank!"

He raced over to where she stood slapping her thighs and I tried to push aside her strange answer about the property. After sticking my foot in my mouth about her parents, I didn't want to pry. Hell, it was probably their cabin, and my nosy questions just ripped open the obvious wound again.

"I'll start the fish," I said to her while she tossed the ball for Hank.

"Okay!" she called back.

After getting the fish placed on the tinfoil, I set it on the grill and sprinkled it with seasoning before putting butter and a squeeze of lemon on it. The vegetable packets I'd made up earlier got tossed on the grill beside them. When everything was set, I grabbed my mug of wine and walked over to where she stood waiting for Hank to return with the ball. All I wanted to do was step up behind her and wrap my arms around her like I'd done last night, but I stopped myself and stepped beside her instead.

"He'll never stop, you know."

"Who, Hank?"

"Oh, yeah. If you let him have his way, he'll make you throw that ball until one of you drops dead."

Laughing, she took the ball from him again. "Last one, Hank." With a grunt, she whipped the ball and Hank blasted off after it.

"Not a bad throw."

"Thanks."

"For a girl."

When she turned to meet me, I was already smiling.

"Dick."

"I've been called worse."

We exchanged another laugh. It had been startling to laugh when she first dropped into my life. But over the past few times we'd hung out, it started to feel natural again. It no longer surprised me to hear the sounds coming out of my mouth. She coaxed them out with such ease. For the first time in five months I started to feel like myself again... like I was going to make it and find that happiness that had walked out the door with Matt and Nikki. In fact, with Cassie, I felt better than myself.

"Did you fish today?" she asked, then shook her head before I could answer. "Duh. Of course, you did. It's cooking."

Laughing, I shrugged. "Well it didn't jump onto the grill by itself."

"Well, you do have Hank pretty well trained. Maybe you can just command fish out of the water and into the flames."

"Now wouldn't that be a talent."

"Well, however it ended up on that grill, it smells really good."

She was right. The fish was cooking fast, and it would be ready soon. "Let me get the table set up and we can have dinner in a few minutes. Make yourself comfortable."

"I'll be right here," she said, sitting down on the porch swing.

While she rocked herself on the swing my grandfather had built, I hurried to set up the small table on the deck. Two plates, silverware, and two glasses of water completed my setup. I thought about putting out a candle, but that looked like I was trying too hard. And even though I was warming to the idea of having her around, I wasn't quite ready to take things to the next level.

Baby steps.

After plating the fish, green beans, and corn, I waved her over. "Come eat."

Debating on pulling out her chair, I decided against it. My mother would have smacked me upside the head, but I was still balancing on that line right between casual hangout and date. Candles and pulling out chairs definitely said date.

"It looks amazing, Jake."

"Not too shabby for a guy who can't actually cook, huh?"

"Can't cook? What do you call this?" She laughed.

"Grilling. I can grill like a son of a bitch, but cooking..." I sucked the air through my teeth.

"Don't worry. I can't cook either. Like... *at all.*"

"No?" I took a bite of my fish. Good. It turned out well.

"Not at all. When I lived in..." She paused. "Chicago, I only ate delivery food and out at restaurants."

"How are you faring with food in Door County?"

"Not well." She laughed again. "I'm pretty much starving to death. I can't eat anything at the Ox because it has carbs and is fattening. The grocery store is hella expensive, and I don't know how to cook." She took a bite of her fish and I watched her face while I held my breath.

"Okay... but this. *This* is scrumptious. You weren't kidding! Wow, Jake!"

"You like it?"

"It's so good! Maybe I don't need the grocery store at all! You can just teach me to fish. Then I just need to get some veggies and I'll be all set."

"I've got *tons* of vegetables in my garden. Seriously. Help yourself any time."

"Seriously?" She looked up.

"Yes. You'd be doing me a favor. It's right over there." I pointed to the huge plot I'd planted with everything I could find at Jerry's Flowers this spring. It had been therapeutic. Not to mention my mother told me she'd skewer me if I didn't keep up on it for her when she visited.

"Wow! I will take you up on that. Vegetables are freaking expensive!"

"My garden is your garden."

"Thanks, Jake." That soft smile melted me like the slice of butter sliding down the side of my corn cob.

We ate our meal and watching her cut the kernels of corn off the cob sent me swaying back over to the side of the line where I wanted this to be a date. She looked so cute struggling with the corn.

"You can just bite it off the cob you know."

"Then it gets stuck in my teeth." Her face puckered. Then she smiled. There in the middle of her teeth was a piece of corn.

"Is that so?" I asked, choking on my chuckle.

"Yep."

"Interesting. Because you have a little something right there in your teeth. Oh. Shocking. A piece of corn."

With saucered eyes, she covered her face and turned away. When she turned back her ivory skin was the color of the hot coals. "Oops."

Our dinner consisted of more laughs and when we were done my stomach hurt. This time it wasn't from eating too much food like we'd done last night. It hurt from laughing.

"Can I help with dishes?" she asked when we stood up.

"Nope. Beautiful thing about grilling is I just need to toss out the tin foil and I'll take care of the plates."

"You sure?"

"Yep. Let's grab the bottle of wine and go watch the sunset."

"I'll get the cups."

After setting the dishes in the sink, I pressed my hands on the sides of the counter and took a deep breath. I was barely hanging on. Being this close to her without touching her, tasting her, was torture. Every laugh, every damned breeze that came by and wafted her perfume had me desperate to pull her into my arms. And that smile. Even with the corn in her teeth she still looked so beautiful. Being with her felt like tumbling down a cliff, desperately grabbing for rocks or vines to stop my plummet. But did I want to fall?

I walked to the porch and saw her and Hank sitting down on the dock. Trying to steady my nerves, I held that bottle of wine for dear life and walked across the yard to join her. When I got there, she had her shoes off and her bare feet dangling in the water. The amber color of the sky was already transforming into an arresting blend of oranges and pinks.

"It's so beautiful," she said while I settled beside her. Kicking off my own shoes, I rolled up my jeans and joined her, dipping my feet in the lake. Hank flopped down at her side, resting his head across her lap.

"It is. I come out here and watch the sunset most nights. But with a beer instead of wine." I shrugged then poured more wine in her glass.

"It's so peaceful here. Door County in general. Everything moves at such a different pace."

"Do you like it? Some people love it. Some people can't wait to get back into the fray."

After a moment of thinking she looked up at me. "I love it."

Her eyes fell to my lips. A soft breeze blew a piece of hair across her face and I desperately wanted to reach out and brush it away, capturing her face in my hands and finally tasting those lips that tempted me every time they moved. Eyes mirroring my desire looked up at me. The sunset danced inside them as they pulled me in, and I felt myself give up my futile attempt to stop this fall. The last fingers of my determination let go of my lifeline and I leaned toward her.

Cassie pushed toward me and I reached out, sliding my hand across her face. Leaning up, her lips brushed against mine. When they touched, I felt the free fall start. The dam of emotions inside me burst open as I pulled her lips into mine. Passion exploded between us while I let my lips wander free. One taste. One touch. I was hers to command. Her arms wrapped around my neck, and she dissolved into me.

Pulling her body against mine, I deepened our kiss, and with it, all the things I'd tried to bury bubbled up to the surface. Raw and exposed, the power in our kiss ignited me from the inside. But with the heat of the flames flickering between us, memories of the scalding pain she could bring resurfaced. As we became lost in each other, flashes of my pain broke through and I found myself scraping my nails on the side of the cliff, desperate to stop the descent.

As amazing as it felt to have her lips devouring mine, as much as I wanted to sweep her in my arms and never let her go, the weight of us crushed down on me. Eventually she would hurt me. Crush me. Destroy me. I wasn't ready. I wasn't ready to go through this again. I couldn't.

Clawing at my lifeline, I begged my lips to release hers. I pleaded with my arms to let go and my legs to take me away from the pain that awaited if I let myself continue the free fall with her. When I was certain her hold on me was too strong and I would never be able to break free from the feelings for her that held me captive, I pushed back, breaking our kiss.

"I can't. I'm sorry," I breathed, barely able to exhale the words I didn't want to say. The words I had to say. "I'm not ready."

The pain and confusion in her eyes threatened to pull me back under.

"Jake, I'm sorry. I thought—"

"I can't. I'm sorry."

Unable to look at her without pulling her back into my arms, I jumped up and hurried back to the house with Hank trailing behind me. I couldn't turn around. I couldn't look. It was too soon. It was all too soon.

Slamming the door to my house, I pressed back against the wall. Sadness, anger, and resentment collided inside me. Not only had Matt and Nikki stolen my happiness in the past, they'd stolen it in the future. Even while I held Cassie in my arms, I pictured her in Matt's. Visions of her cheating on me, humiliating me, breaking me... they flooded my mind. I had nothing to give and everything to lose. The only thing I had left in this world was fear and loneliness. I was destroyed, and even my feelings for Cassie couldn't put me back together again.

My lips still burned from his kiss. Heat radiated from the spot on my chin where his soft stubble had rubbed when our passion finally exploded. But it was my heart that burned the most from the sting of rejection. While I sat on the dock struggling to comprehend what had happened, I fought the tears stinging my eyes.

Did I do something wrong? Did I only imagine that he wanted to kiss me?

I could have sworn I saw it in his eyes. It was there. Desire. Yearning. And when our lips met, I felt it. You couldn't make up the passion that crackled between us. It had been more intense than any kiss I'd ever had. But as quickly as it came, it disappeared. Just like the range of emotions I saw in him in our short time together, hot then cold, on then off, our kiss had mirrored our emotional dance.

I'm not ready. His words haunted me. Ready for me? Remembering now what he'd been through, what had happened to him, I closed my eyes. He was scared of getting hurt again. It had to be. The flames burning between us that I wanted to dance in? Those same flames terrified him.

Starting up the dock to pound on his door and demand he not run from the connection developing between us, I slowed to a stop. His great fear was being hurt again. And I wasn't being honest with him. Hell, he didn't even know my real name. His greatest fear... was me.

The shackles of my situation held me fast in place. I couldn't reveal my identity... not yet at least. And I couldn't continue lying to him, playing out his greatest fear. No. He was right to flee from me. Perhaps on some deep-down level he knew. He knew I was like Nikki. A liar.

The ground beneath me shook, or maybe it was my legs, but I knew as much as I wanted to barge in there and demand he not give up on us, I took off racing for my car. Hot tears burned down my face while I gave in to my situation and climbed behind the wheel.

Desperate to tell Jake my name and why I was here, I remembered the company and how much I wanted to make my grandpa proud... to pick up the reins where my father left off. Looking at the house, I swallowed down the last of my tears. No. This was my punishment, my purgatory. I couldn't move forward. I couldn't go back. All I could do was wait here until Grandpa decided I'd paid my penance. Proved my worth.

Maybe then I could tell Jake the truth. Force him to face the feelings between us I knew were real. But now... now I needed to give him space and keep my head down until I was back in the good graces of my grandpa. With one last look at his house, I turned the key and put the car in drive. A cloud of dust flew up behind me while I tore down the driveway and tried to get as far away from Jake Alton as I could... even though it was less than a mile. This was going to be torture.

CHAPTER FOURTEEN

Jake

The Fourth of July sun beat down on me while I finished cleaning up my boat. Grumbling, I hosed off the bloody remnants of my early morning charter trip I'd agreed to against my better judgement. Looking at the sea of people packed into Baileys Harbor for the parade, I regretted not charging double. Hazard pay. I hated crowds, and I really hated the annual Fourth of July parade in Baileys Harbor.

With the parade blocking off the routes, I'd had to park up the road on E and walk down this morning. Now the crowd stood between me and my truck and the peace and quiet of my home. Debating between sitting on my boat alone all day until they left or forging my way through them to get to my house, I grumbled again, hating both decisions.

Deciding on the latter, I slung my bag filled with fishing lures over my shoulder and headed into the crowd. Every time someone bumped me, I struggled to keep my snarls contained. Grumbling and snarling had been about all I could do since I'd left Cassie sitting on my dock two weeks ago. The memories of seeing her standing alone in my yard before running to her car were forever seared into my mind. I cringed at the memory, like I did every time, hoping when I closed my eyes tight it would miraculously fade away. But even in that split-second of darkness, her face remained. Like a ghost who haunted me, her presence stayed with me everywhere I went.

She was the first thing I thought of when I woke up. The last thing I thought of before I fell asleep. When I fished, all I could think about was holding her in my arms while we reeled one in. Eating was ruined because I just pictured her savoring those cheese curds. Drinking wasn't helping. Not only was I avoiding the Ox like the plague, every time I was out at the Coyote Roadhouse or the Pub where I'd taken up refuge, the gossip featured the hot new bartender in town. Even my house wasn't safe because I couldn't look out in the yard without seeing her standing there. The kitchen, den... everywhere was haunted by the memory of Cassie and how poorly I'd behaved.

Sure, I was scared but leaving her sitting on the dock after inviting her to my *home* was unforgiveable. I wouldn't be surprised if the next time I saw her she slapped me across the face. God knows my mother would if she'd seen what I'd done.

"Hell, yeah! You decided to join the party, Jake!" Aaron's voice broke over the crowd while I pushed through.

Groaning, I turned to see him standing with a plastic cup of beer in one hand and a bratwurst in the other. "Hey, man."

"I can't believe you came to the Fourth of July parade! It's about fucking time you got out of whatever new rut you've been lying in."

"I'm not here for the party. I'm just getting back from a fishing trip and these people are standing between the dock and my truck."

"So, we're still in a rut?" He bit into his brat. "It's like you're starring in your own version of Groundhog's Day. Except instead of Bill Murray, you're Kevin Van Dam."

"Nope. Just don't want to be around all these people," I lied. Although it wasn't a rut I was in. It was a pit. A pit of despair. A deep, impossible to scale out of, pit of despair.

"Drink it." He shoved the beer at me.

"No. I'm good."

"Drink the beer, Jake. Drink it. It will help."

Beer didn't help. I knew this because I'd drowned myself in more beers than I could count, and I didn't feel any better. Dangling the beer in front of me like a carrot in front of horse, Aaron continued chomping on his brat.

"Dude. Get that thing out of my face. No beer. No party. Home. I want to go home."

"Well, I've been calling and texting for like two weeks. I haven't even seen you since the fight. What's up with that? Why aren't you at the Ox?"

Dropping my gaze to the ground, I just shrugged.

"Is it the hot new bartender? Jo told me you took her fishing or something? Did you get back on the horse?"

"No." *No, I didn't get back on the horse. I got my foot in the stirrup then panicked, fell in the mud and I'm never getting on another horse again.*

"All right, well if you won't hang here today, you at least need to come to the Ox for the Fourth tonight. It's our tradition. Beer. Fireworks. More beer."

Since I was a kid, I had come down every Fourth of July to watch the fireworks. As an adult, I'd joined the party that brought all the locals out for one debaucherous evening at the Ox. But this year, with Cassie possibly bartending tonight, I knew it was the first year I'd be breaking tradition.

"We'll see," I said to appease him.

"Yeah? You gonna come?"

"Probably. I'll see you tonight."

Desperate to get away and back to the serenity of my lake house, I gave him a smile and turned away.

"I'll see you tonight, man!"

With a backhanded wave, I started back through the crowd. After I was certain I was far enough away to avoid any more of his persecution, I slowed while I searched for the path of least resistance leading to my truck. As I scanned the crowd, I froze when I saw her. Even though I was outside, it felt like all the oxygen had been sucked from the atmosphere.

She was standing with a group of people, a cup in one hand and her other hand waving in the air while she told a story. Her long hair was pulled back into a loose ponytail and it swung with the animated movements that had everyone surrounding her laughing. I remembered how easily she'd made me laugh... something that hadn't happened since the last time I'd seen her. The plaid button-down sleeveless top made her look more local than tourist. My eyes slid down to the legs that went on forever coming out from the bottom of those jean shorts she'd worn the night she came over. With a hammering heart, I looked back up and saw those green eyes staring back at me.

Shit!

Desperate to run, I forced myself to remain steady when her hand lifted in a shy wave. I'd already run from her once and I'd never been more ashamed. Running wasn't who I was, and the hell if I would do it again. It didn't matter how badly I wanted to take out these people like bowling pins while I made a beeline for my truck.

Lifting my hand in an awkward wave, I forced the semblance of a smile. She smiled back, and before I could turn around, she started toward me.

Shit. Shit. Shit.

Compelling my feet to remain glued to the pavement like I was standing in tar, I stilled while she approached. With every step that brought her closer, my heart pounded faster. That roller-coaster ride started up again in my stomach and the free fall was underway.

"Hey, Jake," she said when she arrived, and the soft tones of her voice chipped away at me again.

"Hey, Cassie." I kicked a stone by my feet then forced them to hold steady again.

"Listen, Jake. I'm really sorry about what happened. I shouldn't have kissed you. It—"

"Please. Don't apologize. *I* am the one who needs to apologize. Running off and leaving you out there..." I blew out a puff of air. "It was totally awful, and I am so ashamed I did it. I'm really sorry, Cassie. I totally panicked."

"It's okay." She reached out and touched my arm. That familiar bolt of lightning traveled through me even from the featherlight touch. When my eyes darted to her hand, she retreated, and I felt those agonizing fingers of regret tighten around my heart. "Sorry."

"Please don't apologize. Again. It's me, Cassie. It's all me. I just... I'm pretty fucked up from what went down."

"I get it, Jake. I totally do. And I'm sorry I pushed. It won't happen again."

She hadn't pushed. I'd pulled. Just like I wanted to do right now. To pull her back into my arms and taste those lips I couldn't get out of my mind.

"Even if you aren't ready to, you know, date or whatever," she stumbled. "I don't want you to avoid me. The Ox is your bar. Hell, that seat of yours still sits open waiting for you. Please don't let things that happened, or didn't happen, between us ruin your world. I'm the tourist. You're the native. If anyone needs to go, it's me."

"Don't go." The words came out with more force than I'd intended. "I mean, this is my issue. Not yours. I'll get over it."

"Well, I won't go if you promise to start coming back to the Ox. Jo's gonna kill me if you don't come back. And you know Jo. She can mess me up."

A small chuckle started and just like it had when I first met her, it startled me.

"So, will you come back to the Ox?"

I nodded. "I suppose. I don't want Jo to kill you. And she's got a hell of a right hook. I've seen it."

"And a left I bet."

We laughed together, and just like before, her icepick chipped a little piece away again.

"So, you'll come back?"

"I'll come back."

"Good. I'm getting pretty good at this bartending thing. You ought to see me in action."

"Yeah? I see you figured out how to drink beer, even. Impressive." I gestured to the cup in her hand.

"Yep. I drink beer and I do shots of... wait for it... Jägermeister."

"Holy shit! Not shots of dirty martinis, straight up, extra cold, extra dry, extra dirty?"

"You remembered!"

She laughed and her eyes sparkled. When that happened, it felt like all my loneliness and pain could evaporate. And I'd be whole again.

"Yep." Of course I remembered. I remembered every moment I'd spent with her.

"You doing okay, though?"

The answer was no, but I nodded anyway.

"Good. I'm finally getting the hang of things around here. I've made some friends. They're up for the summer working as well." She gestured to the group of girls she'd been talking to I hadn't met before. "They're really nice and we've been having a lot of fun. They've shown me the beaches, and I even started stand-up-paddle boarding. It's my therapy."

"Like my fishing."

"Exactly. Now I need a coffee cup that says, 'I SUP so I don't choke people.'"

A laugh exploded out of me and I felt the warmth returning to my soul. She was like sunshine breaking through the darkest storm clouds. Feeling her light shining on me melted away another layer I'd worked so hard to construct in her absence.

"So, I'll see you tonight?"

"Sure. Why not. And I really am sorry, Cassie."

"Hey. You're not the only one who got hurt and did some screwed up stuff in the aftermath. I get it. I could write the book on taking a bad situation and making it worse."

"Thanks, Cas. I'm trying. I just need to find my way back."

"You will." She reached out and touched me. This time I didn't recoil. "I did."

We exchanged a smile.

"I'll see you tonight," she said. When her fingers drifted off my shoulder, I had to force myself not to reach out and take her hand.

"I'll see you tonight."

She turned and walked back to her friends, tossing a smile over her shoulder before the crowd swallowed her up.

All it took was one look. One word. One touch. And I was sliding back down the cliff again.

CHAPTER FIFTEEN

Cassie

"Where'd you go?" Lucy asked when I got back to my group.

"Just bumped into a friend." Jake wasn't just a friend, but even though I now considered Lucy and Josie just that, I hadn't told them about my almost-romance with Jake. Knowing it wasn't going to happen for us, I didn't see the point in reliving the ache of his rejection. Only Poppy knew what had transpired because she'd curled up in my arms that night while I cried and recounted the whole tale.

"You need another beer?" Josie asked.

"No, I'm good." I lifted the half-full cup and smiled.

We'd met at the Ox last week. Josie and Lucy were roommates in college who came up here to work for the summer. After a few shots during my shift we'd gotten to talking, and they'd invited me to join them at the beach the following day. Avid paddle boarders, they'd taught me how to do it and even lent me my own for the summer. Outdoor sports, well sports at all for that matter, had never been my thing. But being on the water and enjoying the peace and tranquility of this little town had been just the thing to help heal my heart from Jake's scathing rejection, and the loss of my parents I still struggled with every day.

I looked back through the crowd, but he was gone. Seeing him today hurt more than I'd been prepared for, but I hoped I'd kept my feelings hidden away. Easy and breezy. That's what I'd gone for. In reality, agony and misery were what I'd felt when those azure eyes had stared down at me. And those lips. Now that I'd tasted them all I wanted to do was launch back into his arms.

But he was still hurting. And that I understood. The searing pain of loss coursed through me as well, but in a different way. It was death for me; betrayal for him. Guilt mounted on top of my loss is what had sent me to the bottom of the bottles after I lost my parents. But for the first time in two years I was dealing with the pain I'd hidden from in a mist of parties, drugs, and alcohol. Even though I'd been more than reluctant to come to Door County, I was finally healing here. Grandpa had been right, and I owed him my eternal gratitude for helping me find my way back.

"Hey, I'll catch you guys tonight at the Ox. I'm going home for a little while."

"You sure?" Lucy asked. "We were going to head over to go watch the band by the docks."

"Yeah, I'm sure. I need to make a call and get some rest before tonight. If it's as wild as you guys say it is, I'd better take a break!" Moderation. That was my new motto while I found the new balance in my life.

Josie laughed. "It is. Go nap. Rest. We'll meet you at the Ox at eight."

"I'll see you then."

After finishing my beer, I walked back to where my beast was parked on the side road up from the Blue Ox. When

I climbed inside, I pulled out my phone and pushed my grandpa's number. It rang twice.

"Cassandra?" he answered.

"Hey, Grandpa, it's me."

"You okay?" The intention threaded through the words. It had been two weeks since we'd talked, and I knew he was still expecting me to toss up the white flag and beg to come home. But that was just it. This place now felt like home and returning to New York was the farthest thing from my mind.

"I'm great, Grandpa."

"Really?" Shock settled in his voice. "You're doing good?"

"I'm doing great. I just wanted to call and tell you thank you. You were right. I needed this. For the first time since my parents I feel like myself again."

"I can't tell you how happy I am to hear that, sweetheart."

The fact I could even bring them up was a monumental step for me, and I knew he understood that.

"I love it here. I'm making friends. My job is pretty great and I'm making enough money to get by. A lot of people up here work two and even three jobs just to make ends meet. It's unreal how hard they have to work just to pay rent and buy groceries."

"I'm glad you're starting to understand the struggles of the other half. Not everyone has a trust fund waiting to support them. When I was your age, I was lucky to have a roof over my head."

"I see that now, Grandpa. You were right. I never appreciated it before."

"I'm glad to hear it. If you take over Davenport Industries, a lot of hardworking people will depend on you to take care of them and ensure them jobs to support their families."

"I understand that now."

"Good. Very good, Cassandra."

"So, I work. A lot. Poppy and I are getting by in our little cabin. And I've started SUPing and really love it. It's therapeutic for me."

"SUPing? Is that a new drug?" He growled.

Laughing, I was shaking my head even though he couldn't see it. "No, Grandpa. It's stand-up paddle boarding. I go out on the lake on a big board and paddle around. It's good exercise, relaxing, and it's given me so much time to think. I love it."

"Oh, good." He blew out a breath. "Sounded more like the latest designer drug."

"No more drugs, Grandpa. I don't need them anymore. Door County has changed me. I mean, I still struggle with the guilt, and I miss my parents all the time, but I can move forward now. I feel lighter."

"I don't know how many times we have to tell you that it wasn't your fault, Cassie. You have no reason to feel guilty. They wouldn't want that weight on you."

I was nodding, but again he couldn't see me. "I know. I'm working on it, Grandpa. I just wanted you to know I was doing great and I think you'd be proud of me. They'd be proud of me."

"I am proud of you, Cassandra. So proud. Proud enough I put the sale of the company on hold until we can figure out if this is the right path for you."

"You really were selling it?" Part of me thought it was just a threat.

"Yes. Edward Garvey was going to purchase it with the promise to keep all the jobs and continue running the company like your father and I had all these years."

Garvey. He'd been the Chief Business Officer of Davenport Industries for the past thirty years. Even though my father and grandfather respected and trusted him, there was always something about him that raised my hackles. I didn't trust him and the thought of him taking over the company if I failed only deepened my resolve to climb out of this hole I'd dug myself into.

"Don't sell to him, Grandpa. I've got this. When I get back, I will show you I can do this. I can run our company and make sure it stays in the family."

"I hope so. Let's give it some more time and then we'll see."

"I love you, Grandpa. I'll call you later."

"I love you, too, Cassandra."

We hung up, and I pressed my head back against the rest. Part of me wanted to stay here in Door County forever and give up the dream of running Davenport Industries. The other wanted to take up the helm my family had forged for me and do the job I'd dreamed of since I was a child. The one I'd worked so hard to prepare myself for and threw away in the wake of my parent's passing.

With the weight of my decision settled on my shoulders, I drove home to play with Poppy and go for a paddle on Kangaroo Lake.

"You missed!" Josie taunted when the bimini ring I'd tossed swung left and missed the hook on the bull's nose.

"Damn it!" I laughed, stepping out of the way.

"My turn!" Lucy took my place.

"I'm going to check on Jo and Jamie and make sure they don't need me." With the Fourth of July crowds, the town had been packed all day. And apparently the Blue Ox was the bar all the locals flocked to on Fourth of July night to watch the fireworks happening over Lake Michigan at dusk.

"You guys sure you're okay?" I called over the bar to where Jo and our co-worker, Jamie, were hard at work.

"We're good, Cassie!"

"You sure? I don't mind jumping back!"

"Three people is too tight back here. We're good with two," Jamie said as he slid up beside me, handing a bottle of beer to the guy on my left. "Not to mention the money is amazing tonight."

Grumbling, I nodded my head. I'd actually wanted this shift, but since Jo and Jamie had seniority over me, they got first dibs. Watching the bills flying over the bar had me itching to get back there.

"Just go across the street to the Beachfront Inn and watch the fireworks. You can cozy up on their beach and get a front-row view of the fireworks at Anclam Park. They'll be starting soon!" Jo called before diving back into the beer cooler.

"Okay. Don't say I didn't offer." I shrugged.

I kept scanning the bar looking for Jake, but he hadn't shown. Maybe our armistice today had just been for show and he still intended to avoid me like the plague. Sadness settled over me thinking about him avoiding his friends and his bar on my account.

"You guys watching the fireworks?" I asked when I got back to Josie and Lucy.

"Nah. We'll be here drinking." Lucy raised her glass.

"Are you?" Josie asked.

I shrugged. "Yeah. Why not. I'll be back."

The last time I'd gone to watch fireworks, I'd been a kid sitting on my dad's lap. My mom had spread out a blanket and the three of us clapped each time an explosion lit up the sky. The thought of watching fireworks without them caused that lump to swell in my throat again, but it felt like part of my healing process to experience it again and let their memories flood back over me.

After leaving the Ox, I crossed the street and walked through the parking lot of the Beachfront Inn. Children splashed in their outdoor pool, their innocent laughter carried away with the warm summer breeze. As I walked past, I remembered the way my father used to lift me over his head when I was a child playing in the pool at our summer house in the Hamptons. He'd launch me through the air only to scoop me back up before I splashed into the water below. I looked over and saw a man holding his son in the air, sweeping him across the water while the little boy squealed with the same joy I used to have. Smiling, I kept walking, hoping that little boy would always cherish this memory of his summer vacation and of his father the same way I would always cherish mine.

When I made it to their little stretch of beach, I paused to inhale the intoxicating smell of the lake. Darkness hovered just above the strip of light settling into the horizon. The fireworks would start soon. Careful not to step on the people scattered along the beach, I found an opening just down the way. When I got there, my feet stuttered to a stop when I saw Jake standing alone staring at the sky. As I debated on bolting before he saw me, his head turned, and our eyes connected.

Too late now.

With the same soft smile I'd given him when I saw him earlier in the day, I walked to his side.

"Fancy meeting you here," I said, followed by a nervous chuckle.

"Yeah, I guess." His own nerves were apparent in the way he shifted his feet.

"I can go somewhere else if you want. I didn't know you'd be here."

"No. No, it's fine." Though he said the words, the intent behind them was missing.

"Are you sure? I can totally find another spot."

He blew out a deep breath and shook his head. "No. Stay."

The fear in his eyes shifted and that look I'd seen in them before slid into its place. It looked like a war waged inside him, and I recognized it because the same one waged inside me.

"Okay," I answered and stepped to his side.

Silence settled between us while we stood staring at the darkening sky. When the tension was thick enough I could slice it with a knife, I took a deep breath and spoke.

"I haven't seen fireworks since I was a kid. With my parents."

He turned to me, and I saw the recognition in his eyes. He'd seen how difficult it was for me to talk about my parents that night at his house.

"Is it hard?"

I nodded. "Yeah."

"I haven't missed a Bailey's Harbor fireworks in my life. Even as an infant, my parents brought me here. They've been friends with the owners of this hotel for ages, so they always saved us a spot. And we watched fireworks together every year until they moved away. They aren't like, gone, or anything, but I still wish they were here."

I stared up at him.

"It's stupid, right? I'm like a grown man who still watches fireworks alone and misses his parents." Rolling his eyes, he shook his head.

"It's not stupid." I touched his arm. It was the third time today my hands went rogue and reached out. "It's not stupid at all."

Another silent exchange passed between us. The battle in both of us shifted, and I didn't make any attempt to fight it. A firework exploded and snapped our attention toward it. Sparkles illuminated the sky while bursts of color lit the world surrounding us.

Memories of my mother's laughter echoed in my mind, and I could almost feel my father's tight squeeze while he held me and pointed to the sky. It had been two years since I'd lost them, but for the first time since it happened, I wasn't numbed by drugs and distractions. I let myself feel the grief I'd fought to suppress. While I felt their absence deeper than I had prepared for, a tear slipped out of my eye and slid down my cheek. Another explosion lit the sky and Jake glanced down at me. With teary eyes, I looked back up at him. Before I could shed another one, his arm slipped around my shoulder, pulling me in tight. I pressed against his chest and wrapped my arms around his waist. That feeling of safety and protection I'd gotten in my father's arms once again settled over me in Jake's embrace.

"You're okay," he whispered and pressed a gentle kiss to the top of my head. "I've got you."

With tears streaming onto his t-shirt, I watched the colors exploding around us. So many emotions surged through me, igniting like the fireworks crackling across the sky. Guilt. Sorrow. Loss. Safety. Security. And that emotion only Jake could elicit inside me.

When the fireworks stopped, the crowd applauded, but Jake and I stood in silence, my face still pressed to his chest.

"Are you okay?" he asked.

I looked up to see concerned eyes searching my face.

"I'm okay. Thank you. That was harder than I thought."

"I'm really sorry for your loss, Cassie. I'm just glad I could be here for you."

"Thank you, Jake. It means a lot to me." Not wanting to slide out of his embrace, I held myself against him for a moment longer. Sniffling, I wiped my eyes. "Sorry I cried on your shirt. I feel so pathetic."

He snorted and tucked a piece of hair behind my ear. "You have every right to be struggling right now. I, on the other hand, am a grown man watching fireworks alone. I'm the pathetic one."

"You weren't alone," I said, then looked up at him.

A long swallow slid down his throat and a soft smile lifted his lips. "Thanks, Cassie."

God, I wanted to kiss him. It took every ounce of my willpower not to lean up and press my lips against his. That same look returned to his eyes, but last time I tried it ended with me sitting alone on a dock. Aching. Forcing my lips to keep to themselves, I sighed and smiled.

"Well, I guess good night?" As I spoke, hope sprang into my chest.

"Do you..." He paused and sighed. "Do you want to come over and have a bonfire with me? I'm not really in the mood to be jammed in a bar with a hundred hammered people."

I nodded with more enthusiasm than I wanted. "Yes."

"Okay." He smiled. "Good. Why don't you go get Poppy and I'll get the fire started? The dogs can play, and we can have a few beers... now that you drink beer."

"Deal." I grinned back.

"Okay."

"Okay. I'll see you at your house."

Forcing myself to pull from his embrace, I started down the beach. Even though deep down I knew it was wrong to pursue something romantic with a man who didn't even know my real name, I couldn't stop myself. Denying what was going on between us was no more possible than denying gravity. We'd already crossed the line and there was no going back. Now I just needed to figure out how to tell him who I was without putting my dream of taking over the company at risk.

CHAPTER SIXTEEN

Jake

My Bluetooth speaker played the soft sounds of country while I tossed another log on the fire.

"What am I doing, Hank?" I asked him while he panted at my side. But this time I knew what I was doing. I was no longer denying myself the happiness that hovered within my reach. The same happiness I'd been too scared to grab onto, instead pushing it away. But seeing her so vulnerable in my arms tonight made me realize I wasn't the only one who'd been in pain. And if she could fight her demons and try to heal, so could I.

Headlights coming down my driveway sent my heart racing again. It wasn't just the headlights illuminating my life. It was Cassie. She was like a beacon guiding me through the storm, and this time I wouldn't sail away from her light. I would let it show me the way.

"Hey, Jake," she said when she came around the side of my house. "I saw the fire and figured you'd be out here."

"I'm glad you could make it." I looked to the little dog clutched in her arms. "And Muskybait, too."

"Jake," she warned with a smirk. Hank appeared at her side now, leaping in the air around her. Poppy squirmed, desperate to get down.

"Let her down. He won't hurt her."

"Let me just hook up her leash." She fumbled with the pink strap in her hand.

"Just let her down, Cassie. She'll be fine."

"What if she runs off?"

"She won't run off."

"But the coyotes."

"Hank will protect her. Just relax. Let her be a dog."

Worried eyes met mine, then she bent and set Poppy down. Instantly, the two dogs started their game of tag. With lolling tongues and enthusiastic bounces, they raced around the yard taking turns chasing each other. Cassie bit her nails while she watched. Chuckling at her, I cracked a Spotted Cow and extended my arm. "Drink this. It will help."

Letting out a sigh, she grabbed the bottle and took a long swig.

"I just worry so much that she's going to get hurt."

"You can't protect her from the whole world and deny her the happiness of being a dog. Sometimes you gotta just let go and hope for the best."

The minute I said it I shook my head, realizing I could have been talking about myself. Just like Cassie guarded that dog, robbing her of a full life in the process, I was so worried about getting hurt I was robbing myself of a chance at happiness. Cassie was my version of a coyote.

While she watched them tear around, she took another sip of her beer.

"I still can't believe the martini drinking carb-hater is guzzling beer."

"I've changed a lot since I've been here. It turns out life really is better with carbs." She shrugged before we broke into laughter.

"That's what I've been saying. Come on, sit."

Pulling out a folding chair, I stood behind it while she settled in. This time it was a date. It was firelight instead of candlelight, but just like my mother taught me, you hold the chair for the girl. After she leaned back and kicked off her shoes, I pulled my chair up beside her and sat. Kicking off my own shoes, I rested my feet on the log in front of us.

"So," I said, taking a swig of my beer. "We meet again."

"So, we meet again."

We each took another sip of our beer, our tentative gazes darting between each other and the fire.

"Look. I panicked last time you were here. I just really want you to know again how sorry I am. That's not me."

"I know, Jake. It's okay."

"Have you heard what happened?" I knew she had. Small towns and all.

"Yeah. I heard. I'm really sorry that happened to you. Getting cheated on sucks."

"Yeah. It does. But it's no excuse for how shitty I was just leaving you on the dock. Trusting someone again after what I went through is hard. In fact, I'd planned on never doing it again."

That softness in her eyes dissipated for a moment and she took another swig of her beer. "I've been through a lot myself. If anyone gets it, it's me. No one can blame you for being gun-shy."

"Yeah. And it wasn't just that I got cheated on. It was my best friend. It was like a double whammy. I guess it just took me longer to recover this time."

"It's been two years since my parents died and I'm still not okay. Loss sucks, no matter what kind it is."

Her parents. She'd brought it up, but I didn't know if I should ask.

"It was a plane crash."

"What?" I asked, turning toward her after she said the answer to the question lingering in my mind.

"They died in a plane crash. It's really hard for me to talk about."

"I can't even imagine, Cassie. My loss is nothing compared to what you've been through. I just lost a girl and friend. You lost your parents."

"I did a lot of stupid shit after it happened. A *lot*." She blew out a puff of air. "Shit I'm still paying for now. But I'm trying, Jake. I'm trying to be a better person and to move on with my life. But it's hard."

I nodded along. "Don't I know it. Moving on is really hard."

We sat together in silence for a moment and I watched the flames licking the logs while they crumbled. A glance over to Cassie found those eyes that had haunted me these past two weeks searching mine. The way the light illuminated her face had my hammering heart pounding even faster. God she was beautiful.

A new song started on the radio, and when I heard the lyrics start up, I closed my eyes and chuckled. *Let Me Down Easy*. Of course, it was. The song that had me thinking of her every time I had heard it since I met her was now the soundtrack to our quiet moment. The powerful lyrics fueled me with the confidence I'd struggled to find. This time I wasn't going to screw it up.

Standing up, I reached out a hand and stared down at her. "Dance with me."

With a slack jaw, she looked back up at me. Holding my breath, I awaited her answer. It came when she reached out and took my hand. When her fingers closed around mine, I finally let out a long exhale. A gentle tug pulled her to her feet and into my arms. Feeling her arms encircle my neck, and the weight of her body press up against mine chased away the last of my fears. I had nothing to lose. Not even my heart. She already had it.

Together we swayed to the sounds. The full moon hung over our heads while the flickering embers floated up before drifting back down around us. Just feeling her in my arms erased all the pain, all the lies, and all the agony that had been my life lately. Everything about this moment told me this is where I belonged. With her. As the song came to an end, she looked up at me. My heart stalled out underneath the desire in her stare. Casting aside all my doubts, I reached down and slid my hand under her chin. While I tipped it up, she rose on her toes, our mouths drawing together like magnets.

Just before our lips finally touched, a loud splash drew our attention to the lake. The full moon showed Hank bouncing up and down in the water sending droplets spraying into the sky, then a small yip traveled up from the water.

"Poppy!" Cassie screamed. "She can't swim!"

We broke our embrace and raced toward the water. Hank barked, and I could hear the panic in his tone. When we reached the dock, I saw the faint outline of Poppy in the water below me. Ripping off my shirt, I dove into the water after her. Emerging with a gasp, I searched the water for her little dog.

"Poppy!" I heard Cassie screaming from the dock just before she plunged in after me.

"Poppy!" I called, my eyes scanning the surface of the water. Hank swam past and Cassie popped up beside him.

"Where is she? Poppy! Poppy! Jake! Find her! Please!"

I dove under, searching the blackness and finding nothing. Desperate to find her, I stayed under until I choked for the relief of a breath of air. When I popped up, I saw Cassie treading water beside me, the little dog safe in her arms.

"I found her! She swam to me!"

"She can swim?" I asked, gasping for breath.

"Apparently she can." Cassie kissed her head. "My little Princess Poppy can swim! She's okay!"

"Good God. I thought she'd drowned, and I killed your dog." The panic pushing my heart to near bursting finally let loose.

"I thought a Musky got her!" She panted while she broke into laughter.

"Poor little Muskybait."

"She's not Musky bait!" A splash of water slammed into my face.

"I know! I'm teasing! Well go on. Let's see her swim."

"Are you sure a Musky won't eat her?"

"I'm sure, Cassie. There aren't any in Kangaroo Lake. And I promise, she's too big for any fish to eat."

Poppy struggled in her arms. With a sigh, Cassie released her grip and the little creature cut through the water like a seasoned swimmer. Hank paddled up beside her and the two swam in circles before paddling back to shore and tumbling in a heap as they rolled through the yard.

"Are you okay?" I asked, swimming up beside her where she made it to water shallow enough to stand.

"Yes. I think I had a heart attack, but I'm okay."

Finding my footing in the sand, I walked the last few steps to where she stood wringing the water from her hair. Droplets slid down her shoulders and rejoined the lake. The way the full moon illuminated her wet skin sent a surge of passion coursing through my veins. It pulsed with my desire for her, like she'd somehow gotten inside me, and every fiber of my being belonged to her, and only her.

When I stopped in front of her, our eyes connected. I gave her no time to speak, or even breathe. Sliding my hands along her face, I pulled her into my kiss and caught her gasp in my mouth. This time I wasn't sliding down the cliff, desperate to stop the descent. I launched off it and enjoyed every second of my free fall while her tongue met mine.

Our bodies pressed together while her arms encircled my neck. Every agonizing second I'd been away from her dissolved with the power of our kiss. The heat from her body pressed up against my bare chest sent a throbbing sensation into my soaking jeans. With every swirl of her tongue and grasp of her hands on my shoulders, I felt her ripping away the last of the walls I'd built around myself. Like a tornado tearing through me, she sent all my reservations flying away. And I was happy to see them go. If being with her meant feeling like this, then there wasn't anything in the world that could keep her out of my arms.

She was the hand that pulled me from the ashes. The voice that guided me out of the dark. The touch that soothed the last of my ache away. To me, she was everything. And now she was mine.

"Jake," she breathed as our kiss softened. Warm breath ghosted my lips, and I claimed hers once again. Lifting her body up against mine, I slid my hand down her back, pulling her tighter while she slid a leg around mine. The heat burning between us could have boiled the water swirling around our legs. It burned away all my fears, all my reservations, and I deepened our kiss.

Her hands slid to my chest, splayed palms caressing the muscles and exploring their way down my abs. Groaning, I pulled her tighter, desperate now to finish what those looks had promised. Running my hands down her arms, I felt the small bumps prickled on her skin.

"You're cold," I whispered between kisses.

"I hadn't noticed," she answered, sliding her tongue back inside my mouth.

I softened my embrace and pulled back those lust-filled eyes boring through me. "Let's go inside."

"Okay," she answered, and her smile told me everything I needed to know.

Sweeping her into my arms, I devoured her lips again, then carried her back to land.

My fingers clung to the sinewy muscles of his shoulders while he carried me across the yard. Even in the dim light, I could still see every impressive bulge and defined cut of his body. It only increased the rate of my heart fluttering against my ribs.

"Hank! Poppy!" he called while we passed the fire. I saw Hank come tearing across the yard with Poppy in tow.

When we reached the door, Jake set me down while he fumbled to open it.

"It sticks," he said, the waver in his voice giving away his nerves. The same ones banging around inside my stomach. After bumping it open, he held the door. Stepping inside, I watched Poppy and Hank tear in past me. Jake followed and closed the door behind us. We stood together on the wood floor with water dripping off us, forming pools at our feet.

Biting my lip, I reached for him. It was all the encouragement he needed. I gasped when he caught me around my shoulders and pulled me into his kiss. Our limbs tangled together while his kiss invaded me again. A welcome conqueror I had no desire to resist. The siege on my mouth continued until we broke apart as he pulled my shirt over my head.

Bumping into walls and furniture, we devoured each other as he moved me through the house, our clothes dropping piece by piece while he guided me up the stairs. For every second our mouths had to come apart, they returned with more power than the last. I hadn't even noticed I was now in the bedroom until I felt the bed press behind my knees. Opening my eyes, I saw Jake standing above me. The moonlight slipped between the slats of the blinds and the soft glow of the clock illuminated his body. For the first time I saw him clearly. It was better than I'd imagined. And I had imagined perfection.

His chest grew with every deep breath while he stood in his boxers and examined the matching bra and panty set I still wore. I reached out and touched the rippled muscles covering his stomach. Dragging my finger along the lines, I watched his eyes close tight while he exhaled a deep breath. Letting my fingers wander free, they explored every inch of his tanned, taut torso. Before I could explore any lower, his kiss upended me again.

With a gentle shove, my back hit the bed. He towered over me, the desire and passion in his eyes heating my body everywhere his eyes roved. Pressing a hand on either side of my head, his biceps bulged beneath his weight while he lowered himself over me. A gentle kiss brushed my lips and drew another one of my soft moans.

"Jake," I whispered before his tongue pressed inside my mouth. The gentle touch after such a carnal explosion was a shock to my senses. My hands found their way to his back and spread out over the bulging muscles I couldn't see but imagined rivaled the ones in the front.

While he continued exploring my mouth with his kiss, his fingers drifted down my shoulder and continued to my breasts. Cupping one in his hand, I exhaled my relief to finally have his touch where I needed it. With a gentle squeeze, he deepened his kiss, and I melted into the mattress. The material of my thin bra gave him no trouble while he slid his hand beneath it. Rough fingers brushed my nipple, and I whimpered at his touch. Continuing his soft exploration of my body, he moved to the other one, repeating the soft circles that had heat coursing between my legs.

As if he could read my mind, his fingers drifted down my stomach and grazed the top of my underwear. Ready to beg for his touch, I sighed when his fingers disappeared under the silk without my need to plead. When they touched me where I needed him most, I grabbed his face while I moaned into his mouth. They moved against my heated skin in rhythm with the tongue continuing its invasion of my mouth.

"Cassie," he breathed before sliding a finger inside me.

"Oh, my God." The fire he'd lit in my body surged to heights I worried would incinerate me. A soft buzz started in my ears while his fingers played a song that had me ready to scream the finale. When I was sure I couldn't take another second of his talents, I felt the pressure in my body release with one final swirl of his fingers. Clinging to him while I rode the wave, I held his mouth with mine, whimpering into it the sounds of my ecstasy.

As I panted below him, his hands returned to the side of my head and he hovered above me. Satisfaction and pride collided with the desire swirling inside those azure orbs. After catching my breath, a soft smile lifted my lips, and a desire to give him the same pleasure he'd given me brought my hands to his chest. As I pressed him over, he fell to the side and rolled onto his back. Holding his gaze with my own, I straddled him, pressing myself against the wet boxers that did nothing to hide the sizeable bulge straining against my silk panties.

Reaching behind my back, I unclasped the hook on my bra. When it slid off, exposing my breasts, his eyes dropped to examine them. I could see his muscular chest lifting with quickened breaths while he took me in. Moving on top of him, I pressed my soaking underwear against him while he closed his eyes and groaned. The friction between us had me already climbing back up the mountain I couldn't wait to plunge down again.

"Damn, Cassie," he breathed while I rocked above him. Certain now he needed me as much as I needed him, I stopped my hips and slipped off the bed to stand before him. Eyes begging for my return met mine. Inch by inch, I slid my panties off my hips and let them drop to the floor. When his gaze fell between my legs, it sent a surge of heat coursing back through me. Leaning over, I took ahold of his boxers and inched them down. When his cock sprang into sight, I bit my lip. The perfection I'd imagined his body held didn't disappoint when I saw it.

Reaching out a hand, he took mine and pulled me down into his arms. Our wet, naked bodies tangled together while he rolled over on top of me. The force of his kiss pressed my head back into the bed, and my hands moved to the rigid cock straining against me. Taking it in my hand, I slid up the length of it, feeling it bulge when he growled his pleasure. All I wanted was to feel it inside me.

Softening our kiss, he lifted himself away, pulling open the bedside table. Emerging with a condom, I waited while he put it on in silent anticipation until he was back between my legs. With a gentle kiss, I felt it brush up against me, sliding through my heat and making me dizzy with desire. As his kiss deepened, I grabbed ahold of his back and pulled, begging him to enter me. When he pressed against my entrance, I pulled harder until he slid inside.

Our conjoined moans drifted away on mingled breaths. Clinging to his back, I held tight while he moved inside me. The heat between us rose to scalding while he continued to press deeper into my body. Each thrust of his hips sent me farther up the mountain, and the fast tempo of his breath told me he was climbing it with me. Our sweat-slicked bodies slid against each other while we dissolved into one. No longer able to tell where he stopped and I began, I closed my eyes and let the pressure increase until I was sure I would explode again. Digging my nails into his back, I screamed out my release, and his low groan followed. We clung to one another while the last waves of our passion coursed through us. When Jake collapsed on me in a boneless heap, I wrapped my arms around him.

"Oh, my God." He panted before rolling onto his back and pulling me into his arms.

Pressing a kiss to his chest I used as a pillow, I let out a shaky breath while his grip around me tightened. "That was spectacular."

"It was so much better than I'd imagined. And I'd imagined incredible."

"Right back at you." I giggled.

"I'm so glad I pulled my head out of my ass. You're amazing, Cassie."

Cassie. Hearing him say that name yanked me back to the reality in which he held a woman in his arms he didn't know. Guilt flooded through me. I'd made myself a promise on my way here tonight I wouldn't pursue things with him until he knew who I was, but I'd lost all my resolve when those lips had touched mine. I needed to tell him the truth. I had to. He'd been lied to enough, and I didn't want to be another reason he didn't trust anyone. Now to figure out how to tell him the truth.

Strong arms held me tighter as I pressed myself along the length of him. Tonight, was about us. But tomorrow I would call Grandpa and explain things, then tell Jake the truth. And I could only hope he would forgive me.

CHAPTER SEVENTEEN

Cassie

The morning light shining through the slats in the window landed right in my eyes. Groaning against the unwelcome assault, I clamped them shut harder then rolled over with a grumble. Jake's arm tightened around me and I sighed when I remembered where I was. And who I was with.

"Where do you think you're going?" he asked.

Smiling, I rolled back over to see those sparkling eyes staring at me. "Nowhere now." I pressed a soft kiss to his lips, but he slid a hand behind my head and deepened it to one that got my pulse racing once again. "Three times last night wasn't enough?" I quirked an eyebrow.

A mischievous smile curved his lips. "Not even close."

Laughing, I looked over and saw Poppy curled up in his other arm.

"Don't say anything," he warned when he saw the enjoyment on my face.

"Don't say anything? You're snuggling with Poppy. It might be the cutest thing I've ever seen in my life!" The excitement in my voice stirred her and her snores softened while she peeked open one big eye.

"Shhhh. You'll wake Muskybait," he whispered. With a big yawn, Poppy snuggled deeper into the other nook of his arm, mirroring the one I was in on the opposite side. We both burst out laughing when a loud snore rippled through the room and she fell back asleep.

My heart swelled to bursting seeing my tiny dog safe in the muscular arms wrapping around us both.

"Could you be any more perfect?" I sighed and pressed my head into his chest, placing a soft kiss on the chiseled pec that made a perfect pillow.

"I'll be even more perfect after I get done whipping you up my famous omelet."

"I thought you didn't cook?"

"I've got a few things in my kitchen arsenal. Meet me on the porch and we'll have breakfast out back." After kissing the top of my head, he gently lifted still-sleeping Poppy and set her down beside Hank who was passed out at our feet. Like a limp rag doll, Poppy didn't budge even when Hank pulled her in tighter with his nose.

The bright sunlight finally gave me the full effect of Jake's naked physique. He walked to the closet, and I watched from beneath the covers until his perfect ass disappeared beneath the jeans he tugged up. When he headed out of the room without a shirt covering his impossibly chiseled abs, I smiled. Breakfast would be even better sitting across from that.

After a long stretch, I climbed out of bed and looked at my still-soaked bra and underwear crumpled on the floor. There was no doubt the rest of my clothes scattered through the house like crumb trails to our lovemaking were likely water-logged as well. I walked to the closest and fingered through the t-shirts all lined up on hangers. Settling on the one I thought he'd appreciate most, I pulled it over my head and giggled when it fell almost to my knees.

Drowning in the camouflage tent, I headed downstairs and found him in the kitchen cracking eggs into a bowl. The sight of his shirtless body in the kitchen had me ready to yank him back upstairs to bed. He turned to look at me, and a wide grin appeared when he looked at my getup.

"Now *that* is a good look for you!" He laughed, and I gave him a little twirl. "I can't imagine a better t-shirt for you."

He gestured to the photo of the antlers across the chest with the words "I Love Big Racks" written beneath them.

"I thought you'd appreciate it." I smiled and padded across the tile then slid my arms around his waist.

"I do love big racks."

"Is that so?" I arched an accusatory eyebrow and peeked up at him.

"Well, I love *your* big rack. And *only* your big rack."

"That's better." Rising on my toes, I gave him a kiss before heading out to the porch. I saw my purse still sitting on the desk, so I stopped to grab my phone and check my messages before heading outside.

Three missed calls and a barrage of texts awaited me. I didn't need to look to see who'd been messaging me in the middle of the night. For the past four days Donovan, Liza, and the rest of my former "six-pack" had been hounding me wondering where I was. I had hoped by now they'd just replace me and move on, but late-night cocktails and drug-induced ragers had them calling me to their side.

Liza: *Bitch, where are you????*

Donovan: *Baby! Are you in rehab or something? Why aren't you answering us???*

Liza: *Party in Rio THIS WEEKEND! You need to come! Cassandra! Where the hell are you?*

The string of texts went on, each inquiring about my whereabouts and trying to entice me out of hiding with promises of parties and adventure. There was a time when I would have been hopping on the next jet to join them, but not anymore. Now I couldn't think of anywhere in the world I would rather be than right where I was. With Jake. For the first time in years it felt like my world was finally right-side up again.

Putting my phone on airplane mode to keep them from interrupting my time with Jake, I shoved it back in my purse then made my way toward the back porch. Hank and Poppy trotted down the stairs side by side, so I held the door while they scampered out into the yard.

The smell of the fresh air up here still shocked me every time I stepped outside. And today it smelled even sweeter. It was something I'd never realized I was missing until I came here. That and stars. In Door County, at night the sparkling light of a million stars sprinkled the sky. According to Jo, the absence of city lights is what made them so visible here. Whatever caused it, it was something I was grateful for, and I hoped they would never stop making me stare at them in awe.

Settling onto the chair at the table on the porch, I tucked my knees up inside the t-shirt. I wrapped my arms around my legs and smiled while I stared out over the yard at the sparkling water that greeted me. I could get used to this. To

Door County. To this house. To waking up next to Jake every day. For the first time in as long as I could remember I felt peace. True peace.

"Coffee, baby?" Jake said from behind me.

"Oh, yes!"

He wrapped an arm around my shoulder and a cup of coffee in the "I'm a Hooker" cup appeared. Bursting into laughter I tipped my head back and looked up to see him beaming at me. Jake leaned down from behind me and planted a kiss on my lips. "Here you go, Hooker."

"I've got a nice rack *and* I'm a hooker. You are one lucky man."

"The luckiest." He kissed me once more before I took the cup of coffee. "Eggs will be out in a minute."

With a happy sigh, I settled back against the chair and sipped my coffee. This was happiness. There wasn't a better way to spend my life than right here with him. But just as I envisioned learning how to bake in this house while our dogs raced around the yard, and maybe someday children, I felt my happiness flutter away.

I still needed to tell him who I was. The struggling bartender was actually an heiress set to inherit billions of dollars. The girl driving around in the rusted-out beast normally traveled by private jet. That property he had asked about, the one he loved so much, was mine. Or would be someday. I still had a company I was set to run. A company in New York. Jake never wanted to leave here, and now... neither did I. But I also wanted to take up my mantle in our company. There were so many obstacles standing in our way.

I could only hope we could find a way to balance out our two lives. That was, if he could forgive me for the lies.

"Breakfast is served!" he said triumphantly as he appeared.

When he placed the plates on the table, I forced a smile back onto my face.

"Fresh veggies from the garden, and eggs from my friend's farm down the road."

"It looks amazing, Jake."

"Let's hope it tastes good, too."

Taking a small bite, I closed my eyes and moaned. "Yummy!"

"Yeah? It's okay?"

"Better than okay! This gives Nancy a run for her money."

"Who's Nancy?" he asked, then took his own bite.

Struggling to swallow after I realized my slip, I coughed then bided my time while I chased it with a swallow of coffee. I couldn't tell him Nancy was my private chef in New York. "Um, Nancy is a friend who used to make us breakfast a lot. Who taught you to make omelets?" I changed the subject immediately.

"My mom. She said every man needs to be able to make at least three things well. Omelets were one of my specialties."

Grateful he'd dropped the Nancy conversation I took a deep breath, then another bite.

"Do you want to go boating with me today? I don't have any charters. You, me, Hank, Muskybait all go out for a little relaxing lake day?"

"That sounds perfect, Jake. I just have to be back for work at five."

"No problem. A boating day it is." He beamed.

He was lighter today. Like the weight he'd been carrying around on his broad shoulders fell off in the night. The dark cloud that seemed to hover over him faded away, and instead he radiated warmth and light. It felt like a side of Jake reserved for me and me alone. I only hoped that he would still radiate it after I told him what I'd been keeping from him.

We finished breakfast, and I kissed him goodbye so I could go home and change for our boat day.

"I'll pick you up in an hour."

"I'll be waiting," I said, dissolving back into his arms. It was only an hour, but already I missed him.

After one last kiss goodbye, I drove home and collapsed on the couch. Knowing I couldn't keep lying to Jake, I pulled out my phone and dialed Grandpa.

"Davenport residence," Eleanor's voice greeted me.

"Hi, Eleanor! It's Cassie."

"Cassie? Oh! Cassandra! Oh, hello sweetheart. How are you?"

A happy sigh started the sentence. "I'm amazing, Eleanor. So very happy."

"I can't tell you how good it is to hear that. Your Grandpa said you've been doing great. We're so proud of you, honey."

"Thank you. That means so much to me. I've learned so much here. And I'm happy for the first time in longer than I can remember. This was so good for me."

"Good for you, Cassandra. You deserve it."

"Hey, is Grandpa around? I need to talk to him about something."

"He's in board meetings all day today. But he'll be home around five."

"Shoot. I work at five."

"Work. It's still shocking to hear you say you have to go to work!" She laughed.

"I'm finally over the shock," I said, joining her laugh. "Now I kind of like it!"

"Well, good for you! A hard day's work is good for the soul."

"Well, I miss you. And Grandpa."

"We miss you, too. I'll tell him you called."

"Please do. I really need to talk to him tomorrow."

"I'll make sure he calls."

"Take care, Eleanor."

"You too, Cassandra."

We hung up, and I groaned. I was hoping to discuss my situation of keeping the truth from Jake so I could tell him on the boat today. But without Grandpa's blessing I didn't dare break my promise. I'd let Grandpa down enough already. Just one more day and I knew I could convince Grandpa lying to Jake wasn't right and get him to agree. I'd come so far, letting Jake, and maybe Jo, know who I was wouldn't send me backsliding to the life I'd left behind. The one that paled in comparison to the one I was living now.

CHAPTER EIGHTEEN

Jake

"Everyone in?" I asked, glancing over to Cassie who held Poppy in her lap beside me. Hank was lying by my feet where I stood holding the wheel of my center-console.

"We're all in!" she answered. The hot July sunshine lit up her golden hair, but it was her smile shining the brightest.

Pushing the throttle forward, we started slowly out of the marina until I got out past the 'No Wake' zone. As soon as we cleared the last buoys, I pushed the throttle forward. The bow of the boat lifted, and the wind whipped through our hair while we cruised out of the harbor. Cassie's smile only grew and matched mine. It was rare that I boated for pleasure and not fishing, but today I wanted to enjoy the weightless feeling Cassie had given me. And there was no better way for me to soak in the joy she'd given me than a day floating beside her on the lake.

Since succumbing to my desire last night, the battle waging inside me was over. Even though I'd thought happiness and love weren't in my future, one night with Cassie had changed it all. One kiss, one touch, and I knew she was worth the risk. Not that I could have resisted her even if I'd tried. This was one battle I'd lost before it even started. It was lost the first time I looked into those emerald eyes.

As we cruised along the shore, I pointed out all the landmarks dotting the landscape. As busy as things got in Door County in July, there was always a reprieve when I was out on the water. Having spent my life out here, I didn't pay much attention to the impressive sights. They had become part of my daily scenery. But seeing Cassie's eyes devour every inch of them had me pausing to remember the true beauty of this place. It was almost as beautiful as her.

"What's that?" she called over the wind. Her finger pointed to the top of the white lighthouse jutting out from the small clump of trees on the island.

Pulling back on the throttle, the boat settled into the water until we bobbed on top of the soft waves. "Cana Island Lighthouse."

"It's so cool!"

"It's over one-hundred-fifty years old. That lighthouse has steered ships around Baileys Harbor for over a century."

"It's awesome."

"We can climb it sometime. They open it to the public all summer long."

"Really? I would love that!"

"Then consider it a date. This looks like the perfect place to anchor for a while."

It was quiet here. The majority of the boat traffic was closer to the marina, and the view of Cana Island Lighthouse stretching above us in the distance provided the perfect backdrop for our day.

I dropped the anchor over the edge of the boat and waited until I felt it catch. When I turned back, Poppy and Hank shared a spot in the sun on the stern seat, each stretched long while they absorbed the rays. Cassie was stripping off her shorts, her tank top already in a pile at her feet. The sight of her in that tiny pink bikini had my erection pressing against my board shorts in seconds. She pulled out an oversized towel and flipped it in the air, letting it settle onto the floor of the boat. Kneeling down, she smoothed it out before lying on it. That bulge in my trunks only grew looking at her sprawled out before me.

"Do you need some sunblock?" she asked, holding up a bottle.

"I'm good. I don't burn."

"I don't want wrinkles." She scowled before putting some in her hands and rubbing it on her face. Unable to remain even several feet away, I moved to her side and settled down beside her. The sun already heated the towel, and it felt warm beneath me while I rolled onto my side.

"I'll put it on your back," I said, itching to caress her soft skin.

"Thanks, Jake." After handing me the lotion, she rolled onto her side. The tiny string holding her top on stretched tight across her back. With a secret smirk, I started rubbing the lotion into her skin, sliding my fingers to the bow and giving it a tug. It gave no resistance as it unraveled.

"Jake!" She laughed, clutching the top to keep it from falling off. "You ass!"

"No one but me can see you down here. The sides of the boat are shielding us."

"Except for all the tourists with binoculars climbing the lighthouse." Looking over her shoulder, she quirked a brow before letting out a defeated sigh. Releasing the forearm holding her suit in place, she let it free. With one more tug on the knot around her neck, I watched the top fall to the floor. The sight of her exposed breasts had me heated to scalding.

"Better?" she asked with a coy smile, rolling onto her back to give me a full view.

"Perfect," I whispered, then leaned down and captured her lips with mine.

Her moan pushed into my mouth when my fingers drifted across her nipples. Those soft hands of hers spread across my back and pulled me down into her. Letting her guide me, I settled over her and kneeled between her legs, our lips continuing the dance I knew I'd never tire of.

"Someone will see us," she lightly protested when my fingers moved to the ties at her hips holding up her bottoms.

"There's no one out here but us," I whispered back when I gave one a tug. It unraveled, and she whimpered while I pushed her bottoms off to the side. Only one strip held them in place, and I brushed across her heat while I moved to it.

"Oh, God," she breathed when my fingers teased her bundle of nerves before moving to undo the other tie. When it came undone, I pressed the ties aside and looked down to see her bottoms fall away, showing me the soft smooth skin that begged for my touch.

Thick lashes batted over desire-laden eyes while she looked up at me. My own desires were ready to explode with just one look. Barely able to contain my own pleasure,

I pulled a condom out of my pocket and put it on while she panted below me. Lowering myself between her legs, I pressed at her entrance. Her parted lips pulled me toward them, and I captured them with mine while I pressed inside. Deeping our kiss, I pushed inside her, and that dizzying wave of ecstasy pulled me back under again. Our bodies connected, our bond deepening with every thrust of my hips and every frantic grab of my back while she pulled me into her. Never had I felt the power of so many emotions rushing through me than I did when I was inside her. Overwhelmed with emotions, I closed my eyes and let the waves wash over me while she cried out my name again.

Collapsing in a heap beside her, I pulled her into my arms. "That was so much better than fishing," I breathed.

Laughing, she pressed up against my chest. "I hope that isn't what you do on your charters!"

"Nope." I kissed her head and closed my arms around her. "That is for you and you alone."

"Lucky me." She chuckled.

In this moment, I was certain there had never been a time I'd been happier. Hell, I bet there wasn't another man on the planet happier than me. Or luckier, I thought while I looked down at the beauty draped across me. My intentions of treading lightly into this new relationship were blown away. I'd gone headfirst off that cliff and I was enjoying every second of falling for her.

"Jake? You there?" A voice called across the water. With wide eyes, Cassie and I shot each other a look. Hank barked and his big tail wagged while he bounced on the seat he and Poppy had been snoozing on.

"What the hell?" Cassie whispered while we fumbled to pull the towel out from under us. "You said we were alone!"

Just as we got the towel over our naked bodies, a boat pulled up beside us.

"Jake! You on there or did you fall over, and I need to call the Coast Guard?"

Aaron. Figures.

"I'm here, Aaron. Go away!" I called back to him.

The motor on his boat softened while it slid up beside us. I saw his bearded face appear over the edge while he peered with wide eyes into the bottom of the boat where Cassie and I lay covered.

"Whoa!" Aaron laughed. "You *are* on the boat. And back on the horse I might add." A sly smirk lifted his furry lips while a triumphant nod tipped his head up and down.

"Shut up, Aaron," I called back, trying not to laugh while I held the towel tight around Cassie.

"I saw the boat, and it looked abandoned. I just came over to check on you. I see you're okay. *Very* okay." His grin grew.

Two men and a young boy appeared behind him and all eyes showed white when they saw us.

"Divert your eyes, young 'un," Aaron said, covering the wide eyes of the teenage boy staring at us. "It seems they're okay and we can be on our way. Jake's got other things on his mind than fishing today."

"Oh, God," I groaned while his charter clients stared at us.

"Back to fishing we go! And no... we won't pull a woman like that out of the water. But I can put you on the salmon for sure! And let's be honest... salmon are a hell of a lot less trouble than women."

The charter group laughed while Aaron gave me a sly nod.

"Get out of here," I growled, but the laughter hovered just beneath the words.

"We're going. We're going. Well done, man. Well done." He crossed his arms and smiled down at us.

"Go!" Cassie and I shouted in unison.

"All right, all right... I'm going. You two have yourselves a wonderful afternoon." He winked then disappeared over the edge and back onto his boat.

The motor chugged while he pulled away. Cassie and I exchanged a horrified glance and then dissolved into laughter.

"Alone?" she said through her hysterics while slapping me on the shoulder. "Alone? You said we were alone! He almost saw me naked!"

"I'd have had to drown him. No one sees you naked but me." I laughed and peeked under the towel. "That is all mine now."

"Then don't make me get naked out in public where your friends are gonna see me!" She slapped me on the shoulder again. I broke through her feigned resistance and pressed a kiss to the lips she pursed shut.

"You can try, but it's not gonna work." I kissed her again, feeling the firm lips soften then give in to my persistence. Our tongues reconnected while she melted into my demands. She sighed the sweet sound I loved hearing her make.

"I'm getting dressed," she said between kisses.

"I'm sure he won't come back. Maybe just one more—"

"Jake!" she scolded then tugged the towel away, leaving me naked on the floor of the boat. Scurrying to pull up my shorts, I laughed while she leveled me with a glare.

After tying her suit back together, I slapped her on the bottom and kissed her cheek. "There. You're safe."

"Thanks, baby." She leaned back and brushed a kiss on my cheek. It amazed me how every word from her mouth and every touch could send me into a whirlwind of emotions that ignited the darkness inside me, drowning out every painful memory I had.

Hank saw a duck flap past and land in the water beside the boat. With a powerful push he flew over the edge. The splash soaked us both and Cassie screamed her displeasure.

"Hank! You ass!" she called while he padded toward the duck before it flew off. Poppy yipped, the nub of her docked tail wiggling in excitement.

"Poppy, don't!" Cassie said, noticing her intent. Before she could reach her, Poppy launched off after Hank. "Poppy!"

"Don't worry. I promise. No fish will eat her."

"You're sure?"

"I'm sure. Let them have fun. It's hot out. I bet the water feels good."

The two dogs paddled in playful circles around the boat, and I tipped my head, glancing sideways at Cassie. "You know. It *is* hot out. The water looks pretty refreshing. Swim?"

"No. I'm good. I think—"

Before she could finish, I scooped her in my arms. Her scream echoed across the lake when I launched us over the edge. Plunging beneath the surface, I held her tight until we bobbed to the top. Her horrified gasp came when we emerged.

"You asshole!" she yelled, slapping my shoulder while we tread water. The dogs swam over, happy grins parting their mouths while they circled us.

Laughing so hard I struggled to breathe, I pulled her into my arms and shut her mouth with a kiss. Her resistance shattered, and she wrapped her arms around my neck. Together we floated, wrapped in each other's embrace. The weightless feeling I experienced in the water paled compared to the way she made me feel, like I could just float away.

When our kiss broke, her soft smile gave away her enjoyment of our impromptu plunge.

"Told you it would feel good."

"I'm never going boating with you again."

"Liar." I kissed her again. "I hate liars."

The smile dissipated and she turned, swimming back to the boat.

"Where are you going?" I called, swimming after her.

"The boat! I'm cold!" she called back.

I watched her struggle to climb back up, realizing I'd forgotten to put down the ladder. Laughing at her failed attempts, I swam behind her and hoisted her on board.

"There's a ladder over there. Just hook it on the edge in those clamps," I said while I continued treading.

Here face appeared over the edge while she propped her hands on her chin. "Hmmm. Let me just think about that."

"Cassie!" I laughed.

"Cold?"

I was cold, though I wouldn't admit it. "Nope. But unless you want your little dog to drown, you'd better get that ladder down so we can get them up."

"Poppy!" Her eyes fell to Poppy who was still happily paddling away with Hank. "Okay, okay!"

After she put the ladder on, I climbed up and called Hank. He scaled it with ease, years of practice guiding his way. Poppy swam up behind him and I leaned down and scooped up the little ball of fur.

We spent the rest of the afternoon curled up in the sun, laughing and napping before the clock told us it was time to get her in for work. When I had the boat docked again, we drove home, and I kissed her goodbye before she climbed back out of my truck.

"Don't fall," I said when she opened the door.

"I'm never going to live that down, am I?"

"Nope." I grinned. "I'll still be warning you when you're ninety."

With a flush in her cheeks, she smiled and grabbed her beach bag and Poppy, climbing out of my truck carefully. Before closing the door, she blew me a kiss.

"I'll come in and see you tonight," I said.

"You'd better." She smiled and slammed the door. I waited and watched until she was safely inside her cabin. With a smile that rivaled any kid at Christmas, I drove away, counting the minutes until I could see her again.

CHAPTER NINETEEN

Cassie

It was hard to keep from skipping behind the bar at the Ox tonight. Over and over, flashes of those magical moments with Jake invaded my mind. Every touch, every look, every second I'd spent in his arms was seared into my mind. Hoping he would arrive soon, I alternated between staring out the window and watching the seconds ticking by on the clock.

"What is your deal tonight?" Jo asked.

"Huh? What do you mean?" I looked away from the window to find her arms crossed while she arched a brow.

"You're giddy. You're staring out the window. You can't stop humming."

"I'm humming?" I hadn't even noticed. But I'd been told I did it in times of extreme happiness... which hadn't happened in years.

"Yes. Humming." A quizzical gaze swept over me while she pursed her lips in a smug smile. "You got laid."

"What?" I choked out.

"Yep. I know that look. You. Got. Laid. Who was it?" She leaned in.

"I did not!" The heat rose to my cheeks and drew her knowing gaze. *Busted.*

"Jo! Can we get a round of Fireballs?" Tony called from the end of the bar.

"This isn't over," she said, before turning her attentions back to the customers.

Grateful for the reprieve, I blew out a sigh. Would Jake want me to tell her? I wasn't sure, and I didn't want to overstep any imaginary boundaries I wasn't aware of.

The door swung open, and I craned over the heads at the bar. When our eyes met, those familiar butterflies swept through my stomach again.

"Hi, Jake," I said, while he walked up to the one open stool always sitting vacant for him.

"Hey, Cassie." His smile nearly sent my stomach through the floor.

"Whiskey and coke?"

"Yep."

Our words didn't say it, but the looks between us had me ready to dive over the bar and cover him with kisses. I hurried to make his drink so I could keep my hands from grabbing his face and planting one on him.

"Hey, Jake," Jo said while she moved over to him. "Welcome back! It's been a couple weeks. I almost sent out a search party. How are you?"

"I'm great." He smiled. "How are you?"

Jo furrowed her brow. "Great?" She leaned closer, examining his face like she searched for something nefarious. "You're *great?*"

"Um. Yeah?" he answered, and his eyes slid to me.

"You're never great, Jake. Not in the twenty-plus years I've known you. You're fine. You're okay. You're good at times... but never great." She gasped and slapped the bar. "You got laid!"

Jake choked on the sip of the whiskey and coke I'd just delivered.

"And *you* just got laid!" Her eyes darted between us while that sinister smile curved her lips. "You laid each other! Ha!"

We both stared at her with mouths agape. A quick glance to one another and we dissolved into laughter.

"Who are you, Sherlock freaking Holmes?" I asked as I shook my head.

"I'm a bartender. Bartenders know *everything.*" Waggling her eyebrows, she gave us both a triumphant stare.

"Well, I suppose the cat's out of the bag. Considering Aaron busted us on the boat today, it was only a matter of time before tongues in town start wagging. So yes, Jo. Cassie and I are... together." He looked at me as if for confirmation on that last part. Nodding, I confirmed that we were much more than just a lay. So much more.

"That's so awesome. I'm taking full credit."

"Don't hurt yourself patting your own back, Jo," Jake teased.

"Whatever. I did this. Me. You're welcome." With a half-bow she backed away. I saw the excitement in her eyes, but for a split-second I saw her prior warning flash through them when she locked eyes with me. That "if you hurt him, I'll kill you" stare shot through me. But I didn't want to hurt Jake. In fact, I wanted nothing more than to make him happy.

"Well, looks like we're out in the open," Jake said. I leaned on the bar next to him. "Are you okay with that?"

"Very." I grinned. Sliding his hand into mine, I gave it a squeeze.

"Good. Because in a small town you can't really get away with much for long. And I have no intention of hiding how I feel about you."

"I wouldn't have it any other way."

We leaned forward and met in the middle of the bar, our lips brushing together for a soft kiss.

"Oh, hell no! No making out at the bar!" Jo scolded and bumped me while she passed by.

"Sorry, Jo," I sighed while our lips drifted apart.

"Don't make me spray you horny kids down with the water on the gun."

Jake shrugged. "That wouldn't stop us. We can still make out in the water. Been there, done that."

The memories of the two times we'd made out in the water together pushed back into my mind and I sighed.

Laughing, Jake pushed off his stool, giving me a playful look before walking to the jukebox. When he leaned up against it, the way his ass looked in those jeans sent that familiar wave of desire coursing through me again.

"Can I get a Captain and coke?" a customer down the bar asked, pulling my attention away.

"Sure. Of course." I glanced at Jake once more before heading to the ice well with a happy sigh.

As I shoveled ice into the glass, the quiet bar filled with the familiar notes of the song I'd heard only once in my life. Until now. He'd played it last night when he'd asked me to dance. He turned around and leaned back against the jukebox, crossing his arms while he stared straight through me.

My hand slipped on the glass I held, and it crashed to the floor in an explosion of rum and soda. The rolling ice echoed through the bar, and I gasped as I dove to grab the still-intact glass. When I stood up, Jake was back at the bar, leaning on it grinning.

"I've still got it," he said, causing me to burst into laughter.

"You certainly do." It felt like that first night I'd seen him. The promises dancing inside those azure irises caused me to lose my grip on the glass again, but this time I caught it before it made another embarrassing decent to the ground.

"Yep. Still got it." He grinned while he slid back onto his stool.

"Is this going to be a problem? I can't have you throwing Cassie off her game the rest of the summer," Jo teased.

"I'll be sad if she stops dropping glasses when I come in. I intend to have you dropping glasses for many years to come."

The look that passed between us was a silent exchange that meant he felt what I was feeling. It meant we were more than a summer fling. It meant I wasn't just a lay to him. The look broadcasted that we shared something, and we were both in this together. For the long haul.

"Bachelorette party incoming," Jo said while she glanced out the window.

"What?" I asked, still unable to climb out of Jake's intense gaze.

"We got a limo and a couple of glitzy hos. I'm guessing bachelorette party."

Groaning, she moved away from the window.

"Better cover your groin, Jake. We all know bachelorettes love you."

Rolling his eyes, he curled back up into that same hunched ball he'd been in when I first saw him. I was happy to know he had no intentions of flirting with the women who would be filling the bar with their Beyoncé, off-key singing, and copious number of RumChata shots I'd learned accompanied every bachelorette party.

The door opened, and I saw the eyes of every person widen when the newcomers drifted to the door. Curious what these girls were wearing to cause such a reaction, I finally pulled myself away from Jake. When I saw what they were looking at, my heart plummeted to my feet. Two women in scandalous dresses stood preening in the doorway. Two women I knew well. Liza in her skin-tight glittering gold mini-dress and Jessica in a Versace gown with a plunging neckline were causing all the fuss.

"It must be wrong. This can't be the place." Liza said to Jessica while she stared at her phone, then scoffed at her surroundings. "No way Cassandra is here."

Before I could dive under the bar to avoid their searching eyes, Liza's locked with mine.

"No way! It worked! Hey biyatch! We found you!" Liza shouted and hoisted her bottle of champagne triumphantly in the air.

Fumbling for words, or the ability to disappear, I froze behind the bar.

"Cassandra! She's here, guys! It worked!" Jessica called out the door.

My eyes slowly moved to the door, and I saw James and Richie step inside. Dripping in designer clothes with their perfectly styled hair, they smiled when they saw me. And right behind them was Donovan. When he appeared, the song Jake had played for me came to an end, and now I worried we would too.

This can't be happening.

"Baby! We found you!" Donovan shouted, waving at me where I stood glued to the floor. My eyes moved to Jake's and after he took them all in, his brow furrowed while he looked back to me.

"You know them?" he asked.

My mouth wouldn't respond. I stared at him, struggling to find the words, any words, to say.

They moved through the bar, each staring in shock at their new surroundings. "What *is* this place?" Richie said while he touched Captain Bailey as he passed by. Donovan took no time examining his surroundings. He and Liza came around to the entrance of the bar, and he stepped behind it like he owned the place.

"Are you *bartending?*" Liza asked when she realized I was actually behind the bar. "Like *working?* No way! We need a selfie! A Cassandra's working selfie!"

She launched to my side and leaned in with Donovan, snapping a shot while they smiled, smooshing my face between theirs as I tried to push the phone away.

"Insta!" she said while she clicked away at her phone.

"Don't. Please don't post it." My eyes darted between them and Jake.

"We've been looking for you *everywhere!*" Donovan said while he stepped up and slipped an arm around my waist. I was too shocked to fight him. "Your old gramps wouldn't say a thing, and you wouldn't respond to us, so we thought you were in rehab. But then James was telling the story about that time in Ibiza when you got so hammered we couldn't find you, so you had us put that tracking app on your phone so the next time you blacked out and woke up somewhere weird we could find you. Sure as shit, we opened it up and there you were! In *Wisconsin!* We thought it was a glitch, but we took the jet anyway, because well, why the fuck not? So here we are and sure enough, you're right where it said you'd be! What are you doing here, baby? You're not really *working,* are you?"

All I could do was stare at Jake. There were no words to explain away the lies I knew he would put together in seconds. The lies I had hoped to clear up tomorrow, so he didn't find out this way. The lies I knew would rip him away from me.

"Holy shit!" Jo breathed. "You guys are 'The Six-Pack'. That's where I know you all from. I've seen you on the internet before and you..." Her eyes widened when she looked at me. "That's where I know *you* from. I knew you looked familiar. You're Cassandra Davenport."

It felt like the world Jake had turned right side up flipped upside down again. Everything spun around me while my eyes moved from Jo, to Donovan, then Liza, and finally back to Jake.

"What?" he asked, confusion furrowing his brow. "What's going on?"

"Jake," I whispered. "I can explain."

"She's not Cassie Sinclair, Jake." Jo growled. "She's Cassandra Davenport. A fucking billionaire socialite playgirl." Her penetrating gaze moved through me while her eyes narrowed. "What is this? Is this some reality show and you've got cameras in here? Some rich chick hacking it in the real world and making fun of us local-yocals?" Jo looked around for cameras, but then her eyes locked back on with mine. "What the fuck is Cassandra Davenport doing here? And why the fuck did you lie to us?"

"Jo, I can explain."

"Wait. Your name isn't Cassie Sinclair?" Jake asked, shaking his head.

"Cassie Sinclair?" Donovan chimed in, laughing. "Who the fuck is Cassie Sinclair, and who the fuck is this guy, Cassandra?"

"I'm Jake Alton. Who the fuck are you?" He growled, rising from his stool.

"I'm her boyfriend. Donovan." His arm slid around my waist and I finally convinced my feet to move. Pulling from his grip, I shook my head.

"No. Jake. This isn't what it looks like."

As I stared at the agony in the depths of his eyes, it felt like his hand wrapped around my heart and crushed it into dust. "It looks like you lied to me about who you are and that you have a fucking boyfriend!"

"Who is this guy, baby?" Donovan asked. When he said the word baby, Jake's eyes narrowed.

"Don't call me baby." I spat, then turned my attention back to Jake. "Jake. I swear I was going to tell you. I just couldn't yet. But I was going to."

His head was shaking while he backed away from the bar. "No. I can't. I can't believe you lied to me, Cassie... or Cassandra. Or whoever the hell you are. How could you do that after... everything you know about me?"

He turned and pushed through the gathering crowd.

"Jake!" I called, rushing after him. When I made it to the door, I saw him jump in his truck. I raced after him, but all I caught was the smoke from the burning tires while he peeled out. It felt like the smoke surrounding me was from the life I'd planned now engulfed in flames.

After standing in the road watching until his taillights disappeared, I stumbled back into the Ox in a daze. An eerie silence had settled over the customers, and every set of eyes stared at me while I moved between them back to the bar.

"Seriously, Cassandra. What's going on?" James asked while I brushed by him.

"Are you seriously like, working here or something? We thought you were in rehab and we were coming to bust you out," Richie said, but I ignored him and kept moving.

"Cassandra?" Jessica asked as I stepped back behind the bar.

"You guys need to go," I whispered, barely able to form the words.

"Baby, what's up?" Donovan reached for me, but I stepped out of his grip.

"Go."

"Cassandra? What the hell is wrong with you?" Liza stepped to his side.

They all stared at me. Seeing them again... their over-done makeup, expensive clothes, glittering jewelry, and the vacant look in their eyes reminded me of the life I'd left behind. The life I'd never wanted. Because of my extreme grief, I'd fallen into it and I'd let them keep me there even when I'd wanted out. It had been too hard to say no. Too easy to let the drugs and the parties cloud my mind and my heart, protecting me from the pain I didn't want to accept. But now, seeing them with clear eyes, I knew I could never go back to that life again. This was the life I wanted. A life here. With Jake.

And now, because of them, I saw the life I truly wanted slipping out of my fingers.

"Cassandra?" Donovan said while I stared at them, blinking.

"Get out!" I screamed, startling even myself with the force of my words. "All of you! Go! I don't want any of you in my life anymore! Please. Go. Leave me alone. Just leave me alone!" Tears broke through and burned a trail down my cheeks.

"Cassandra," Donovan said, reaching for me one last time.

"Go. You're all bad for me. This," I waved a hand over them, "isn't what I want. It's not who I am. Just, please go. Go. Go!" I screamed, hurt and rage rising inside me. Anger at the death of my parents. Anger at the way I'd thrown away my life. Anger at these people who fueled my grief with drugs and alcohol. And the anger that I'd lied to Jake and he would never forgive me.

But mostly, anger at myself. I'd lacked accountability in my life for far too long. That ended right now.

"Okay, okay, we're going. Whatever, bitch," Liza snapped, then pulled Donovan by the hand. I caught the glares of all my old friends while they walked out the door, and I hoped, out of my life. When the door closed behind them, I let out a deep breath. I'd finally been strong enough to tell them no. This time I chose myself, and the life I knew I could have without the temptations of a quick escape.

Standing at the entrance to the bar with tears streaming down my face, I turned to Jo. "Please. You have to let me explain."

"The only thing I have to do is not kick your ass because I don't feel like going to jail tonight, and I have a feeling you and your money come with a lot of lawyers. But if you don't get the hell out of here in the next thirty seconds, I'll take that jail stay. I told you if you hurt Jake, I'd kill you. So, consider this your head start, *Cassandra*."

"Jo, please."

"Go get on your jet and go back to your shitty little world."

"That's not what I want anymore, Jo. This is the life I want."

"Then don't. I don't care what you do. All I know is you'd better get the fuck out of here. And stay the hell away from Jake. He didn't deserve this, and you don't deserve him. Now go."

A sob wracked my shoulders as I nodded. I stumbled out the door and jumped when it slammed behind me. It sounded like the door to the new life I'd imagined slamming as well.

I looked down to the street to see my old friends climbing into their limo, and five sets of eyes glared at me while they pulled away. Liza rolled down the window and screamed bitch for good measure, and it only solidified my desire to never see them again. How I'd spent so much time blinded by my grief that I'd ever considered them friends was something I didn't know if I'd ever understand.

I didn't want to be like them. I *wasn't* like them. And now that I'd tasted how wonderful real life could be, I knew I'd never follow them down that road again. Their limo wound around the corner and I stood staring at it, watching the last of my old life disappear.

And just like my grief and guilt, I hoped they would stay gone for good.

Desperate to talk to Jake and explain myself, I climbed into my car and drove to the docks looking for his truck. When I didn't see it, I texted him while I sat on the side of the road, but it went undelivered. He'd shut his phone off. On my way home, I drove to his house, but he wasn't there either. Knowing I'd blown it, and knowing Jake wasn't the forgiving type, I let the tears stream free while I drove back to my cabin. When I got inside, I collapsed on the bed and curled up with Poppy in my arms. She was all I had left.

CHAPTER TWENTY

Cassie

Poppy's soft snores vibrated against my ear. Opening my eyes, I saw her smooshed face pressed against me. The damp spot from my tears lingered on my pillow, and before I had a moment to breathe, the tears came again.

I'd ruined everything.

Letting my grief settle over me, I held Poppy tight while I cried into her soft fur like I had until I fell asleep last night. I'd tried Jake's phone dozens of times, but it went straight to voicemail each time. Jo returned my apology text with a simple and concise "fuck you" and I knew she hated me as well.

Why wouldn't they? I'd lied. I'd barged into their world and lied about everything. But what they didn't know was why. They didn't know my family's legacy was on the line. That the stipulation of my redemption was that I do it without the benefit of my name or money. I know my grandfather hadn't considered the ramifications of living a lie, and neither had I until my feelings for Jake grew into something deeper than I'd ever felt before.

Wiping my tears, I rolled over and picked up my phone to try Jake again. I'd called him a dozen times last night, desperate to explain myself, but each call went straight to voicemail. Hoping maybe there was a text or a voicemail from him, I held my breath while I clicked it on. Instead of a missed call from Jake, I saw a missed call from Grandpa. Clicking the buttons, I tapped on my voicemail and listened to the stern voice on the other side.

"Call me. Now."

Groaning, I dialed him up. Now what.

"Hello?" he answered.

"Hey, Grandpa. It's me."

"Well, if it isn't Cassandra."

I furrowed my brow at the unchecked aggression in his voice. "What's wrong, Grandpa?"

"What's wrong? What's wrong is you've been lying to me. And I believed you."

"What are you talking about?" I sat up.

"You didn't think just because I don't know anything about all that social media crap that I wouldn't have someone watching it?"

"What?"

"Your *friends* are up there. There was a photo on that Instachat or whatever it's called. You promised you wouldn't get tangled up with them again."

"No, Grandpa," I argued. "I'm not. They just—"

"I don't want to hear it!" he shouted. "You led me to believe you were up there making money, learning about life and real work. That you broke ties with those treacherous, spoiled misfits. But it seems you lied. Again! I told you that cutting ties with them was part of the deal. A deal you have now broken. You couldn't even make it a month without calling them back to your side. Them and their drugs and their scandalous ways!"

"Grandpa! That's not true! They just showed up!"

"Lies! I'm done with your lies, Cassandra!"

"But I'm not lying," I whispered with a trembling lip.

"Well, it's too late. You can't be trusted. I failed you. But I won't fail my company. I'm selling it to Edward Garvey because I can trust him to care for my employees and my legacy."

"No, Grandpa. Please. Just let me explain."

"I've had two years of your explanations. Your commitment is free. You're welcome to leave Door County now. It doesn't matter anymore. It's over, Cassandra."

I was still recovering from the blow last night and his callous words felt like a slap on the other cheek. Before I could argue back, he hung up. Tears continued streaming while I stared at my phone. Yesterday I'd never been happier, my life finally headed in the right direction. Toward a certain and worthwhile future. Today I had nothing left. Just when I started putting myself back together, the cruel hand of fate yanked the rug right out from underneath me and now I didn't think I'd ever be whole again. Everyone I cared about was wreckage in my wake and I didn't know who to turn to. I had no one left and the emptiness inside me threatened to swallow me whole.

After an hour of sobbing into my blankets, I heard the memories of my father's voice in my mind. He used to comfort me when I cried, but every time I did, he would say the same thing.

"Cry your tears, but then remember, tears solve nothing. Instead of crying over your situation, give me three ways you can fix it."

Instead of allowing me to wallow in self-pity, he'd force me to problem solve my way out of the grief. And sure enough, every time he presented me with the challenge, I found a solution. My tears would dry up and I would march off to solve the cause of them. That wasn't how I'd been living my life since their death. All I did was run farther and farther from my problems and pain. Even though all I wanted to do was cry, it wouldn't repair the rifts I'd torn between myself and the people I cared about. Imagining my father holding my hand and pulling me up, I rose from the bed and took a deep breath.

My grandfather couldn't sell Davenport Industries to that shady bastard, Edward Garvey. It was my birthright, and I could run it better. I knew I could and now I just needed to prove it. And tears weren't the solution. After wiping them away, I tossed some clothes in a suitcase, fed Poppy breakfast, then carried her and my suitcase to the car. Pulling out my phone, I dialed the one person I hoped would still help me.

"Cassandra?" Eleanor asked when she answered the phone.

"Yes. It's me. Eleanor, I need a plane ticket home," I said into the phone while I started up the engine.

"I don't think that's a good idea, Cassandra. He's really upset."

"That's exactly why I need to see him. This is all one big misunderstanding. I have to explain it to him and make him understand that I didn't ask them to come here. They just showed up. I swear it. Please. Send the jet. Buy a ticket. Get me a train. Just get me back to New York. Today. Please."

"Okay, Cassandra. I'll book you a flight out of Milwaukee and have the car service pick you up at JFK." I heard the reluctant tones in her voice, but if I was going to fix things with my grandpa, I was going to do it face to face. Like a woman capable of running a billion-dollar corporation would do.

"Thank you, Eleanor. Thank you so much. Just text me the details and I'll see you soon."

We hung up while I drove down my driveway and onto the road. When I saw Jake's driveway, I turned in. I was going to make things better one person at a time. But when I pulled up, no truck sat in the driveway.

I put my car in park and reached into my purse, pulling out my little notepad. If Jake wouldn't take my calls, maybe he would read a letter. After scribbling down my apology and begging him to call me and let me explain, I folded it up and walked up his front steps. With a deep breath, I shoved it underneath the door. It wasn't much, but it was a start.

Swallowing the lump in my throat while I refused to cry, I pulled back out. When I passed the marina, his truck wasn't there either. Though I was desperate to see him, I didn't have time to wait. Stopping my grandpa from selling his company was my priority today and getting Jake to forgive me would have to be next.

Hoping I was making the right decision, I guided my car through Baileys Harbor. Just a month ago this had all looked so foreign to me, so frightening. A new world so different from my own. But now it looked like home. All the quaint stores lining the roads. The sweeping views of the water that caught my eye when I drove by. The Blue Ox towered over me while I drove past, and I remembered how odd I'd thought it looked in this small town. Now it was one of my favorite places and one I hoped I could come back to soon.

Forcing my foot to stay on the gas, I drove out of town toward Milwaukee to catch my flight. It was my last chance to prove to my grandpa that I really had changed.

My limo pulled up to our apartments. The driver opened the door, and I stepped out. Taking a deep breath, I held Poppy close while I straightened my back like a rigid rod. If I was going to show Grandpa I was capable of handling this company, I needed to do it like a businesswoman… not a blubbering granddaughter begging for forgiveness.

"I'll send your bags up," the driver said while he dipped his head and stepped out of my way.

"Thank you," I answered and started toward the steps to our building.

"Miss Cassandra! Welcome back!" Archie said as he swept open the door.

"It's great to see you, Archie." I paused to kiss him on the cheek. He dropped his eyes to the ground, concealing his shy smile.

"Is Grandpa here?"

"He is. Do you need an escort up?"

"No, thank you. I can do this on my own." With a deep breath I went to the elevator and pressed the button. I was on my own now, and I didn't need Archie holding my hand.

After the ride to the top, I stepped out and paused at the sight of my old surroundings. It was a drastic change from the little cabin I'd come to love so much. This used to feel like home to me, but now I felt like a visitor in my old life. Now my cabin felt like home. Door County felt like home. Jake... Jake felt like home.

Forcing his memory from my mind, I focused on one problem at a time. Right now it was my grandpa. With a stilling breath I started down the hall.

"Cassandra? You made it!" Eleanor said, stepping out of the sitting room.

"Eleanor!" I pulled her in for a hug, squishing Poppy between us. "I missed you!"

"We missed you, too."

"I didn't do what he thinks I did, Eleanor. I swear. I was so happy up there."

"I believe you, Cassandra." She squeezed me tighter. "I can already tell that you've changed."

"I have changed, Eleanor. So much. But Grandpa doesn't believe me. I really need to see him. Is he in his office?"

Nodding, she gestured to his office door.

"Does he know I'm coming?"

She shook her head.

"Thank you for getting me home. Can you watch Poppy while I talk to him?"

With a nod, she took the sleepy bundle from my arms and held her tight. "Good luck."

The soft warning in her eyes didn't deter me. Heaving another breath, I marched down the hallway and knocked.

"Enter!" he called.

Pushing open the door, I peeked inside. His head was down, staring at paperwork.

"Grandpa, it's me."

Slowly, his gaze rose until it settled on me. It wasn't my sweet Grandpa staring back at me. It was the powerful man who single-handedly created a billion-dollar company. A man who commanded respect in any room he entered. It was the look I was certain his adversaries had been on the receiving end of more times than not. This time, it was directed at me.

"Cassandra. I'm surprised to see you here." He steepled his fingers while he leaned forward on his desk.

"The conversation we need to have is better face to face."

"Is that so?" he asked, arching a brow.

"It is." I strode in with confidence I didn't yet have, but hoped I radiated.

"Then please sit." He gestured to the chair. His surprise at my formal behavior didn't go unnoticed.

"Thank you," I said, sliding into the leather chair.

"What can I do for you, Cassandra? Need some money?" An accusatory stare met mine.

"Not at all. I was doing just fine on my own, without your money *or* their money."

"Is that so?"

"It is. And you should know I didn't invite them, nor did I reveal my location. It seems they used a tracking app on my phone to find me. I sent them away and told them I didn't want to see them again."

He scoffed. I didn't blame him for not believing me. Years of my lies and excuses had laid a path that led him to the easiest conclusion... I was lying again.

"I want to make you proposition."

"And what on earth is it you want to propose?"

"Let me run the company for six months, under your guidance. If in six months you don't think I can do it, then sell it to Garvey."

"It's too late."

"It's not too late. I know you don't believe me, but I swear to you I was fine on my own up there. I made my own money, friends, and I learned so much about how hard people need to work. You and father have been training me on the business side of running Davenport Industries since I was in diapers, you know I can do that part. What you didn't know was if I still had it in me. I do. I swear I do."

"Cassandra, it's—"

"I admit it." I stopped him, seeing the wrong answer in his eyes. "I was a wreck after my parents died. You know I blamed myself and the guilt was more than I could bear. But that's not an excuse for my behavior. I was wrong, and you were right to throw me out on my ass. I needed it. And what I also needed was to remember my father's words to fight my problems head on, find solutions, like a true Davenport. My solution is test me. Train me. Stand over my shoulder and critique everything I do. I welcome it. Learning from you would be the greatest gift you could give me. Please Grandpa, don't sell the company. Test me. I won't disappoint you."

This time I saw the shift in his eyes. The wobble in his resolve. A long sigh followed, and we sat in silence while I let him ponder my proposal.

"Cassandra. I love you. More than you could ever know. But it's too late. I met with Edward this morning and we've already started the process to officially sell the company to him. I gave him my word, and my word is my bond. I won't go back on it now. Edward Garvey will take the reins. I have faith he will take care of my employees and my legacy."

It felt like the air got sucked out of the room. Struggling for my next breath, I lifted my chin. "I see. Well, I'm sorry to hear that. I did what you asked of me down to the letter, and I hurt people in the process. People I've come to care about. But I don't blame you for giving up on me."

A softness washed over his face. "I didn't give up on you. I would never do that. But I gave up on waiting. I'm exhausted, Cassandra. The energy of my youth has left me, and I don't have what it takes to run this company anymore. I'm not a strong leader anymore. Putting my pride aside, I know it's time, past time in fact, to hand it over. And you're not ready. I'm sorry, Cassandra."

Even though it felt like my dreams were shattering, I understood. How could I not? I'd given him no reason for confidence in me, and he'd done what he had to do. Protect his company and his employees. If I'd been in his position, I'd have done the same thing. Any good businessperson would have.

"Can you forgive me?" he asked.

"Of course, I can. Can you forgive me?"

Leaning forward, his weathered hand reached out for mine. I took it in my own and squeezed. "I love you, Grandpa. Even though I think Garvey is a treacherous snake," I narrowed my eyes, pursing my lips together while he chuckled, "I do hope he takes Davenport Industries to new heights."

"Yes, he can be a bit of a devious one, but he's never turned on me. He's been loyal for decades, and our directions have always been the same. I trust that he will take care of my company."

"Then I'm glad for you, Grandpa. You deserve to retire. I'm sorry I messed it all up."

"I'm sorry I didn't stop you sooner, Cassandra. It's as much my fault as it is yours."

Shaking my head, I squeezed his hand again. "No. You may have given me an endless supply of money to behave the way I did, but even if you hadn't, I would have found a way. It's my fault."

"And about the money, Cassandra. I'm not cutting you off. You'll still receive a sizeable allowance until your trust fund kicks in. I would never turn my back on you."

Sitting back, I sighed. "I don't want it."

His eyebrows shot up. "Excuse me?"

"The money. I don't want it. I want to take care of myself. Make my own way, just like you did. Who knows, maybe I'll start my own Davenport Industries." I arched a brow, and he burst into laughter.

"Are you sure? You don't want any of our money? I mean, the trust is yours in a couple years, but I am happy to support you until then."

I shook my head. "I don't think so. It's time I stood on my own two feet. Even though you didn't believe me, I really was making it okay on my own. I doubt I have a job to return to, or a boy for that matter, but I have to try."

"A boy?" He pursed his lips.

"Yes. But a good one this time. He's a fisherman."

"Really? A fisherman?"

I nodded. "Yes. And I hurt him, Grandpa. I need to go make things right. I need to fix my messes. All of them."

"Tell me about your time in Door County."

We sat in his office for hours while I told him all about my mishaps, about my time with Jake, the Blue Ox, and all the things I'd learned. When I'd finished, I felt the rift between us repairing, and I hoped that when I returned to Door County in a few days, after spending some much-needed time with Grandpa, that I could get them to forgive me as well.

CHAPTER TWENTY-ONE

Jake

"Are you sure you put whiskey in here, Jo?" I grumbled, sipping on my drink.

Jo rolled her eyes. "It's over half whiskey, Jake."

Leveling her with a stare, I pushed it forward. We sat in a silent standoff for a long moment before she sighed and grabbed the bottle of whiskey, filling it back up to the top.

"There. Happy?"

"Not even close," I answered, then took a long gulp.

"So, this is it for you again? Grumpy and alone? Sworn off love and happiness?"

"Yep."

With an exasperated sigh, she tossed up her hands. "Well, that's just great, Jake. Sounds like a kick-ass life."

"It will be just fine. At least I won't have to go through that shit again."

"I get it. It sucked. She lied to us. But you can't let that tramp push you back into that pit of despair you love to wallow in."

"I'm not wallowing. I'm accepting my life alone. How I want it. How it was *going to be* until you pushed her on me."

"So now this is my fault?"

"You said you were taking full credit for the hook-up, so now you can take full credit for the aftermath."

"Fine. It's my fault. I did it. Sorry, I wanted to see you happy. I'm the asshole here. Now, can we get back to the part where you're smiling again?" She plastered on a fake smile and waited for me to join her. All I did was grumble and take another sip of my drink.

"I give up." She shook her head and walked away to serve another customer.

"What's up, man?" Aaron asked as he pulled up a stool beside me.

"Nothing."

"You okay? I heard a rumor that the little hottie was some rich celebrity or something?" His eyes widened while he waited. Of course, Aaron would think the lie from Cassie was no big deal... or Cassandra, or whatever the hell her name was.

"I don't want to talk about it."

"Dude. You like, dated a celebrity. A *hot* celebrity. You've got to spill!"

Spill? What the hell did he want me to spill? That I got trampled by a woman again? Lied to again? Had my heart stomped on again? It was all happening *again*. I dove off that cliff, and instead of floating beside her I'd gone headfirst into the dirt. The pain from her betrayal cut deeper than anything I'd ever imagined.

I'd known Nikki the better part of a decade and her loss paled in comparison to the loss of Cassie. Even though I'd just met her this summer, the feelings she evoked had consumed me. They didn't take years to grow on me. No.

They snuck up on me. Like a match to a can of gasoline, my feelings for her had exploded in seconds. And as much as I tried to douse the flames with beer and whiskey, they still raged inside me. Though this time the flames from my anger matched them. A lethal combination of dueling fires burned inside me now.

Threatening to burn me alive.

I took another sip from my drink. "I don't want to talk about it."

My new mantra. I said it to Jo. I said it to Aaron. I'd repeat it to anyone else who asked me about Cassie. And I *didn't* want to talk about it. I couldn't.

Jo leaned in and appraised my solemn face. "At least she's gone, Jake. Word has it she left with those rich friends of hers. No one has seen her for five days. I still wonder if it was like a reality show or something?"

"Dude! If it was, I'm so going to be famous!" Aaron smiled. They both peered around, still looking for the cameras they were convinced had been installed at the Blue Ox.

I wasn't entirely convinced it *wasn't* some reality show. What other reason would a billionaire socialite have to live in a dilapidated cabin, drive a car that saw its best days decades ago and take up bartending at the Blue Ox? It didn't make sense. Then thoughts of my stupidity in falling for her being broadcast across the world tightened the knot in my stomach. Even with my affinity for tying and untying knots when I fished, I couldn't undo this wadded up lump no matter how hard I tried. Was I just part of the plot?

Convince some dumb redneck to fall for her equals ratings gold?

"Well, if it is a TV show, they need to have us all sign those agreements to be on it, so I guess we'll know if they show up," Jo said.

"I'll sign!" Aaron smiled.

"I won't. No fucking way." Shaking my head, I felt a little better knowing they couldn't exploit my broken heart and embarrass me not only in my small town, but to everyone in the world.

"Oh, come on, man!" Aaron bumped me with an elbow. "Take one for the team."

"Aaron," Jo warned. She shook her head and silenced him with a stare.

"Are you really that torn up about this?" he asked, finally noticing my lack of enthusiasm in this turn of events.

"I'm fine," I grumbled.

"Dude. I'm sorry. I didn't know. I figured you just met her, got a quick lay to get back on the horse. No harm; no foul."

I didn't answer. Why couldn't I have just done that? Why did I have to go and fall for the girl, like a lovesick schmuck? Wondering why I somehow lacked that gene most men had that allowed them to sleep with random girls without a modicum of attachment, I took another sip of my drink. A big one.

At least she was gone. Having to see her around town would have been cruel and unnecessary punishment. She was probably laughing about me with her friends at some swanky club in Paris right now.

"Oh, shit," Jo said, as she looked at the door.

Aaron and I, along with the other dozen people scattered throughout the bar, followed her gaze to the door.

Shit is right.

Cassie stood in the doorway. Her eyes met mine and that surge of power her gaze induced in me pulsed through my veins once again. I cursed it while I struggled to keep my mouth closed.

"What are you doing here?" Jo asked, her protective nature over me surging while she stepped around the bar to my side. Even though I'd spent our childhood beating up bullies who picked on her and tossing out guys at the bar who got too handsy with her, this time I was grateful it was her protecting *me*.

"I came back to apologize to you guys. To Jake." Her eyes remained locked with mine and I struggled to force my own away. So many emotions collided inside me underneath her sorrow-filled gaze.

"Get the hell out of here, *Cassandra*. You've done enough damage already," Jo argued.

"Please. I just want to apologize and explain myself."

"We don't want to hear it."

Grateful Jo seemed to be pulling the words out of my mouth, I sat in my stool unable to speak or move away.

"Please, just let me explain."

"Let me guess," Jo said, pressing her finger to her chin. "You got bored with your glitzy life, took a bet or signed up for some stupid reality show, then came up here to live amongst the little people. To make fun of us and call back to your friends with stories of how pathetic we all are without our jets and limos and five-thousand-dollar shoes."

"That's not what happened, Jo. I swear."

"Seriously, Cassie. We don't want to hear it. You lied. You hurt Jake. And I told you what would happen if you did."

Now Jo's protective ways made me feel like a small child rather than a grown man.

"Just go, Cassie," I finally managed to say. "I don't want to hear it."

"Jake, please." She stepped toward me and touched my shoulder. It wasn't that I didn't want her to touch me that had me shooting up off my stool and out of her grasp, it was that I did. Even with all her lies, the electricity in her touch still affected me like it did before. It still ripped through me and had me desperate to pull her into my arms. But not this time. This time I wouldn't forgive the woman, eat up her lies, then let her humiliate me over and over again.

No fucking way.

"Go, Cassie," I commanded.

"I'm not leaving until you let me explain myself!"

"Fine. Then I'll leave." Pushing past her, I stormed out into the streets and made a beeline for my truck. Maybe it was childish to run, but I didn't care. I couldn't be with her and not succumb to my desire to taste those lips again.

Slamming myself inside my truck, I pressed my head into the steering wheel. Why couldn't she just stay gone? Let me get on with my life? My life alone.

The dome light flicked on and I heard my passenger door open. Looking over, I saw Cassie fumbling to get inside.

"You've got to be fucking kidding me," I growled when she planted herself beside me.

"Please, Jake. You have to let me explain," I begged while I closed the truck door, sealing us both inside.

"Apparently I *do* need to lock my doors even in Door County. Get out, Cassie."

"Jake, please. I'm not leaving until you let me talk."

The hurt and pain in his eyes tore me apart. I'd been the cause of it. This time, I'd put it there and not some random faceless woman who'd fled the scene of the crime. The last thing I'd wanted to do was hurt him, yet it was exactly what I'd done. He was the first man in my life who set my soul on fire, who cared about me for *me*, and I'd destroyed him.

"I don't *have* to let you explain anything. You lied. Period. You know how I feel about lies. Now get out."

"I do know how you feel about lying, Jake. I swear I do. But I had to lie. I was trying to save my company. It was a requirement for me redeeming myself that I not tell anyone my real name. I was planning on telling you as soon as my grandpa said I could."

Shaking his head, he scoffed. "What are you even talking about?"

"If you'll let me explain, it will all make sense!"

"No. It doesn't matter. I don't care about whatever stupid excuse you have for lying to me about who you were. There isn't an excuse in the world to make what you did okay. I trusted you. I cared about you. Hell, I was *falling* for you! And I didn't even know your fucking real name!"

Tears burned behind my eyes while I braced against his anger like the hurricane I knew it would be.

"My parents died."

"So that's your excuse? Your parents died, so you come up here and lie to us?"

Shaking my head, I reached for him, but he pulled away. "No. Two years ago, my parents died. And I went off the deep-end, Jake. I went from a good girl, grad school high honors, and the heir to my family's company to a complete disaster. Drugs. Parties. You name it, I did it. Before they died, taking over that company was all I had ever planned on doing, but I thought it would be years away. When my father retired. But after he died, my future fell into my lap while I was stunned by tragedy."

He'd let me get this far without stopping me, so I kept on, hoping he would finally let me explain.

"I wasn't ready. Not only was I too young, I was overwhelmed with my grief. I handled it poorly. Poorly is an understatement. I was a shit show, Jake."

"I've seen the photos online now." He glared across the dim lights of the dashboard.

"I'm not proud. And neither was my grandpa. He toughened up and cut me off. Taking away my chance to step into my father's shoes and run the company. So, I begged for any way to show him I was capable of taking the reins. And his solution was to send me away, on my own. No money, no help, and no using my identity as a crutch. No favors based on my name. If I told *anyone* who I was, my family company was gone, and he'd consider me a failure. But I swear I was planning on telling him I couldn't lie to you anymore. I'd even called him that day to ask him if I could reveal myself to you, but he was in meetings. I promise Jake; I never intended to hurt you. I didn't know what to do. If I told you, I betrayed him. If I didn't tell you, I betrayed you. I was so stuck."

Silence settled over us and I inhaled, glad he'd stopped screaming at me to get out of the truck.

"You need to know that I *want* this life. I don't want to go back to who I was. Parties, drugs, and a life filled with empty people who would sell their soul for money. This is where I want to be. Here."

He scoffed. "Sure, Cassie. The second you win your way back into his good graces you're out of here."

"No. That's not true," I reached for him again, but he wrested himself away. "I already *did* win my way back into his good graces. That's where I went. Home to New York. Even though I was too late to claim my place in the company, I earned his forgiveness. And I chose to come back here. To you."

"I don't even know what to think right now, Cassie."

"I know it's a lot to take in. And I did *not* want you finding out that way. I thought I'd cut them all out of my life, but they found me anyway. I swear I was going to tell you the next day."

"So, what exactly was your plan. With us?" He glared. "You said you were just here to earn your way back into the company. So what, you were going to have a fling with me and then just haul ass out of here the minute you proved your worth? Leave me here while you fled back to the city?"

"No." I shook my head and sighed. "I don't know. I wanted both. And I was trying to figure out a way to have both. You, Door County *and* the company. I wanted to fulfill my dream, my father's dream, and step into his shoes. But I wanted to live here. With you."

"Bullshit." He rolled his eyes. "It's such bullshit, Cassie. You would have taken off in a second."

"That's not true! I would have figured something out! But it doesn't matter now. The company is gone. Sold."

"So that's why you're back." He snorted. "Your plan failed, so you came running back here hoping I'd forgive you. Your second choice."

"Jake. I swear to you I wasn't going to bolt once I inherited the company. This is where I want to be. With you. Right here in Door County."

Those blue eyes burned through mine. Searching. I could only hope he could see the truth inside me. My feelings for him were real. My desire to be with him was real. It was the most real thing I'd ever had in my life.

"Please, Jake. I know I fucked up. Again. It seems to be all I've been able to do since my parents died. Hell, I'm even the reason they're dead. It was my fault. They died, and it was my fault." The tears broke free and saying those words out loud ripped back open the wound I knew would never fully heal.

Even though I knew he was furious with me, seeing my tears softened the anger inside his eyes.

"How was a plane crash your fault, Cassie?" he asked, quieter now.

"Because they were flying to me. I'd gone skiing in Vail and fell, breaking my leg. When I called them from the hospital, I begged them to come be with me. Grandpa was away on the jet, so they chartered a plane and were flying to me. It crashed, Jake. And they died. They died because I went skiing down a hill I wasn't ready for. They died because I made them come. They died because of me."

Sobs shook my shoulders. Saying it out loud, admitting it to Jake felt like unloading a burden I'd carried alone these past two years.

"Cassie, it's not your fault," he whispered. His hand brushed against mine. When he squeezed it, I cried harder.

"It *is* my fault. They got on that plane because I begged them to come. They died because of me."

"Hey, hey," he said softly, scooting toward me. Wrapping an arm around my shoulder, he pulled me into his chest. "They died because of a plane crash. You didn't control the plane. It happens. Life. Death. It just happens. And it's no one's fault. You can't blame yourself, Cassie. You couldn't have known."

"I *do* blame myself! It's all that I could think about until I found the escape, the crutch of booze and drugs I've leaned on for two years now. And even though I still blame myself, I finally found peace up here. With you. I started to heal."

"You're not to blame, Cassie. I can't imagine what you've been through. But you're not to blame. You need to forgive yourself."

He held me while I cried. Knowing he was the type of man who could comfort me even amid his anger made the agony of my lies to him burn deeper.

"I'm so sorry, Jake. I'm so sorry. I messed everything up. Again." I sniffled and peered up at him. This time it wasn't anger burning through me. It was understanding. Kindness. I leaned up, closing my eyes while I pressed my lips to his.

"I'm so sorry, Jake," I whispered against his resistant lips. But he didn't pull away. I pressed my lips to his again. This time they responded. Soft at first, a reluctant return of my kiss. I pressed deeper into him, wrapping my arm around his neck. Passion exploded from his kiss when he pulled me against him. I whimpered into his mouth when our lips collided, the power of our connection crackling once again between us. But then he froze in my embrace.

"No," he barked, ripping himself away.

"Jake." I tried to reach for him again, but he shook his head, wiping his lips while he stared out the window.

"No. I can't. I'm sorry, Cassie. I'm sorry about what you went through. But I can't do this. Not again. I— I don't know what to feel right now. I don't even know what to believe, or how to make sense of this. I just need time, or space, or... I don't fucking know what I need, but I just... I can't."

"Jake, please."

"Go, Cassie. Please. Just go." Tears shimmered in his eyes and caused mine to flood unchecked again.

Nodding my head, I sucked on my lip still tingling from his kiss and opened the door. With teary eyes, I looked back at him once more before climbing out. He didn't look at me, and I wondered if he'd ever look at me without hurt in his eyes again. He'd already been so damaged, and I'd torn apart what was left of him.

"I'm sorry, Jake. You have to believe me," I said, before I closed the door.

Silence was his only answer. When I stepped back, the engine roared, and he drove off, leaving me standing in the road. Struggling to keep from running after him or crumpling into a heap, I heard my father whispering in my ear again. Crying wouldn't fix this. It wasn't going to make Jake forgive me or pay the new bills I'd have out on my own. And it wasn't going to bring my parents back.

Even though I didn't know if I could ever truly forgive myself for their deaths, I knew to finish the process of healing and fix all the damage in my wake, I needed to try. This was a fresh start for me, and I felt like they each stood holding my hand, encouraging me to take the first steps toward redemption. I was too late to save the company, but I hoped I wasn't too late to save myself.

With my new resolve coursing through my veins, I turned back toward the Blue Ox. Maybe Jake wasn't ready to forgive me, and Jo may kill me when I walked through those doors, but I needed a job and I needed her forgiveness. Hoping to win both, I marched inside.

"You've got to be kidding me," she groaned when I came through the doors.

"Jo. I need to apologize to you."

"Don't want to hear it." She turned her back and pretended to fuss with the beer bottles.

"You're short staffed now. And that's my fault. But if you'll let me explain myself to you, and what really happened, maybe we can find a way to work together. Or I can at least help you until you replace me. Unless you feel like working doubles in the middle of the busiest month of the year." I arched a brow and held my ground.

Rising slowly, she turned to meet me. "Fine. Speak. But if we get to the end and I don't like what you've said, I get full permission to punch you. And you don't get to call your fancy lawyers and throw me in jail."

Struggling to suppress my smile, I nodded. "You have yourself a deal."

With an eye roll, she crossed her arms and raised her eyebrows. "Well. Go on then."

After exhaling a long sigh of relief, I started from the beginning.

CHAPTER TWENTY-TWO

Jake

My muscles ached from the fight that salmon put up during my evening charter tonight. I'd welcomed the battle to help unleash all the anger Cassie's return yesterday had built within me. Just when I'd thought I could start healing and move on, she'd marched back into my life. Like a wrecking ball, she'd blown everything to pieces.

With the call of whiskey pulling me in, I stumbled up the steps to the Ox. Being a Saturday night in July, the bar was packed, and I felt bad that Jo would be alone. This would have been a shift Cassie was on if she still worked here. But there was no way I could sit here with Cassie behind the bar again, so even though it sucked for Jo and meant slow service for the night, I looked forward to a Cassie-free night at the Ox to unwind and help forget her.

"Hey, Jake!" Jo said while I slid into my stool. "You missed happy hour. You're in late tonight."

"Yeah. Evening charter ran late. I'll take a –"

"Really? You still think you need to order a drink? I'm pretty sure you've been drinking whiskey and cokes since we had our first one sophomore year at that field party out on Logerquist Road."

"You're probably right."

"I think I still have prickles embedded in my skin from when the cops raided, and we tore through those juniper bushes."

If I'd been in a better mood, I would have laughed. Matt, Jo, and I had run for an hour when cops busted in on our underage party. It was the first time any of us had gotten drunk. But remembering my friendship with Matt only pushed the knife deeper in my back. It seemed everyone wanted a turn twisting the blade these days. At least Jo was still a loyal friend.

"So, there's something I need to tell you," she said as she dropped the drink in front of me.

When I looked up, her eyes shifted, and the brazen confidence Jo wore like a cape flitted away. Biting her lip, she glanced toward the door to the kitchen. It opened. The second I saw the blonde hair I started off of my stool.

So much for Jo being a loyal friend. She hired her back?

"Jake. Just wait." She grabbed my arm and pulled it down to the bar with strength surprising for someone her size.

"Are you fucking kidding me?" I growled. "She's back?"

"Jake. You really should listen to her story."

"I *did* listen to her story. That sucks about what happened, but the bottom line is she lied to me. I've been lied to by women enough!"

"Come on, Jake. Life isn't so black and white. That girls been through some shit. I think she means it when she says she wants to make a life here. And if I can find it in my hardened heart to forgive her, maybe you should at least consider it."

I shook my head hard. "No. I can't."

Cassie stepped behind the bar and our eyes connected. How she could still send my stomach tumbling into the abyss after everything she did shocked me more than the sight of her still working at the Ox.

"Jake. Just hear her out."

"I don't need to hear her out again. You're short of help. You hired her back. I get it. But that doesn't mean I need to sit here and get tortured by her. I'm out of here."

"Jake!" Jo pleaded while I ripped my arm away.

"I can't, Jo." Hanging my head, I pushed through the crowd out onto the front porch. Even my sanctuary was ruined now. The Blue Ox had been my bar. Matt got the Cornerstone. I got the Ox. Now Cassie had it and I felt one more thing being taken from me. The door creaked when it opened behind me.

"Jake."

Cassie. Of course, it was. I groaned and stared out at the street. "Don't Cassie. It's fine. I'll go."

"I don't want you to go, Jake. I want you to forgive me."

"I can't." I couldn't look at her. One look into her teary eyes last night shattered my resolve. One taste of those lips and I almost couldn't stop. I didn't dare look into her eyes now. One look and I knew she could strip away the last of my defenses and send me hurtling off the cliff again. Not this time. I couldn't take another crash to the ground.

"Jake." She brushed her fingers against my arm. "If you won't forgive me, I'll quit. I'm not going to ruin your life any more than I already have. But I wish you could find a way to forgive me. If I'd have known I would fall for you, I never would have lied the first day we met. I swear."

Fall for me? Oh, God. I wanted to turn around. I wanted to look into her eyes and see if they were filled with more lies or maybe, just maybe, this time the truth.

"I'll do anything to prove it to you. Just give me a chance, Jake."

With my eyes boring through the pavement, I heaved a breath. Could I? Could I trust her one more time? But then I remembered the pain. The agony. The shame I'd felt in falling for her lies before. Her lies I'd endured while still reeling from the aftermath of betrayal from my best friend and Nikki. No. I couldn't take another round of devastation and get deceived again. Shaking my head, I shrugged away her hand. "I can't."

I heard her soft cry while I hurried down the stairs and into the darkness. *Don't look back,* I commanded myself while I rushed down the sidewalk. I didn't dare stop at my truck. If she climbed inside again, I knew I'd have her pressed up against the door, my lips leading the charge in destroying my last shred of resolution. Instead I kept walking, kept moving, as far away from Cassie as I could.

When I finally slowed down, I was at the docks. My boat bobbed in the water just up ahead. Deciding peace and quiet on the water was just what I needed to calm down, I started down the docks toward my boat. The silhouette of a man casting into the water slowed my feet. As I got closer, my slowed steps stuttered to a stop.

Matt.

"You've got to be kidding me." I groaned. Was the universe playing a cruel joke on me? Nowhere was safe tonight. Cassie commanded the Blue Ox, and it seemed Matt had hijacked the docks. *My* docks.

"Jake?" Matt asked, looking over from where he reeled in his line.

"I'll go," I grumbled, turning away.

"I'm sorry. I didn't know you'd be down here. I'll go. I just wanted to fish a little tonight. It's been a while."

Fishing these docks together was something he and I had done countless times since we were kids. Spinning on my heel, I started away. "Whatever. I'll go. This is just the *perfect* end to my fucking day."

He set down his rod and jogged to my side, stopping in front of me.

"I wouldn't get in my way, if I were you." I leveled him with a glare while he blocked me from leaving.

"Jake. I have no right to ask for your forgiveness. None. But I'm asking anyway. I miss you. I miss us. And I know I don't deserve it. But can you? Can you forgive me?"

A laugh ripped out of me. Bending over, I pressed my hands into my thighs. At this point in my night, laughing was all I could do now. The unexpected reaction sent Matt back a step, and it surprised me as much as it did him.

"More people wanting my forgiveness tonight." My laugh deepened. "You know, the really messed up part about this, Matt? I'm neck-deep in shit right now, and the *one* person I know could pull me out of it is you. If you hadn't screwed my fiancée, I'd be asking you to meet me on these docks and fish it out while you helped me dig myself out of the hole. Because that's who you were to me. My best friend. My brother. The person I relied on most in this world. But here we are. I'm drowning, we're on the docks, and I can't even talk to you about it because, you know, you crossed the fucking line!" I laughed harder.

"Jake," he said, pressing a hand on my shoulder. "Talk to me."

With a powerful shrug, I sent him back a step.

"Don't touch me. You aren't my friend anymore. You gave up that right when you betrayed me."

"I get it. I do." He lifted his hands but held his ground. "But I need to tell you something. This is the first time I've gotten a chance to talk to you— the first time you'd listen to me. And I just need you to know that I didn't sleep with her."

"What?" I choked out the word.

He blew out a puff of air. "What I did was still unforgiveable though. I... I kissed her. That I did do."

"Jesus," I whispered. "Why the hell didn't you tell me that?"

All this time I'd believed the rumors. Matt had screwed Nikki. Everyone and anyone were saying it. And it wouldn't have surprised me. At least on her account. She'd done it before, so it didn't take much for me to think she'd done it again. But thinking *he'd* gone that far had been the surprising part.

And now it turned out he didn't. I struggled to make sense of it. Did that mean I should forgive him? Still be furious he'd kissed her? My mind reeled as I tried to digest this new information.

"Dude, I wanted to tell you. I tried. I left messages for you and told anyone who would listen that it didn't go down that way. But you apparently deleted my messages without listening, and no one else believed me. And I did cross the line, so when people started twisting the truth and the rumor mill warped what had really happened, I stopped fighting it and trying to explain that wasn't what happened. Because it didn't matter in the end. Kissing... sex... it was all a betrayal to you. Plain and simple."

I scrubbed a hand down my face trying to process his words.

"I still don't expect you to forgive me. I may have stopped things before they went any farther, but I never should have gone there in the first place. But that doesn't mean you can't still talk to me. If you're in shit, I can help you out. No one on this planet knows you better than I do."

I ignored the pinch in my gut. "That's the worst part. I know you do. I know you would know just what to say to help me find my way out. It's not that Nikki cheated on me that hurt so bad. It's that it was with you, and because of it, I lost you as my best friend."

I shook my head, the pain of that night I found out slamming back into me.

"I'm so sorry, Jake."

"You didn't even have the balls to tell me. I had to find out from rumors around town. Honestly, at first I didn't believe it because I *knew* you wouldn't do that to me. There was no way. The first time I heard that you'd banged her, I actually laughed it off. Then twenty minutes later Nikki showed up at the bar sobbing and begging for forgiveness, confirming my worst nightmare. I barely heard a word she said other than 'Matt and I didn't mean to hurt you.' After that, I left. Haven't talked to her since. She told me everything I needed to know in that sentence. It broke me, man. You betrayed me, and you didn't even man up and tell me. You know better than anyone how much I value honesty. Hell, I may have even forgiven you, if you'd have just come to me."

He stared at the ground. "I know, Jake. I know. It was so messed up. I was drunk and–"

"I was drunk?" I laughed again. "That's the big excuse? You may not have slept with her, but you still kissed her. My fiancée!"

"... and I thought I had feelings for her."

Those words shoved the laughter back down my throat and I turned to face him. "What?"

He heaved a sigh. Sorrow-filled eyes rose to meet mine. "I thought I had feelings for her. After she moved here freshman year, I had the biggest crush on her. I'd finally given up on my childhood dream of Jo ever wanting me as more than a friend, and I kinda moved those feelings over to Nikki. But she wanted you. And I was happy for you. I was. So, I sat on the sidelines and watched you with the girl I thought I wanted. And I did nothing. Because you were my best friend. My brother. It was *agony* spending all that time, all those years, watching you two together. But I was happy for you."

With a slack-jaw, I could only stare at him, blinking.

"When you got engaged, it killed me. Deep down I'd always expected you'd break up, then I'd get your blessing to ask her out. That one of these days it would be my turn. Every time you broke up, I waited for the right moment to ask your permission, but then she always came running back to you and it was too late."

Conflicting thoughts tumbled in my head. "I... I had no idea."

"I know. I didn't want you to. I thought she made you happy. But that one night, I was so drunk, and she kissed me. It was wrong, and I knew it. But it felt like I was under some kind of spell. After all those years of wondering what it felt like to be you, to feel her kiss, it was finally happening. And I let it. I was drunk, sure. But I knew what I was doing, and I couldn't stop myself. And yeah, I stopped it before it went farther, but it took everything I had in me to push her away. God. I'm so stupid."

We stood locked in a silent stare. Matt couldn't take what he'd done back, and even if he could, his betrayal had ultimately led me to Cassie. To something real.

"You thought you had *feelings* for her?" I stammered. "Shit."

With a shrug, he nodded. "*Thought* being the operative word. Turns out she's a pretty shitty person and I spent a lot of years dreaming about a girl who didn't exist." He snorted. "But just because I had spent all those years coveting her, it doesn't make what I did right. Or okay. Or forgivable. But I just wanted you to know why. Not that you'd understand. You'd never have done that to me. No matter how much you wanted the girl."

He was right about that. But there was one thing I understood more than he knew. The power a woman could wield over your good sense.

"You should have told me how you felt about her, Matt."

"How do you tell your best friend you want his girl?"

"Well, kissing her was definitely not the best way." I arched a brow.

Sucking the air through his teeth, he gave me a sheepish grin. "Yes. I can see that now. Hindsight and all."

My soft snort snuck out, and the corner of my lip almost pulled into a smile. I missed his sense of humor.

"So. Now you know. And if it makes you feel any better, after years of thinking she was the girl I wanted, of fighting my attraction to her, it turns out we wanted nothing to do with each other. I'd been wrong all along. So, all I got out of my massive fuck up was a shattered life without a friend in the world."

I scowled. "I know how that feels."

"Not good."

"Nope. Not good. Though, I would be lying if I said I didn't find some enjoyment in the fact you got your heart crushed, too."

"It is well-deserved." He rocked back on his heels and clucked his cheek.

"Very well-deserved."

The water lapped at the dock and I heard a fish breach the water. We both looked toward the sound. "Fish are biting tonight," Matt said.

"Yeah?" I asked, now itching to catch one.

"Grab your pole. We could try to snag a few?"

The weighted question hung between us. With the bulk of my problems settling on my shoulders, all I wanted right now was to have Matt help me sort through this mess. He'd been my sounding board even as children. My partner in crime. And tonight, more than ever, I missed the way he could always help steer me out of the dark.

"Okay," I answered.

His eyes lit up. "Yeah?"

"Don't get too excited. I just want to snag that fish." I pursed my lips.

But even with my hesitant stare, I saw the smile start on his face. "Got it. Just grab your pole. They're biting on white."

With a sharp nod, I turned back to my boat and grabbed my rod and tackle box. Matt cast into the water while I got set up, using the white lure like he'd suggested. A fish grabbed his lure and the whirring of the reel got us both excited while I watched him fight the fish. The line snapped.

"Damn it!" He laughed.

"My turn." I grinned and cast where I'd last seen the ripples.

"You're on." He cast beside me, and we exchanged a familiar smile while we reeled simultaneously. It was the same look we'd shared as boys, then teenagers, and eventually grown men when we'd race each other to catch fish off this dock.

The fish grabbed my lure, and I set the hook.

"Lucky cast!" Matt jibed while I fought him in. "Bet you lose him, too!"

"Watch and learn, Matt. Watch and learn." I battled the fish for a minute before the tension on my line disappeared without warning. "Shit."

Matt's laugh echoed across the water. "Watch and learn? Learn what? How to lose a fish?"

"Shut up." I laughed.

We tied on new lures, and with a challenging look, we both cast back into the water.

"So, you gonna tell me what's got you in shit up to your neck?"

"It's a long story," I grumbled, flashes of moments with Cassie invading my mind.

"I've got time." He glanced over his shoulder while we reeled in the last of our lines. Once again, we cast them back out into the water.

"It's a girl."

"I figured that much. What happened?"

"Well, let's just say I might understand more than you'd know about women stripping us of our good sense."

"Oh, yeah? That good, huh? So, what happened?"

"She lied."

"Little lie or big lie?"

We cast again.

"Big lie."

"Let's hear it."

Before I knew it, I unloaded my problems back onto Matt's shoulders just like I had since we were kids. We stood on the dock, casting and reeling for hours as I told him the whole story. He listened while I told him about the girl I'd found stuck in a porch step under attack from a pine snake. The girl who'd fallen out of my truck. The one who I'd kissed in the lake. Made love to on my boat. The girl I'd given my heart to only to have her crush it to dust. When I got done, finishing up with seeing her tonight, I heard the rush of air come out of his lips.

"Whoa," he breathed.

"Yeah. Whoa."

"That's a whole lotta messed up."

"Yep."

"So now what?"

"Now I have no idea. I move?"

Matt laughed. "You know you'll never leave here."

Shrugging, I cast again. "True."

"Do you love her?"

"What?" I snapped, turning to look at him.

"Do you love her?" he asked again, casting his line.

"I just met her."

He scoffed. "So. You don't have to know someone for years to be in love with them. Sometimes it just takes one look."

I remembered how I'd felt the first time I saw her. It felt like the world had tipped upside down.

"So? Do you love her?"

"I don't know. Maybe?" I answered.

"So that's a yes."

"It's a maybe," I argued.

Matt responded with a laugh. "Look at me."

I turned, and we locked eyes. "What?"

"Do. You. Love. Her?"

Holding his eyes, I started to look away.

"Ah! Look me in the eye and answer me. Do you love her?"

I stood in silence for a moment while mirth danced in his eyes. When I saw her face flashing through my mind again, I sighed. Matt knew me too well. There was no use in trying to lie when I answered the question I hadn't known the answer to just a minute ago. "Yes." The weight of the admission nearly took me to my knees.

"Well? Then what else is there?"

"She lied to me, Matt."

"Oh, come on, Jake. No one is perfect. God knows I'm not, and you've forgiven me."

"Who said I've forgiven you?" I arched a brow.

He only smiled and cast again. "Well, you're going to have to forgive one of us. If you don't, *both* the Ox and the Cornerstone are off limits to you." Waggling his brows, he grinned wider. "And there you'll be... loveless. And whiskey-less."

"Shit." I laughed. "I suppose I do need to forgive one of you."

"Or both?" He turned toward me. "Maybe you need to forgive us both."

Forgiveness didn't come easy for me. Every time I'd tried in the past, I'd been burned. Nikki was the perfect example. Yet when I stared into those familiar eyes, I wanted nothing more than to forgive him. To have my friend back. My happiness back. Well, at least part of it. The other half of my happiness was still slinging drinks at the Blue Ox.

"I'll think about it," I answered, but the look that passed between us was one that needed no other words. After decades of friendship, he knew exactly what I was thinking.

Smiling, he turned back to the water and continued reeling in his line.

A fish bit my line and I snagged it, careful this time not to reel too fast.

"Oh, come on! That one was mine!" Matt teased while I brought it in. This time I was careful not to go too fast, and soon the silvery scales glistened in the dim light when it surfaced by the dock.

"I got it!" Matt said, lying on his stomach and reaching into the water. With a swoop of his hand, he caught it by the gills and lifted it up. We stood grinning at the size of the monster trout he held up.

"Teamwork makes the dream work!" He grinned and pushed it toward me.

"Shit! That thing put up a fight!" I panted as I caught my breath.

"The best things come at the end of the biggest battles."

His veiled words settled over me while he peered at me from behind the big fish. This time I felt like it was me squirming on the end of the line. I'd waged a battle against my feelings for Cassie. I'd run, she had pulled, I'd swam toward her, and she'd kept the tension just right. Even though I'd thought I'd broken free, when I'd seen her tonight, I'd felt the tension tighten again. She still had me on the end of the line. And now I didn't think I wanted to toss the hook. This time, I wanted to give up my battle and let her reel me in.

"Are you keeping it?" he asked.

"No. Toss it back. I've got to go see about a girl."

With a growing smile, he nodded. Leaning over the edge, he put the fish back in the water and rocked it until it burst free. He stood and pressed a hand on my shoulder.

"Go get your happy ending, man. You deserve it."

Staring into the eyes of my oldest friend, a slow nod tipped my head. I felt all my anger and all my hurt dissolving beneath his apologetic gaze. I grabbed him by the shoulders and pulled him in for a hug. We embraced for only a moment before I patted his shoulder and stepped back.

"Thanks, Matt. I needed this."

"Anytime, friend," he said. "If I can still call myself that?"

Shaking my head, I smiled. "You'll always be my friend. My brother. But if you so much as look at this girl sideways, I swear to God I'll finish what I started at the Ox."

He raised his hands against my glare. "Hell. No! Never again! I'd sooner pluck out my own eyes before I covet your girl again. I'm still chewing slow after our last encounter." Rubbing his jaw, he gave me that playful smile I'd missed so much.

Smiling, I gave him a nod. He was worth forgiving. Worth a second chance. The bonds of brotherhood between us were woven too tight.

"Well, what the hell are you waiting for? Bars closing. You'd better go get your girl."

With a nod, I walked off. There was one other person I needed to forgive tonight.

CHAPTER TWENTY-THREE

Cassie

"Seriously, Jo. Go home. I'll close up. It's the least I can do after leaving you short-handed this week." I pushed the rag down the bar.

"You sure?" she asked. The exhaustion shone through her eyes from almost a week trying to keep the Blue Ox afloat in high-season without me.

"Positive. I owe you a lot for giving me a second chance."

"Let's be honest. I was just short-staffed." She laughed, giving me a little well-deserved side-eye.

"Well I'm still grateful for the chance to come back. You don't understand how much this job, and this place, mean to me."

"So, you're really not going to take any money from your grandpa? You could be traveling in jets and limos, and you're going to keep driving that rust-bucket around?"

"It's *my* rust-bucket, and I kind of love of it." I grinned, pulling glasses out of the dishwasher.

"You're a strange bird, Cassie. But I dig it. Good for you to stand up on your own. You know how I feel about rich people, so I'm glad you're no longer one of them."

Laughing, I sucked the air through my teeth. "I mean, I do have a hefty trust fund headed my way someday, but maybe I can change your mind about rich people."

"We'll see. If you can survive on your own for a while, maybe, just maybe, I won't hate you when you inherit your millions." She winked.

"Yeah. It's about time. I mean, I'm sad I lost the chance to run the company, but this will be a good place for me to start climbing up the ladder myself. Just like my grandpa did."

"You really think you could have run a billion-dollar company?" She arched a brow. "The girl who couldn't figure out what went in a gin and tonic?"

Bursting into laughter, I shook my head. "I actually have an MBA from Columbia if you can believe it. Waitressing, bartending, fishing? No clue. Running a company? That I've got down pat. Or, I would have, if I'd been given a chance."

"I'm sorry you missed out on it."

"Me, too. But I can't blame Grandpa for giving up on me. I was a disaster."

"Hey," she said, showing a glimpse of her softer side. "You went through a lot. I get that now. At least he's forgiven you. That's a start."

"Now if I can just get Jake to forgive me." I sighed, wondering if that wish lived in the same forest with leprechauns and unicorns.

Blowing out a puff of air, she grimaced. "That's going to be an uphill battle. But give it some time. He may come around."

"I hope so. I was really falling for him, Jo."

"Falling?" She scoffed. "I saw the way you two looked at each other. The word you're searching for is *fell*. You both fell for each other."

I opened my mouth to argue, but I knew any words other than "I fell for him. Hard." would be a lie. And lying wasn't something I was ever going to do again.

"You're right." I smiled. "But it won't matter if he can't forgive me."

"Just give him some time, Cassie. You never know."

"Thanks, Jo."

"Goodnight, Cassie. Don't forget to lock the door behind me."

"I won't. Goodnight, Jo."

With a wave, she headed out the door. I walked around the bar, stopping to pick up a bottle off the floor. Another one by the pool table caught my eye. Grumbling over how inconsiderate customers were, then laughing since I *was* an inconsiderate customer not long ago, I headed over to grab it. The sound of the door swinging shut startled me.

"Did you forget your keys?" I asked, expecting Jo. When I turned around, I saw Jake standing in the doorway.

"Jake," I breathed, struggling to form words with my breath trapped in my lungs.

The neon lights above the bar illuminated his blue eyes boring into mine. We stood locked in a magnetic stare.

"What are you doing here?" I asked, still struggling to speak.

Without a word, he walked to the jukebox. I watched while he slid in his bill and pressed the buttons on the screen. He turned around and started toward me. Still clutching my beer bottles, I stood trapped like a prisoner in his intense gaze. Before he reached me, the familiar notes from a song I'd now heard twice floated out of the speakers.

Let Me Down Easy. The song he'd played for me before. My heart soared when he stopped in front of me, reaching out a hand.

"Dance with me," he said, and I glanced at his outstretched hand.

Setting down the two bottles, I reached out and took it. Electricity crackled in our touch as he closed his hand around mine. With a gentle pull, I was in his arms again. Exhaling the breath I never thought I could release, I dissolved into his embrace. Strong arms wrapped around me as I clung to him, fighting the tears that begged to fall.

We rocked together in the glowing lights, every sway of our bodies pressing us closer together. His chin settled on my head, and I disappeared inside him. That safety I'd felt in his arms flooded back. My world spun once again, turning on its axis and sliding me back into his life. Into his arms. Back where I belonged.

A soft kiss brushed through my hair and I sighed. Slowly raising my eyes, I found his waiting for me, my own longing reflecting inside them.

"Jake," I breathed.

He slid a hand underneath my chin. "I love you, Cassie."

Those words moved over me. They crept into every wound, every crack, filling the emptiness inside me and erasing all the pain that consumed me. Rising on my toes, I wrapped my arms around his neck. "I love you too."

Before I breathed out the last word, his lips sought mine, capturing my confession with his kiss. Our mouths melted together, his tongue demanding entrance I granted him without hesitation. The passion in his kiss sent my world spinning, and I clung to him for balance. Like a hurricane of emotions, I felt his ripping through me and fusing with mine.

His powerful kiss pushed me backward when he deepened it. I felt the pool table bump against my legs. Towering over me, he pressed me back with his kiss. Lingering lips ghosted mine while his fingers moved to my hips and slid beneath my shirt. Rough hands grazed my sides as he inched it up, the cool air licking my heated skin as he slowly exposed it. Our kiss broke when he pulled my shirt over my head. When I reemerged, I pulled off his shirt, tossing it on the pool table beside mine. Desperate to taste him again, my hands cupped his strong jaw and pulled him back into me.

"I love you, Cassie," he murmured into my mouth.

My answer was another kiss. He leaned into me and I scraped my fingers down the muscles rippling the width of his back. His fingers fumbled with my jeans until I felt the sweet release that meant another type of release would soon follow. Inching my pants over my hips, I wiggled to get free. Releasing my grip on his back, I let my hands roam around his torso until they settled at the front of his jeans, now the only thing keeping us apart.

Feeling his button relinquish its fight, I pulled down his zipper and pushed his pants over his hips. Before he dropped them to the floor, he pulled a condom out of his pocket, and

I panted with desire while he slid it on. With a passionate groan, he pressed me back until I sprawled across the pool table. Waiting. Wanting.

Needing.

When he entered me, our ragged breaths mingled into one. Desperate kisses met mine while he moved inside me. With every thrust of his hips and swirl of his tongue, I felt the connection between us deepen. The need to be with him, to make him mine for always, increased with the rhythm as we moved together. When my pleasure reached unbearable heights, I clung to his back and cried out his name as he moaned out mine.

Collapsing on top of me, he sighed into my hair. Hot breath brushed my neck as I closed my arms around him.

"I love you too," I whispered into his ear.

Turning his head, he locked his gaze with mine. That soft smile I loved so much lifted his lips before they pressed into mine.

The feeling of her naked body pressed against mine soothed away the last of my aches. Long legs wrapped around mine as I held her in a cocoon of safety, pressing soft kisses to her forehead as we lay together on the pool table.

"I can't believe you came back," she whispered, nuzzling in closer.

"I almost didn't. You can thank Matt."

"Matt?" Wide eyes lifted to meet mine.

"Yes. Matt." I chuckled. "It's a long story."

"Well then, remind me to buy him a 'thank you' drink the next time I see him at the Cornerstone."

"Actually. You may be seeing him here now."

"You're allowing him back at the Ox? Wow. You've had a hell of a night," she said, shaking her head. "I can't wait to hear about it."

"It's been a big one. But most importantly, it brought me back here. To you."

With a sigh, she slid a hand under my jaw and pulled me down for a kiss.

"Never lie to me again. Deal?" I whispered between kisses.

"I swear. Never. And I want to tell you the whole story. Everything."

"I look forward to hearing the tales of Cassie Davenport." I chuckled. "Wait. Do I need to call you Cassandra now?" Furrowing my brow, I searched her face.

"No. Call me Cassie. It's what my parents used to call me. And it's who I am now. Or at least who I'm striving to be. Who I know I can be."

"I know you can do anything. Even eat carbs."

Her laughter started as a trickle then her whole body shook while she pressed into my arms. Laughing, I kissed her again.

"If you can face your fear of carbs, I can face my fear of getting hurt."

"I won't hurt you, Jake. I promise." Her laughter subsided, and those green eyes locked with mine. "Never.

I want this. You. I swear to you that you will always come first."

As terrified as I'd been coming here tonight, putting my heart back in the hands of this woman, I was more terrified of a life without her. Some risks were worth taking, and Cassie was one of them. We were one of them. With a deep breath I blew out the last of my anger. At her. At Matt. Hell, even my hatred toward Nikki drifted away. In fact, I was grateful now for her deception. If it hadn't been for her betrayal, I wouldn't be lying here in the arms of the one woman I ever truly loved.

"You going to help me clean up so we can go home and let the dogs reunite? Poppy has been pouting, wondering when she can see Hank again."

"Hank was almost as big of a mess as I was." I laughed and glanced down. "I'll never look at this pool table the same way again."

I stood, pulling up my pants before hoisting her to her feet. We worked together to close up the bar, pausing for a kiss beside her car.

"Your house or mine?" she asked, leaning into my kiss.

"Mine. I'm not sleeping at your house until we get rid of that creepy owl lamp by the bed." With a shudder, I tried to hide my smile.

"Hey! I kind of like that weird owl lamp now!" She laughed and slapped my chest. "It's grown on me."

"I'll see you at my house. Bring the dog. Leave the lamp."

We dissolved into laughter and I hugged her before helping her inside. With one last kiss, I closed the door. Her engine rumbled when she turned the key, and I watched my

Park Avenue Princess chug down the street in her bucket of rust. If it was possible, it made me love her more.

CHAPTER TWENTY-FOUR

Cassie

"Good morning," Jake whispered into my ear.

Just the sound of his voice reignited that fire inside me before I'd even opened my eyes. I snuggled in deeper, pressing my face into his chest while his arm tightened around me. "Good morning, Jake."

Blinking my eyes open, the first thing I saw was Poppy's smooshed face resting on his opposite pec. His muscular arm held her close to his chest, his deep breaths lifting her up and down while her soft snores punctured the quiet of the room.

"Don't say it," he warned.

"It's still the cutest thing I've ever seen in my whole life."

"We are going to need to work on our sleeping arrangements." He laughed. I peeked down to see Hank draped over his lower body.

"I'm literally unable to move. The three of you have me trapped."

"But we're so comfortable." I looked up and pushed my lips into a pout.

"Well then. If *you* three are comfortable, by all means, who cares about me?"

"Exactly," I teased and leaned up, brushing my lips against his.

After slipping his arm out from under Poppy, he brushed his fingers across my cheek before cupping my chin and pulling me in for a deeper kiss.

"Well, if you keep kissing me like this every morning, I suppose it can make up for the lack of sleep I'm in for with the three of you using me like a chaise lounge."

"Deal." I kissed him again.

"You up for a Jake special omelet?"

"Hell, yeah!"

"Good. I've got fresh eggs. Breakfast in bed?"

"Porch. I want to enjoy the view."

After giving me one last kiss, he rose and walked across the room. His naked body held my eyes the entire way. "This view works, too."

With a coy smile, he took his time pulling on a pair of shorts.

"No shirt."

"No shirt is part of the Jake special omelet." He waggled his brows.

He strode out of the room and I pulled the covers up over my head. How was this happening? How had I gotten here? Blissful didn't even begin to capture the feelings surrounding my new life with Jake. Hank disrupted my thoughts when he collapsed on top of me, all one hundred pounds of him crushing into my stomach.

"Hank," I groaned, struggling against him. But one look in those big brown eyes and I gave up my battle. "Good morning, buddy."

After pulling myself out of the pile of dogs and climbing into another one of Jake's oversized tees, I walked downstairs, following the smell of fresh eggs and simmering coffee. Leaning up against the doorway, I watched Jake float around the kitchen. The joy he radiated mirrored my own.

"Your coffee, love," he said when he saw me. A wide grin matched mine when I saw the "I'm a Hooker" cup heading my way. "It's tradition now. It's officially your cup."

"I wouldn't have it any other way."

Jake opened his mouth to speak, then snapped it shut.

"What?" I asked, narrowing my eyes and taking a sip of my coffee.

Rubbing a hand across the back of his neck, he glanced down at the ground before looking back up at me. Once again, he looked like he was about to say something, but instead he chewed on his lower lip.

My heart thumped. He looked so serious. Too serious. "What is it?"

With a deep sigh, he took my hand in his. "This may be fast, and I don't want you to freak out, but what about making something more than that cup official? What do you think about leaving that terrifying cabin you call home and moving in here with me?"

I almost spat out the sip of coffee I'd just taken.

"If it's too fast, I totally get it. I just figure if you're staying up here in Door County, you'll want somewhere less... horrifying to live."

"Is that the only reason you want me to move in?" I set my coffee cup on the counter and slipped my arms around his neck.

With that sweet smile that sent my stomach plummeting to my feet, he wrapped his arms around me. "Not the *only* reason."

"And what's the other reason?" I rose on my toes and pressed my lips to his.

"Partly because I don't want that owl lamp to come to life and kill you in your sleep," he whispered against my lips, and I laughed. "But mostly because I love you and I don't want to miss another morning waking up next to you. Even a few acres is too far away."

"Well," I said between kisses, "if that's the case, then I accept."

"Yeah?" He leaned back and grinned.

I nodded my head, and the look in his eyes made my heart swell to near bursting. "I love you, Jake, and I would love to move in with you."

With a grin so wide it could have torn his face in two, he leaned forward and swept me into his arms. "You make me so happy, Cassie. I love you so much."

I waggled my eyebrows. "Can I bring the owl lamp and all my pink décor?"

His laugh echoed through the kitchen. "Leave the owl lamp. We'll discuss the décor. Maybe we could compromise. A few pink camo accents. Oh, and Muskybait. Definitely Muskybait. Hank would go on strike if you left her behind."

I scrunched up my nose. "Like I'd leave my Princess behind. So, no pink camo. How about since you get your camo man cave, I get a pink lady cave. A new Alton family tradition."

"I like it." He smiled. "The spare bedroom is all yours to cover in every shade of pink imaginable."

"Deal," I said, and he dipped me backward, folding my body against his as he pulled me closer. When our lips connected, I sighed into his mouth, exhaling the last of the hurt that had plagued me these last few years. In Jake's arms I was happy. Healed. And I never intended to leave the safety of his strength.

After we'd gotten our fill of each other's lips, he pulled me back to standing. "Now, part of our new traditions is breakfast on my porch. *Our* porch." He smiled. "Go on out and relax, and I'll bring your eggs soon."

After one last kiss, I picked up my cup and made my way to the porch, forcing myself to contain my happiness and not skip my way there and spill my coffee all over my rack. *T-shirt, you mean your rack t-shirt.* Excited to greet the day from the porch with the views I would get to enjoy every morning, I walked outside and settled into my chair. My phone chirped, and I looked down to see my grandpa calling.

"Good morning, Grandpa!" I answered.

"Well, you're in a good mood."

With a happy sigh I nodded, then remembered he couldn't see me. "The best."

"So, life in Door County is treating you well?"

"I love it here, Grandpa. It's heaven."

"Hmmm," he responded. The tone of his reaction caused my brow to furrow.

"What's wrong?"

Jake walked out and smiled as he set my plate of eggs in front of me.

"It's my grandpa," I mouthed to him and he nodded.

"I'll give you some privacy," he whispered back. Before I could argue he took away the best part of my view and headed back inside.

"Grandpa?" I asked again. "Are you okay?"

"It's not often I have said this in my life. But... I was wrong."

"Wrong? About what?" I took a bite of my eggs and muffled my happy moan.

"Garvey. It seems he was planning on breaking apart my company like a dead car and selling off the parts. It would have left every employee without a job."

"What!" I choked on my eggs. After successfully swallowing them down, I sat forward. "Are you serious, Grandpa?"

"After you told me again how much you distrusted him, I hired investigators to look into him before I signed the final papers. They posed as investors and he made them the offer to sell. You were right, Cassie. Your instincts were right."

"That's awful! I'm so glad you stopped him, grandpa. What are you going to do?"

"What I should have done in the first place. Give you the company."

My mouth opened and closed like a fish out of water while I struggled for words. "What? You want me to take over Davenport Industries?"

"Yes. You have the skills, the desire, it seems the instincts, and now I know without a doubt you have the work ethic. I would be honored to have you take it over."

Jake peeked out the door and furrowed his brow at my shocked expression. "You okay?" he mouthed.

Nodding, I turned my attention back to the call.

"When can you come back to New York?" Grandpa asked.

New York? Suddenly the thing I'd wanted most was the farthest thing from my mind. I didn't want to go to New York. My life was here now. With Jake.

"Grandpa. I'm honored you are choosing me, and I want you to understand that I *do* want this. But if I'm going to do this, I need to find a way to run this company from Door County. I can't move back to New York."

Silence hung between us while I waited.

"I see."

"I've been considering this issue a lot, before I even came back to visit you. How to juggle things. With technology these days, there's no reason I can't work remotely. We have virtual conference calls, the phone, email... it will practically be like I'm there. We have offices in Chicago I can take a helicopter to as needed, and a couple times a month I can come to New York for briefings. But the rest of the time, I work from right here. In Door County."

More silence on his end.

"Grandpa. I want this company. I can run this company. But my life is here now. And I won't trade it for all the money in the world."

I waited, breath held fast in my chest, for his response.

"Then consider me even prouder of you than I already was before this phone call."

"What?" Even though I knew I could run Davenport Industries primarily from Door County, I'd expected more resistance from him.

"You have chosen happiness over money. And you've shown me you are capable of problem-solving. I see no reason why we can't figure out how to run things remotely. In fact, we can even open a small remote office in Door County where you can hire some key staff to help you. Why don't we see if Eleanor wants to visit you for a while and help you get up and running? We'll make it work."

"Are you serious, Grandpa? You're giving me the company? And I can stay here?"

"Nothing would make me happier."

Just when I'd thought I had everything, even more dropped into my lap. Taking up my family's legacy was a dream I would now realize. And I was going to do it right here with Jake.

"I can start after Labor Day weekend. I have a commitment to bartend up here until then. I'm not leaving Jo in a lurch."

"Even prouder still, Cassie. You finally understand the meaning of hard work and the importance of keeping your word."

Jake peeked out again, this time I waved him out. "Grandpa. I love you. And I can't wait to tell you all the ideas I have for Davenport Industries. I promise I'm going to make you proud. But right now, I have to eat these eggs before they get cold."

"Are they as good as Nancy's?" he asked.

I looked at Jake's ripped body sitting across from me. "Even better. Jake made them."

"You re-caught your fisherman? Good for you." I could hear the smile in his voice.

"Indeed, I did. I can't wait for you to meet him."

Jake arched a brow and my smile grew.

"I look forward to it. I love you, Cassandra. We'll talk soon. Enjoy your breakfast."

"I love you more, Grandpa. And thank you. I won't let you down."

"I know you won't."

We hung up, and I stared at my phone for a moment before looking over to Jake. He shoveled a bite of eggs into his mouth while he looked at me expectantly.

"Well? What did he want?"

"Um. To give me the company."

His chewing stopped and his eyes bulged while he looked at me. "You're kidding."

Shaking my head, I bit my lip while I fought my smile.

"Holy shit, Cassie. That's amazing. It's what you've always dreamed of."

"I can't believe it, Jake. I'm going to get the chance to prove myself and continue my family's legacy."

I saw the light leave his eyes before they dropped back to his plate. "I'm really happy for you, Cassie. I am. I'm just... what about... us?" He looked back up.

I let my smile free. "I'm going to run the company from right here in Door County."

"What?" His eyes bulged wider. "Are you serious?"

Smiling, I nodded and took a bite of the eggs. "Yep. You think I'm going back to New York and giving up having these eggs every morning? Not likely."

Setting down his fork, he leaned forward on his elbows. "Are you serious. You're staying *and* you're running the company?"

"Yep."

"Wow."

"Yep."

We were back to one-word conversations, just like when we'd started.

"As long as you don't mind me hopping off to Chicago on our helicopter when I need to, and a once a month trip to New York on the jet, then yes, I will have both."

"Our helicopter? A private jet?"

I took another bite of eggs. "Yep."

"Holy shit."

"So, are you good with that?"

After a momentary pause, he reached forward and took my hand. "I will never stand in the way of your dreams, Cassie. As long as you don't shove me into a tuxedo and force me to live in New York, you have yourself a deal."

"Cover that up with a tuxedo?" I waved a finger at his shirtless body. "Also not likely."

He grinned. "Then deal. So, you're staying."

"I'm staying."

He pushed out of his chair and stepped to my side. With a powerful pull I was back in his arms. Bending me back, he sealed our love with a kiss.

"Want to know the best part of this?" I whispered between kisses.

"What's that?"

"That property you love so much? The one I live at?" I paused and smiled. "Or *lived* at."

"Yeah?"

"It's mine. Grandpa signed it over this week along with two hundred acres across the street."

The way his body froze, I was certain he would drop me.

"Jake?" I asked, trying to rouse him from his shock. "You okay?"

"Do you mean to tell me you own almost two-hundred-fifty acres on Kangaroo Lake. Two-hundred-and-fifty acres that will never be developed into condos, or a hotel, or a resort?"

"Yep." I grinned. "It's all ours. Even that crappy little cabin."

"Hank! Did you hear that!" he called to the lab that raced around the yard with Poppy in tow. "You dogs have your own wildlife preserve!"

Ignoring his joy, Hank kept on running and Jake turned his attentions back to me.

"I love you, Cassie. And I always will."

"I love you more."

When his lips pressed down on mine, I knew that not only had I learned to live like the other half, I'd found my other half.

Did you enjoy this romantic romp through Door County? Check out the next book in the *Door Peninsula Passions* series, *The Other Room!*

THE OTHER ROOM
Door Peninsula Passions Book Two

Will an unwanted roommate turn into an unexpected romance?

After more than two decades of being best friends, I never thought I'd call Matt my nemesis. But that's exactly what he'd become after he'd gone and done something so stupid, I didn't think I could ever forgive him.

My vow to hate him forever started to fray when avoiding him like the plague was no longer an option. After I took pity on him and he came to crash at my place, the close proximity to the man I once adored started wearing down the walls I'd put up.

As Matt struggled to win back my friendship, I struggled with something even more daunting... ignoring the growing feelings for him that were becoming anything but anger.

I just had to stay strong... stay mad.

Ignore that perfect, charming smile...

Ignore the way he could still draw laughter from me like no one else could...

Ignore those intoxicating eyes that continued pleading with me to forgive him...

Ignore those feelings I didn't want to have... the feelings I *couldn't* have for the man who I'd vowed to hate—feelings growing so hot and intense they threatened to burn our little cabin down.

I had to fight them, and I would... it'd just be a whole lot easier if only he'd put a damn shirt on.

Visit www.katherinehastings.com to find it or learn more about my other books, including romantic comedies, romantic suspense, paranormal romance, historical romance, and more.

THANK YOU FOR READING

I hope you enjoyed *The Other Half*! The greatest gift you can give a writer is your review. If you enjoyed this book, I would be forever grateful if you'd take the time to leave a review. Find out more about my other books and upcoming releases at **www.katherinehastings.com**.

You can also get new book releases, sales, and free book specials delivered right to your inbox by signing up for my Enews!

Get social with me and join me on:
Passion Posse Reader's Group: www.facebook.com/groups/passionposse
Facebook @katherinehastingsauthor
Instagram @katherinehastingsauthor
Twitter @khastingsauthor
Follow me on:
BookBub
Goodreads

Made in the USA
Middletown, DE
11 June 2022